Jibutu:
Daughter of the Desert

Also By Lenora Rain-Lee Good

Novels

My Adventures As Brother Rat

Jiang Li: Warrior Woman of Yueh

Yadh, the Ugly

Madame Dorion: Her Journey to the Oregon Country

Poetry Books

Blood on the Ground:

Elegies for Waiilatpu

Radio Plays

The Cure

Dream Scars of Velara

Grizz

Soc "Box — (handwritten)

Jibutu:
Daughter of the Desert

Ride your Sliwa! (handwritten)

Love, (handwritten)

A Novel

LENORA RAIN-LEE GOOD (handwritten signature overlay)

A Silver Sage Book

Published by
Silver Sage Press
P. O Box 456
Purcellville, VA 20134

SilverSagePress@icloud.com

Author: Good, Lenora Rain-Lee
Title: Jibutu: Daughter of the Desert

ISBN: Paperback: 978-1-63320-059-3

ISBN: ebook: 978-1 63320-061-6

Publisher's Note:
This book is an original story and entirely fiction.

Cover Art:
Bust of Face of Extinction,
Pphotograph by the sculptor, Julie Hawthorne

For my good friend, Jane Roop.
You are missed.

Chapter One
The First Night's Dream

Dreams show Truth; dreams show Dross.
The Dreamer must work to separate the one from the other.
And be wise enough to know which to keep,
which to throw away.
— *Roose, Healer of Yaylin School*

"WHAT IS YOUR NAME?" The faceless voice yelled at me. A woman's voice, I think.

"Jibutu. I am called Jibutu. Who are you? Where are you? Show yourself." I saw nothing but sand as it blew past me.

"I ask the questions. I will give you a new name. I will take yours. You are to be called Teh...! Teh...! Tih...!" The faceless voice stuttered, as if she could not speak the whole name.

"No! I am Jibutu." I shouted to be heard over the raging sand.

Why would this unseen person, want my name? Why would I want another name? A small kernel of fear entered my heart.

The sand swirled about me, carrying the voice away. I looked down upon a tattered shelter that offered no protection to a dying woman and her newborn baby. The baby lived, though barely. The woman looked over her shoulder; panic filled her voice as she screamed, "Run! Must run! You will not have her!" Then she looked at the baby, and up at a man who stood in front of her, waiting.

My own panic rose, I cried out, "I become a healer. Live until I find you."

1

The woman held the baby up to the man who took it. She murmured, 'Teh...' then collapsed in the sand, dead.

The faceless voice, now almost too soft to hear continued, "Her name is Teh.... Your name is...."

The man wrapped the hungry babe in his arms, mounted his sliwa, kicked its scaly sides, and urged the great lizard to run at its fastest speed back to his tribe.

There, the women gathered in a tent, and passed the babe, the tiny girl, from one to the other, until the babe had fed from the breasts of the women and knew their smells, knew their warmth, and knew their love. One woman lowered the babe to her belly and said, "Child of my womb...."

Then the babe was taken to the men, who passed it from one set of arms to the next, swearing to protect her, and keep her safe forever. One man held her to his loins. I heard him say, "Child of my loins...."

And so the baby was adopted into a tribe of the desert. The faceless voice whispered, with love and longing, "Teh.... Teh.... "

I opened my eyes, safe in the tent of Healer Roose.

"What did you dream?" she asked.

"I...I don't know." I wanted to think on it, not tell it. I feared if I told the dream, it might be lost forever. I did not want to lose this, my first dream of the four that were to come with the nectar.

"You *must* know." Healer Roose insisted. "You must master your dreams. You must force them to speak to you, not rule you. Now, tell me your dream!"

Once I told her my dream, she allowed me peace. I lay on my pallet, tired from the ordeal but not ready to sleep. I allowed memories of the past few days to wash over me, to savor them. To remember them. Perhaps they would help solve the mystery of my dream.

Chapter Two

Follow the Star Path; it will lead you to light.
Follow the Light; it will lead you to truth.
Follow the Truth; it will lead you to freedom.
— Lu Ahnah, the Lost Shaman

FROM THE TIME I WAS A SMALL CHILD I knew I wanted to become a healer, and now I walked that path. Of course, I had no idea, then, what was involved. But it didn't matter; I wanted to be a healer.

At age five, I moved into the tent of Healer Roose and began my training. She sent me, at times, to other tents for training in the womanly arts of weaving, cooking, and sewing. She sent me to the tents of the workers of hides and carvers of wood and stone. Had I found a new love, I would have been allowed to stay in the new tent and learn their ways; I always came back to the tent of Healer Roose. She always smiled at my return, and praised my efforts at whatever I had learned in those other tents, pitiful as my efforts sometimes seemed.

Most girls of the desert are married by the time they have seen fourteen summers, but as I had already stated my intention to become a healer there would be no betrothal for me. Healers do not marry; once they drink the fermented juice of the death cactus, they become sterile—if they survive. Not many choose the healer's path, for children and family are important to us who dwell in the desert. No one could remember when, or even if, anyone from our tribe had ever become a healer. I did not

3

receive a betrothal feast, but I would have my wedding feast. My reverie broke with the arrival of my mother.

"Jibutu, I have brought you something." My mother, Saba, first wife of Jib, entered the tent. A large smile graced her face. "Here. My wedding skirt. Please, wear it at the ceremony tonight. When we are gathered, I will present my wedding veil to you. As first daughter, they are both yours."

"Thank you, Mama."

The wedding skirt and veil are traditionally passed from mother to first-born daughter, in the hopes of ensuring many healthy children to the new bride.

"This will be the strangest wedding our tribe has ever seen. A beautiful bride, and no groom." Mama tried to make a joke, but the dark patches under her eyes betrayed her—they glistened with tears.

"Mama, don't cry. Please. I know I will never give you and Papa grandchildren, but Corlu will give you many. And tonight, after the ceremony, I will carefully fold your skirt and veil that you may give it to her. They are hers, by right. She is the one who will give you grandchildren."

Mama and I hugged and my excitement seeped through my arms to her heart. As she left the tent of Healer Roose, her step was lighter. When she turned back to me at the tent's opening, I saw her tender smile of love. With a lighter heart, I went back to my duties, preparing for the night's festivities and the upcoming trial by cactus juice.

"Jibutu! Daughter of Jib!" My papa's familiar roar came from outside the tent. "Come, daughter, I have something for you, too!" He stood at the entrance, holding a pair of sliwa ears, specially tanned and dyed my favorite color, red, for tonight's celebration; my marriage to a profession instead of a fine young man. If disappointed by my choice, he did not let it show.

"Here, daughter. I have worked on these for a long time to get them just right. I will present them to you tonight, but

4

wanted you to see them first." He smiled broadly before continuing, "They fit perfectly through the ear slots of your mother's veil."

His strong arms reached out for me. I stepped into his embrace, and any cares or worries I held were banished by his warmth and his love.

"Thank you, Papa. They are beautiful. Corlu will—"

Papa laughed. "Corlu will be jealous. Hers are not nearly so beautiful." He always tried to stir my sister and me into arguing so he could be the peacemaker. And I knew hers would be every bit as gorgeous as mine, but they would be blue, *her* favorite color.

Healer Roose brought me back into the tent. "Jibutu, daughter of my heart, we must prepare you for the ceremony tonight."

⤜ ⋎ ⤛

A huge fire blazed in the center of the place of gathering— by sunrise it would be a smoldering bed of dying coals. The whole tribe circled it, with Mama and Papa in the center of the crowd, nearest the fire. Drums sounded the slow, measured beat used by the hunters as they ride to the desert; also the one used by the brides as they walk to their beloved. It is the same beat, on a lower note, that is used when we carry the dead to the desert for the last time. Perhaps there is a correlation—death of being single to our final death? Healer Roose slowly walked me to stand next to my parents. The drums stopped, and quiet descended upon the gathering.

Healer Roose spoke first, "Daughter of my heart, tonight you will marry not a man, but the Profession of Healing. Tonight your vows are as serious as the promises of marriage. You will not go to the tent of your husband, but to the tent of your profession. The tent of the healer." Mother Roose stepped away, and Papa stepped forward.

5

"Daughter of my loins, tonight you become a woman and may take part in tribal decisions. I tie these sliwa ears to your head that you may always hear the voice of wisdom where it concerns both the tribe and yourself; that you will always hear the voice of the desert and know the way home to your people and your heart. Your husband would not take you from our desert, but your profession may. Do not forget us in your happiness."

Papa beamed with pride as he tied the ears to my head. He held me at arms length for a long time, looking into my eyes, into my soul. The smile never left his face. At last he nodded, released me, and stepped back. Mama stepped to me, took Papa's place.

"Daughter of my womb, I place this veil upon your head so you may always know—and bestow upon others—love and kindness, warmth and shelter." Mama cried as she placed her green veil over me. It matched her skirt, which I also wore. Green was her favorite color, the color of life. A wife of the desert, she seldom cried, but she cried now, quietly, tears barely staining her eye patches. Papa stepped to her and took her hand.

I faced my parents, and then spoke to the gathering, "Tribe of my Father Jib, I accept these gifts. I will not forget any of you, nor will I forget the desert. Know in your hearts that I am now the happiest of brides!"

At my final words, the drums began again, a happy beat, with flutes and stringed instruments joining. The people of our tribe began to sing the songs of weddings, and the feast began. I was married.

"Daughter of my heart," Healer Roose whispered in my ear, "I suggest you not overindulge in sweets this night."

"I promise," I grinned. Of course, I *meant* I promised to eat as many sweets as I could. There were so many, and each was my favorite. I also ate the spiced grains and goat stews and the sliwa meat turned on the spit until cooked through, but still juicy and tender. Papa had killed a young one for this occasion. Truly, I knew the honor bestowed upon me.

The sun burst upon us as dawn claimed the desert. Most of the musicians and merrymakers had long ago collapsed into sleep. "Come," my father said as he tenderly gripped my elbow in his hand, "it is time." He escorted me back to the tent of Healer Roose where I stumbled to my bed before sleep claimed me, too. I woke at sunset.

I love the desert—it is the only home I have ever known and never do I love it more than at night under the full moon, when the dunes turn from dun to blue.

Although our desert is a sea of dunes, it is also a place of beauty. A tough grass grows in clumps here and there on the dunes and different cacti grow, enough of each to feed our goats, which in turn feed our giant lizards—the sliwa—and us.

Around the oases are fields of fast-growing melons we plant when we arrive. Soon after harvest, we travel on. Sometimes there are orchards, small but valued—if the springs produce enough water. The desert is harsh, but also bountiful for those who know how to reap its bounty.

My tribe, the Tribe of Jib, has claim to five oases. We travel from one to the other so that none is depleted. We are nomads and like to travel for the sheer joy of moving from place to place.

I stood on the dune crest and looked down to my left, where my tribe, my family, and my friends slept in peace. The breeze of the night desert carried a slight chill; I wrapped my robe about me and, at Healer Roose's voice, turned to the right and followed her.

"Come, Jibutu. We have only a short time for you to find and harvest the blossoms of the death cacti." Healer Roose slid down the dune toward the open desert where the cacti grew if one knew where to find them. Cactus that could heal; cactus that could kill. Only when the flowers opened under the light of the full moon would their poison weaken enough to become a path

7

to truth. Harvested at any other time, they would kill whoever touched them.

I heard the night birds call to each other, some warning of our approach, others announcing they had found food. Small animals scurried through the sand to feed and return to their dens before those same night birds saw and swooped down upon them. Larger animals, including a few small and wild sliwa came close, and apparently decided we were too big to tackle. For the most part, the night remained silent. The stillness disturbed by the whisper soft swish-swish of our feet as we waded through the sands. I touched the arm of the older woman and pointed.

"Very good, Jibutu. You have found the first death's bloom. Which box shall you put it in?"

I smiled as reached into my sack and pulled out one of the small, stiff sliwa-hide boxes my father made and dyed for me for this very purpose.

"Love. This first fruit of my night shall go toward the love I hold for you and my family and all people."

I took the long, slender curved knife from Healer Roose, carefully wove my hands and arms through the sharp and poisonous spines and with a single slice, cut the flower from the cactus. Gently, I caught the flower as it fell, and gently placed it in the yellow box of love. I then placed that box into a second carry sack so the empty boxes would not rest against the filled boxes.

Healer Roose smiled. "Love is a good start. Now, we must continue. We need to find five more cacti, five more flowers. Come." We walked deeper into the desert. We had to complete the task before we could turn back toward the tribe.

⤛ ⩊ ⤜

"You have done well, Jibutu. I believe this is the quickest harvest I have experienced. We finished well before the flowers closed for the night." Again, only the soft swishing of our feet through sand broke the silence of the desert as we walked home.

8

Small animals scurrying about their business in order to be safe in their dens by first light added a soft backdrop of sounds to our steps. Even the breeze had tired of play and gone to sleep.

I never tire of looking at the night sky, black as my mother's hair, and filled with sparkling stars. But this was not a night to dawdle or search for elusive paths between the stars; this was a night of haste and inward thinking. This night I would not strive to listen to the song of the stars, but would actually begin my journey to find the paths to travel to them—or at least to their truths.

"Hurry, Jibutu. You must have the flowers in your bowl, and the bowl ready to greet the first rays of the morning sun."

Back in Healer Roose's tent, I knelt upon my cushion, removed the boxes from my carry sack, placed them in the order in which they were filled, then washed my hands in the fresh, pure water Healer Roose, my adopted mother, my heart mother, poured over them.

The bowl in front of me was one I carved during my time in the tent of the stone carver, from a piece of red rock I found on a trip with my father. It had taken many months to carve, along with the matching lid, but I was proud of its simple beauty. From this bowl would come the drink of my life and truth—or insanity and death. I had learned well at the tent of the carver of stone. My bowl was simple, as I hoped my life would be.

Although Mother Roose harbored a slight fear that I might die, I remained unafraid and confident as I began the ritual of preparing the fermented drink. "From this box, I remove the flower of love that I may never forget to love one and all and that I may receive and accept their love of me. I place this flower into the bowl of life." I lifted the flower from the box with tenderness so it did not bruise and placed it in the bowl. "From this box, I remove the flower of family, that I may never forget my small family is part of the larger family, that we are all connected, one to the other, by life, by death. I place it into this bowl of life."

When the boxes of health, truth, loyalty, and freedom had all been ritually emptied into the bowl of life, I carefully poured fresh spring water over them. I carried the bowl to the waiting table outside the south side of the tent and placed it there, covered, so it would steep in the heat of the day's sun. As I set the bowl down, the first rays of the sun exploded over the dune, the strong rays kissed my red bowl. It glowed in the sunlight; the veins of yellows and whites seeming to dance as the light caressed it.

"Now, child, you need to visit your family. Your mother has prepared your breakfast. It is the last meal you may have with your family until you have returned from your dreams, so eat well, enjoy their company, and return before the sun reaches its zenith. There is still much left to do."

"I hope there won't be a huge breakfast. I'm still full from my wedding feast." I grinned at Healer Roose. Never had she, or anyone else, known me to refuse food. Especially if it was sweet, or my mother had made it.

Mama had prepared my second favorite breakfast. At the caution of Healer Roose, she did not prepare my most favorite breakfast of fried cakes and date syrup. This time she had grains with vinegar and spiced meats, and a dark, almost bitter, tea. The breakfast one normally eats before a journey or a hunt.

My parents, too, feared I would not survive the ordeal; I could see it in their eyes. They did not want to send me into the desert to die, or lose my mind; they did not want to return my lifeless body to the desert if the nectar killed me. They put on brave faces, and we laughed a lot, but I could tell.

"Jibutu, you can still—" Mother choked and a tear escaped her eye.

"Mama, I will be fine. And you will have many grandchildren by Corlu and my other siblings." I took her in my arms and held her until the tears stopped.

"Now, I must return to prepare for this new journey. And you, Mama, must begin to prepare for the feast of my returning."

❧ ❦ ❧

"Jibutu, it is time to wake. The sun has set. It is time to begin."

Excitement bubbled up from my inner being. I knew the danger, that I might not survive the four-night ordeal; but was confident I would. I bathed, and placed the clean robe over my shoulders. I knelt on my cushion, in front of Healer Roose.

"Jibutu, do you wish to be healed?"

All healings begin with the ritual question. When I first began to train as a healer, I thought it a dumb question. Who, I thought, wouldn't want to be healed? Then I began to realize there are those who do not desire healing—those who use their sickness to control others, to gain what they think they want. Being healed requires a personal responsibility that some do not have or want. Sometimes, the healing is the acceptance of what cannot be changed, such as death, or loss; the acceptance of what is.

"Yes, Healer. I wish to be healed."

"Then we shall begin. First, you must remove the lid from your bowl, then mash the flowers into a fine paste that disperses in the water. Use as the pestle the rock you picked up on our journey for the flowers." I had wondered why, on our night journey of gathering, she told me to find and bring a round, smooth rock. I smiled, for I had picked up a red one, which nearly matched my bowl. In the moonlight, it had looked purple.

"Oh, the flowers have turned blood red! They were delicate yellow when I placed them in the bowl." I picked up the rock and carefully, so as not to spill any of the liquid, began to crush the flowers into the water. Never had I smelled anything so

11

sweet. When there remained no solid pieces of flower in the liquid, now the color of blood, I awaited my next instruction.

"Now, Jibutu Daughter, take your new drink bowl, the one I gave you, and fill it with the liquid. Take no more than a fourth from your bowl of life, for there are three more nights. Now, drink—and return to your pallet."

"It's sweet," was all I remembered saying before I collapsed on my pallet, and dreamed.

⚜

The second night, the juice had fermented even more, and was considerably sweeter. I almost gagged as I drank it. Again, sleep came quickly, as did my dream.

Quietly, I slid over the dune crest, and began my descent toward the tent, silent as the White Snake of Death; I angled my way down the dune so as not to bring sand upon me. I heard the boys gasp; then I heard them whisper, "Jibutu, come back. Come back right now! Come back, or she'll kill you!"

I ignored them. Then I heard them call again, this time with desperation in their voices, "If you don't come back, we won't tell your mother where your body is. If you don't come, and come right now...."

I continued to ignore them. What made them think I would listen to, let alone obey, them when I ignored my own mother who I loved very much, as she called me home to do chores I didn't want to do?

I smiled, listened to their whispered threats against me, even now too afraid to come after me. I smiled even more as I thought how I was braver than even my older brother, who was five and would be named tonight. I had a year to wait for my name, but I knew I would never change my name. I would be Jibutu all my life. It would be my girl name and my woman name.

And then the faceless voice, the same one from my first dream, intruded into my safe dream. Angry, she yelled at the

12

boys, "Her name is Teh…. Her name is Teh…." The voice stuttered and I thought I heard sobs. I felt what she said was not the complete name, but I yelled back, "Jibutu! My name is Jibutu!"

Something, someone, hid outside my dreams; it wanted my name. I refused to give it. That something, that someone laughed, "You will learn!" And I knew it would be back and would not rest until it had my name.

Sand flowed through my dreams and memories, but this dream was a safe one. It was my meeting with Healer Roose, and the beginning of my journey. Even though I slept with the cactus juice, I felt safe. I could remember my name; I would survive this night. I would survive this ordeal. The sands beneath my pallet whispered to me: "Jibutu. Jibutu". The sands only drink the lives of those without names.

But someone wanted my name. I sensed a name stealer just out of sight.

And it was determined to steal my name.

I smiled and ceased dreaming.

Chapter Three

Dreams are pathways to truth; they are not truth.
Truth must be refined from the dross.

— *Roose, Healer*

"DAUGHTER OF MY HEART, it is time to get up. You must stir the nectar, and place it back in the sun. And tell me of your dreams."

I rose, washed, and stirred the nectar in my bowl. It had begun to separate, with a clear liquid on top. Perhaps it was the red of the bowl, but the liquid seemed more black than red, more sinister in its appearance and the sense of its potency. Perhaps I imagined it? I placed the bowl on the table; the first rays of the sun again danced upon the lid, warming the contents. I told Roose of my dreams, at least what I could remember.

"Ah, gentle dreams. They will not all be as gentle, Jibutu. You must remain on guard."

"Gentle, but...." My voice drifted off into silence. After several moments, Roose Healer spoke.

"But?"

"I don't know how to explain it. There is a name stealer just beyond my vision who wants my name. A woman. She said I would learn. She said that Jibutu is not my real name. But she could not pronounce my real name. She stuttered. All she could say, again and again, was 'Teh...' And then before she started to cry, it sounded like she said 'Tih,,,'."

Mother Roose leaned toward me, looked intently into my eyes. "Do not let her have your name. You must remain on

14

guard. Now, eat this, and drink plenty of water. Then sleep and prepare for tonight."

She placed a bowl of spicy grains and meat stew in my hands, and a pitcher of water next to me. The fire of the stew finally washed the sweetness of the flower nectar out of my mouth. How Mother Roose loved her spices. I drank the water gladly, and though I had slept the night through, found exhaustion overtook me. I slept until wakened to again stir the nectar, and again drink of it. This time it was sweeter, and darker; my dream visions less friendly.

On this third night, I gagged as I poured more nectar into my bowl. When this ordeal is over, I, who love sweets, may never eat another. I was sicker than before, and this time I knew something wanted not only my name but also my mind. It wanted my memories. It wanted my life.

It wanted *me*.

I was again five summers old. It was the time of my naming ceremony. My mother and I argued.

"Pick a flower name, Jibutu."

"My name is Jibutu."

"That is your baby name. You need a girl name, now. A woman name."

"I am Jibutu. Daughter of Jib. I am his daughter and will always be."

"We shall see." Mother pursed her lips; the discussion was closed. But I had a secret. I had learned to keep secrets from my brothers and Corlu, now I would keep one from my mother, at least until the ceremony

The sun blazed, and then it was time. As each child received his or her new name, the Tribe cheered, and repeated the name three times in a melodious chant. Now it was my turn.

"And what is your daughter's name, Saba?"

15

Before she could speak, the Faceless Voice screamed, "Teh... Teh... Her name is..."

And before she could say my name for all of Tribe to hear, I screamed, "Jibutu. My name is Jibutu!" The gathered were quiet. I heard grains of sand rasp against each other as I turned—then laughter and cheering.

And the Faceless One spoke so only I could hear, "You will learn. You will learn. I have searched long for you, and now that I've found you, Teh.... Teh...."

"Who are you?"

"I am.... I am...."

Within my dream, I knew I was no longer safe. I tried to pursue her, the Faceless One, but sand blew into my face. I could not breathe.

I woke.

I had rolled not only off my pallet but also off the rug. I was face down in the sand, vomiting what little remained in my stomach.

"Drink this." Roose Healer handed me a bowl of jer root tea. My stomach calmed. I began to clean my area.

"Go. Wash. Eat. I will take care of this."

I did not argue. I stumbled from my area, washed, and put on a clean robe, then ate the bowl of spiced grains and meat that waited for me. When Roose Healer sat next to me, I told her of my dream.

"I have no idea what it means. Only you will be able to discern the truth, but you must wait until the fourth dream. It seems your dreams are all connected, and I think tonight you will get the answers you desire."

I shook and gagged as I drank the nectar that night, the fourth and final time. There must be none left, and if I misjudged.... Not only was the nectar strong, but also it was now well fermented. Tonight, I must find and face *the Faceless One, she of the faceless voice*. Whatever or whoever *she* is. Tonight I must

16

survive—or lose my name, myself, my memories, *my life*. I gagged as I drank the last dregs of the nectar. It was hard to swallow, and harder to keep down. My stomach heaved, but I would not retch it up. Never before had sweet been my enemy.

This night my fear appeared as a boiling mass of blacks and reds, like the nectar, stirred in the red bowl I made; and I stood at the edge of a giant vessel, looking down, growing dizzy, as the blacks and reds swirled together. The clawed fingers of my fear reached higher and higher up the sides of the bowl, and I knew I had to step into it, where *she* waited. I sensed, but could not see her. She *waited*.

I stepped.

"Come," the faceless voice whispered. "Come, learn your true name. Learn. Come, Teh.... Teh...."

"My name is Jibutu. Do you hear me? Jibutu!"

She laughed.

With my belly full of the black, fermented juice of the death flower, I could lose my name easily. My birth name was lost when Jib ripped me from my mother's arms. She crumbled to the desert floor and died, trying to defend me. I will never forget! That is why I train to be a healer. I train to save other mothers as I could not save mine.

I will never forget. The cactus flower juice makes it impossible not to remember, as if it was happening now, this moment. My mother is dead. Jib slashed her throat with his knife. Her hot blood sprayed everywhere. It ran down my face and covered my clothing, stinking of copper. It filled my mouth, filled my eyes. My world turned red and I knew I would die, but Jib laughed and caught me up to his mount. He jammed me in front of him and kicked the great lizard in the ribs to make it move.

The lizard, a giant amongst the desert sliwa, ate my mother before he moved. I will never forget.

17

The desert wind seared us with its heat. Jib wrapped his cloak around me and I could no longer see my mother. I could no longer see the blood-soaked sands where she died. The cloak stank of Jib's sweat, and lizard musk, and my fear. I lost my gorge all over the inside of his cloak, and down my front. Jib laughed. I got sicker. But the cloak remained around me. It kept the sun and sand out of my eyes.

My mother lay dying in a pool of her own blood. I begged to go back and get her. Jib laughed. I will hate him until after my death. Jib, Dog of the Desert, killer of defenseless women. I cried out, "Mother. Mother." I heard nothing but a soft, "Teh... Teh...."

Darkness blanketed the earth when we stopped. I heard the women singing, heard them call out to Jib as we arrived. They loved him and were glad he came home. Jib unwrapped me from my dark and stinking prison, dropped me into the arms of Saba, a woman, dressed in the browns and golds of the desert. I was terrified, covered in the blood of my mother.

The women scolded him at sight of me. He was tongue lashed and ignored while I was taken to the bathing pool and gently scrubbed with the finest of sands. They dressed me in clean clothes smelling of sweet herbs. They took me into a tent and all the women of the tribe took turns feeding me at their breasts, but still I cried for my mother who lay dead at the claws of the desert dog, Jib. The woman, Saba, called me child of her womb.

When I was full and quiet, Saba took me back to Jib. He stood with the men of the tribe, and he held me down, at arms length, and called me child of his loins, then showed me to all the waiting men, who swore to defend me, and care for me always.

My days were hot and my nights cool. I missed the safety of my mother's arms. We had only begun our journey, she said, to find her people where I would be welcomed and raised and trained as Moon foretold. But my mother lay dead, buried beneath the sands of the Great Desert. The shifting sands grind her bones to nothing. I will never forget her.

Jib's people embraced me. I learned their language. They called me Jibutu, Daughter of Jib. I learned their ways and slowly the picture of my mother faded from my memory. I will never forget she drowned in the sand, leaving me alone forever, to be rescued and raised and trained by strangers.

The lizard, which ate my mother whole, now comes for me each night. With each new darkness, he nibbles more of me. He feasts on my memories. Each morning I awake whole and refreshed. Tonight is the last night he will come.

After tonight I will no longer drink the cactus flower's juice. After tonight I will no longer remember my mother, who is Jib's first wife and sleeps in the next tent, curled in his embrace. After tonight, my journey will end. I will be an apprentice healer for our tribe.

Now, I cry for my mother, dead all these years, unburied, eaten whole, regurgitated as Moon and her stars, leaving me forever alone on the desert. And never will I forget.

"Teh.... Teh... You will learn." I heard pain and frustration in the voice of the Faceless One. I also heard love.

I moaned on my mat. Someone touched my shoulder. I smelled the acid of my regurgitation. An insistent voice broke through my haze. It demanded, over and over, "Who are you? Who are you? *Who? Are? You?*"

I opened my eyes to a warm and well-lit tent. I could smell my own sour bile on my sleeping pad. I rolled toward the voice, and with what small smile I could muster, replied in a very weak voice, "I am Jibutu, Healer-Shaman Apprentice of Mother Roose."

"Welcome, daughter of my heart, you are home and safe. Return to sleep, Healer Apprentice Jibutu, you need it." I did not require further coaxing. The sun had traveled well past its zenith when next I woke, weak, but alive—and sane. I had not felt the cool cloths as she bathed me, but I woke clean, and on a new sleeping pad with clean, cool sheets.

⋗〜〜 ⋎ 〜⋖

"I do not understand my last dream. It makes no sense. Papa would never kill a defenseless woman, let alone my mother. It makes no sense."

"Come. When you have eaten and feel strong enough, we will go to your father and ask him to explain. I do not understand your dream, but he might."

Still weak from the cactus nectar ordeal, I nonetheless walked by the side of Roose Healer to my mother's tent where my beloved Papa Jib, waited with her. Spiced meats and cool drinks waited. I noted with relief Mama had not prepared my favorite sweets. Even thinking of them made my stomach rumble and try to turn away.

I told of my dream, and after a long silence, Papa spoke. "I rode with an advance party to the Oasis of Samarra to be sure it was clean and capable of supporting our tribe when we migrated there in a few weeks time. When we reached the oasis, we found a flimsy shelter, cut to tatters by wind and sand. A soft moan came from within and we found a woman, almost dead, holding a baby girl. You. The woman had placed a net of stars and moons over your head. She tried to stand, but died as I reached her. I removed you from her lifeless arms. According to the ways of the desert, I slit her throat so her life's blood would feed the sands. We never found out who she was. I brought you home, and gave you to your mother," Jib nodded to his wife, "who cleaned you, fed you, and raised you."

"I knew you couldn't kill my mother!" I said the words, yet the dream was so vivid. The killing so real. I didn't believe the words I, myself, spoke.

"Jib," Mama asked, "what happened to the net? I never saw it. Did you put it in your saddle bag?"

20

He looked at her a long moment, then spoke in a whisper. "I don't know. I hadn't thought of it in all this time. I worried more about getting her to you before she, too, died. I think I left it on our daughter's head as we rode, so she would have something familiar. Perhaps, when I pulled her out from under my cloak it fell to the ground, unnoticed."

"No, husband. Had it fallen, we would have seen it. It must have slid off during the ride, and fallen in the desert."

"Why did my mother die? How did she die?"

"Daughter, she gave birth alone, in the desert. There was food, and water, but perhaps she was too weak to get it. I don't know. All I know is, as she died, she handed you to me."

"Did she say anything?" Maybe he knew my name. My real name.

"Nothing I could understand. Her language was not ours. It sounded similar, but she was weak and I couldn't understand, neh?" He shrugged his shoulders and spread his hands, palms up, in the time-honored way of apologizing.

I sat a long time, lost in my mind. How much of my dream was *truth*? Did Jib kill my mother? But why would he? Life is too precious in the desert. Why would I have the dream if it were not truth?

"Thank you, Father. It is good I know the whole story. Now, if you don't mind, I need to return to my sleeping pallet." I rose and walked away; coldness had gripped my heart. I saw the hurt in their faces as I left, but could do nothing about it. I would never trust him again. He killed my mother and fed her to his sliwa. That was the first time I can remember when I called him 'Father' instead of 'Papa.'

☞～ẅ～☜

"Jibutu, you were not only impolite to your parents this day, you were nasty and rude. That will not do for a healer. Ever."

21

I should have hung my head and apologized, but instead I stared her in the eyes. "He killed my mother. I saw it. In the dream of truth." Anger flared through me, hot as the midday sun.

"Daughter," she sighed as she stood next to her rocking chair, "the dream of truth is for you to decipher, not accept as whole melon. I have known your papa Jib for a long time, and never have I known him to kill a woman. Never have I heard rumor of such from anyone, in or out of this tribe. Never have I known him to lie, even when it would have spared him much embarrassment or saved him trade goods. Think on these words, and act accordingly." She turned her back to me and walked away.

She was, of course, right. My papa Jib is the most honorable man I know. That is why he remains the head of this tribe, why the tribe is called the Tribe of Jib. But I was angry. And hurt. And more than a little confused.

I drank a bowl of tea, nibbled a piece of spiced meat—I couldn't seem to get enough spiced foods to kill the lingering sweet from the nectar—and stood. "I will believe him, because he has never lied to me, or to anyone I know of. I must go and apologize."

She smiled, "You are, truly, the daughter of Jib. And the child of my heart."

I crossed the hot sands to the tent of my mother, Saba, the woman I had grown up calling 'Mama.' I formed the face of contriteness, and spoke the words. I then went to my father and did the same. But I wondered, deep in my heart, Who am I? Who calls me? Will I ever know the truth? Will I ever be able to forgive? Why do I hear fear and anger as well as love and longing?

"Teh.... Teh...," came the ghostly reply, soft, like the caress of a mother as she comforts a hurt child.

Chapter Four

Nothing is lost forever.
—*Lu Ahnah, the Lost Shaman*

THE ORDEAL WITH THE NECTAR left me weak and a little confused, but alive and sane. After meeting with mother and father, for I still could not call them mama and papa let alone think of them that way after finding out they were not my birth parents I was even more confused. Although I knew they were the parents who raised me and loved me, a bond had been broken. I had broken it, but could not repair it.

I tried to quell the cold anger deep within my heart. I fought hard with myself to return the love they continued to show me. I fear I did not do a good job. I returned to the tent of Healer Roose, where I had lived for my years as apprentice and slept for three days without waking.

When I did wake, I felt—different. I couldn't explain how, but I was not the same as before I drank the nectar and I would never be the same again. That was all I knew, and all I could explain. And the heart-coldness had warmed a little.

Mother Roose and I sat in the shade of the raised door flap drinking our morning tea and eating our first meal of the day. Mother sat in her chair; I sat on my cushion. I only used my chair when I wrote on the skins. My writing was better if I used a chair and a table. Life was almost back to normal, or as normal as I would know it for some time.

"Mother, I am curious about the final night, and the vision. Do you know what it means? I mean, beyond what fa—papa said."

"I am sure whatever your papa explained is all there is. If you mean, do I know who birthed you, no, I don't. That is a mystery you will probably never know. But I do wish he had saved the netting; it may have given us an idea of where she came from. I can't imagine such a net, nor why it would be used on a babe, especially in the desert. No protection at all."

That's Mother Roose, always practical. Even the dancers used soft wool, or if they could afford it, spider silk, to wrap their babes. But a net? A series of holes held together with thread? I moved onto a different topic, "Why did I call myself a healer-shaman? What is a shaman? Are you one?"

"A healer-shaman? Why Jibutu, you said no such thing." She spoke the words with an unaccustomed firmness and a strange haste.

"Are you sure? I mean, I was mostly asleep, and drugged, but was positive I said I was an apprentice healer-shaman."

"No, child. You said no such thing. And I advise you strongly not to think of it, or speak of it again. Shamans are superstitious people, who believe in magic, and say they can walk the God Paths to the Stars. No shaman would be allowed to be a healer. Ever. You said no such thing!"

For many minutes we did not speak. My world twisted and turned in unruly chaos. First my fourth night dream and now my Heart Mother telling me I had not said what I am *sure* I said.

To break the silence, I had to ask the question I dared not ask before my ordeal, "How many apprentices die from the nectar?"

Roose Healer sighed, and put her skins aside. "Why, child, all die. No one survives."

I laughed. "That makes no sense, I'm alive."

24

"Yes, daughter of my heart. It makes a great deal of sense. All who drink the nectar die to themselves, and are reborn as new people. Different people. Do you not feel somehow *different?*"

"Yes. But I don't know how."

Roose Healer smiled, "Are colors brighter? Sounds more pure?"

"Yes." I thought a bit more, "Yes, they are. But why?"

"It is the nectar."

"No, I mean, why make it sound like it's a life and death decision?"

"Because, Jibutu, we do not want just anyone to come into the Family of Healers. We want people who are truly dedicated, who will do anything, even give up their lives, to become healers. Fortunately, none have had to go quite that far. Though, sometimes, healers have died because they were healers."

"Has anyone ever lost their mind from drinking the nectar?"

"No one I've known. There are stories, but again, we tell all who enquire that is a possibility."

I thought a bit, then with a slight smile, I asked, "They knew, didn't they? That I wouldn't die, I mean. You told them."

"Yes. I told your parents. It would not be right for them to fear for your safety. After all, you are daughter of their loins, daughter of their milk. And, most importantly, daughter of their love."

"When I am through with my training, will I be sent back here, to work with you?"

"Daughter of my heart, that is a question I can't answer. It depends on where Authority and the staff at the Healer's School determine your assets would be best used. You will be allowed to return home to visit as time permits, but I doubt you will be reassigned here."

"But I want to work with you!" Petulance crept into my voice. I wanted my world to be according to my wishes, not someone else's. Even though I knew it would never be Jibutu's world, I harbored that selfish dream. I would give up sweets to have it my way. At that thought, I smiled, for I never wanted to see, let alone eat, another sweet in my whole life. That wouldn't be much of a sacrifice, I thought, and laughed aloud.

I began, that instant, to drink all of my tribe with my eyes, so I would never forget them. The first eye-drink was Mother Roose. For the first time, I really saw her tattoos, the medicine box of the Healer on her left cheek, and her personal choice of the death flower on her right cheek—light where the scars were in the dark patches under her eyes, and dark where they crossed into the lighter skin. I saw the wrinkles in her brown skin, the crinkles around her eyes from her laughter. I became aware she favored her right knee a bit more than her left. And how she always wore yellow somewhere—her robe, a sash, a hair ribbon. Yellow, the color of love as well as the color of the death flower if seen during daylight, closed against the sun.

"And, when do I leave for Yaylin?"

I looked at Mother's hand as she placed her bowl of tea beside her. When had she grown so old? And thin? I had lived with her for years, had seen her daily, but only now did I truly see her.

"Yaylin is a long way. It is on the other side of the desert. Jib and I decided to wait until Carnival. The whole tribe will be going, and from there to Yaylin is not so far, and he can afford an escort more easily from the carnival to Yaylin. We will leave with the rest of the Tribe."

"Will we be able to partake of Carnival, or only go there in order to leave immediately?" I loved Carnival. It was a time to meet old friends, to see and possibly buy or trade for new things. Things needed, things wanted, things beautiful, and things fun. There were always sweets for the children, and small toys to amuse them as they traveled. It was there that my adventure into healing began. Before I met Healer Roose, I had wandered through the stalls at Carnival, and saw a man making marks on a skin. I watched him for a long time. People came to him, gave him money, and waited while he made the marks. Then they took the skin and left. When no one else waited, he turned to me.

"So, Little One, would you like something written?"

"Written? Is that what you do? You written?"

He laughed and a friendly smile spread across his face. "I write words. What I write is called the written word. What we say to each other is the spoken word."

"Can anyone written? I mean, write."

"Anyone who cares to learn. Come. Here." He pointed to his side, "What is your name?" As he looked into my face, he reached behind him and brought forth a small tray of sand.

"I am Jibutu, sir."

"Ah, Daughter of Jib. Here now, watch." He sprinkled water upon the sand, flattened it with care, then took a stick and slowly wrote my name. "There. Now, you try." He brought out a second tray, dampened the sand, and helped me until I could write Jibutu almost as well as he.

"Very good, Jibutu. Come again next Carnival and show me how well you do." I practiced, daily, and when I discovered Healer Roose knew how to read and write, I bargained with my father for lessons. The price was high. I had to do all my girl chores when Mother asked before I was allowed to go to the tent of Healer Roose. To this day, I do not know what price—if any—Mother Roose exacted from my parents.

It was a natural decision when the time came for me to choose to apprentice under her tutelage. I had dreams at that time of living forever with her, and becoming Healer to the Tribe of Jib—in my dreams, I would be as wise and as respected as my father. How painful is the death of childhood dreams.

"We will be able to partake for a few days, but not the whole time. It depends on when we arrive how long we will stay."

Good. I would have time to see my old friend, the scribe, before leaving.

"Will you come with me to Yaylin?" I had never been to a city. Never had I seen real buildings, only the tents of the tribes. How would I know where to go? Would there be pennants flying so I could tell who lived where? Would I be able to speak their language to ask directions? Would I understand their replies?

"Oh yes, daughter of my heart. I must present you to the school. I must tell them all about you. How disrespectful you are to your elders and teachers. How nasty you are to little children. How—"

"Mother!"

The laughter I so loved burbled forth from her, water of balm from the dry of the desert. "Yes, Daughter, I will accompany you and give them an accurate accounting of your apprenticeship under me, and tell them of your fourth night vision. Together you and I, along with the staff, will plan your classes. Then I may return here or I may be reassigned. So, we must pack everything. You will have your own boxes, but remember, what you pack you may have to carry." It is a rule of the desert—pack the most important things separately from the rest. That way, if you need to carry your own, if there is no sliwa available, you can carry what you need. But I knew there would be, for this trip, the necessary sliwa. Father would see to it.

Indeed my packing was easy. Jib presented me with a gorgeous sliwa-hide box he made. There were no designs burned on it, but the heavens of our home were depicted in the lid with tiny pieces of inlaid woods. I did not know my father could do such things. Never had I seen him do any work with wood or hides, other than what was necessary.

Wood is precious on the desert, and most of our boxes are made of shaped and stiffened lizard hide.

Unless an artist burns or paints designs onto the hide, which they seldom do, the boxes are all gray-green. Sometimes

28

dyes are added to the tanning solution, so they become red or gold or orange, but most people want plain and practical for everyday use. My box was red. The lid a dark blue with the wood chips set into the hide as stars. How could I not respond to such love? Not just the love of my Papa, but the love of my tribe?

"Do not cry, daughter. The salt of your tears will stain the woods." Jib took me in his arms, and held me as he had not held me since I left his care and protection, when I was five. And when his arms went about me, 30,000 bees buzzed within my being, and I knew beyond doubt that Jib was my Papa, and that his version of my birth—and my mother's death—was *truth*.

"What," I sniffed, "if I never see you again? What if I am sent elsewhere?"

"Why Daughter of Jib, you will see me, and the whole of our tribe, every time you look at this box. Everyone contributed a piece of the inlay. And you will know that I, and all in our tribe, love you, and that I, and all of us are very proud of you. You will be sad, but then you will remember our love, and you will again be happy, neh?"

Whatever ice remained in my heart shrank and melted on the sands of the desert. Papa's manner to me had not changed, only my coldness toward him, which he lovingly ignored. Now, in looking back, I understand I must have cost him great hurt, which he, the peacemaker, could not fix. I remembered the bees racing through my body and knew peace and warmth.

So we packed. Everyone was in a frenzy of packing. All clothing and implements not needed for a few days were packed first; necessary items were left unpacked, to go into their own boxes at the last minute. A communal kitchen was set up in the center of the meeting ground; everyone contributed to the giant pot of food and ate from it.

At last, the day of departure arrived, bedding was rolled, tents were dismantled and folded, and the sliwa were loaded with their burdens. We set out for Carnival with great laughter and

29

singing, and children ran and screamed as they chased each other and generally behaved like...children. Happy, healthy, well-loved children.

Carnival is held at a huge oasis that can accommodate all the tribes for a short time. A few people are elected by the tribes every carnival to stay and care for the oasis. This is a great honor, though by the next carnival, the keepers are more than ready to get back to the nomadic life they know and love.

None of the oases will support a tribe full-time, so we go to an oasis and stay a while, then pack up and move to the next one, giving the one just left an opportunity to replenish itself.

We take from the desert, but we also give back to the desert. The desert receives our dead; it receives our respect. The desert is our life, and we are not a suicidal people, so we husband its resources carefully. Each tribe has its own section of desert, so one tribe won't leave and another one arrive too soon, thereby depleting the oasis.

I love traveling in the desert. We move in a wide and long, slow column. Most of us walk next to our sliwa, though the elderly and infirm often ride. Sometimes, the children ride, too. I love sleeping outside under the bright stars. When small, I would jump and try to grab a star from the heavens. One time, when we had reached our destination, I saw a star that had fallen into the pool. I soon joined it as I fell into the same pool while reaching for it.

Papa laughed as he fished me out, and explained about reflections in the water. The laughter of my papa is very special to me. It conveys love of his family, and love of life. I carefully placed his laughter in my heart as well as in my box, along with other memories so I would hear his laugh even when we were apart.

Desert travel can be dangerous. Storms are not uncommon, though not frequent during the time of Carnival. Sand can blow and cover a caravan in a matter of minutes. If there is time, we circle the sliwa and gather in their center, under a flat shelter of sliwa hide. The sand would shred a lesser tent. Even our shaggy goat wool, which keep us warm on the coldest nights, is no match for the sand. But if we are under a sliwa hide, holding it flat as possible, the sand blows across it. Because sliwa will always dig themselves out we each tie one end of a rope to a sliwa and the other end to our wrist so if need be, we can follow the rope to safety. Speed is of the essence, as blowing sand can shred the hide from a human in a matter of minutes. Outriders who do not make it back in time are considered dead unless— until—they return. They can survive, if they get on the lee side of their lizard and not too much sand is blown over them. Or through them. It is always safer to ride with the group.

On this trip to Carnival, the sky remained blue and the horizons stayed sharp and far away. We arrived without incident and set our tents up in our usual place. The Tribe of Jib would be here for a ten-day. Mother Roose and I would be here for a two-day. Then we would each mount a lizard and with an escort make the trip to Yaylin in a three-day. This would give our escort time to get us there and get back so they could enjoy a short time at Carnival and leave with our tribe. Papa said he would wait for their return.

"Come, Daughter. We will not set up with the tribe. We'll take our boxes and go to the Healer's Tent. While here, we will offer our services. We shall wait the two-day and see if any other healers and apprentices arrive to make the journey with us."

Mother Roose led the way through the campsites to the far edge where a large, brightly colored tent with the Healer's flag on top waited. Like our tent with Tribe, it was away from the rest of the new city. I had always stayed with my parents when we came to Carnival; this was my first time to go to the Healer's Tent.

"Roose Healer, come in, come in. Be welcome." A man as old as sand and the same color motioned us into the tent. "And who might this be?" he asked, nodding toward me.

31

"Leys Healer, I present Jibutu, Apprentice Healer. We are on our way to Yaylin. She is to be presented to the school and I will possibly be reassigned. We thought we would stay here until we leave in a two-day, possibly a three-day, and help out as necessary. If our help would be welcome."

"Roose Healer, you know you are always welcome in my tent. Or the tent of any other healer." He paused a moment, a twinkle in his eye, then asked, "Why so formal, old woman?"

"Because, old man, I have an apprentice in tow, and she needs to see some real manners, other than what she learned in her tribe!"

"Well, then, Roose Healer, please bring yourself and your apprentice into the tent. While you put your boxes away and unroll your sleeping pads, I shall pour us each a bowl of cool tea. Then we shall sit and talk. At least until the first fight breaks out in the crowds."

And so we sat and talked and enjoyed our tea until, as Leys Healer predicted, the first fight broke out. Rather we sat, they talked, and I listened. Leys watched me as I worked with the lesser fight injuries, saw what I could do on my own, and how I treated the injured, and thereafter included me in the conversation. Until then, I was merely a child to be seen and not heard.

The sun stood at its zenith the next day when another healer entered the tent. I did not see her come in, but Leys and Roose did. "Mees! Welcome! Come in, come in." As I was in the other room, I continued putting it in order, and let them talk. They obviously were old friends and had much to talk about. Once the room was in order, I decided to just sit and not interrupt. I would have gone to the tent city of Carnival, but did not wish to disturb them.

"Jibutu? Come meet an old friend and school mate, Mees Healer." I walked into the other room and was introduced. She was the healer of the Tribe of Tarlan, and like Mother Roose, she

32

had an apprentice in tow—a young man. And that is how Tems, Healer Apprentice and I met.

Tems was much lighter skinned than anyone I had ever seen. His eyes were violet, not black-brown, and his light brown hair waved rather than curled. Tems stood a head taller than me, and appeared very shy. He was close to my age, and would be one person I would know at the school. I assumed, of course, that we would share many classes.

"Jibutu, why don't you and Tems go into Carnival? I doubt anything will come up that the three of us can't handle, and it will give you both a chance to say final good-byes to friends. We won't leave until the moon is high. Here, Jibutu. Your father gave me a coin to keep for you." With that, Mother Roose handed me a small coin—a coin to spend on whatever I wanted, and with it I could buy several things.

Mees Healer handed Tems a similar coin. I noticed she did not call him 'son'.

"These coins," Tems said, once we were away from the tent, "are from the healers. At least mine is. My father would never give a coin to anyone unless it was for something necessary, like food."

I smiled, "I think you are right. But it pleases them to think we are fooled, neh?"

"Yes, it does. Let's go and see what we shall see. I think it will be a long time before we are again here. So, tell me, how do you come by your name? Isn't it a baby name? Didn't your parents want you to have a woman name? When did you know you wanted to be a healer? What was your experience with the nectar?"

Tems was a shy one, around the healers, but alone with me, he could hardly keep his mouth shut. He asked any question that popped into his head, with no mind to how personal it was.

We talked and found many things in common. He told me his mother's mother had come from a city far away, where their skins were almost white and his mother's skin was lighter than his. Of course, now that he had undergone the Ritual of Nectar, there would be no issue from him, but his siblings are also light. Tems' eye patches were a golden brown, not the dark brown-black of those who live in the desert. At least, I had never seen ought but dark ones.

Tems was fascinated about my fourth night vision. His was nothing like mine, and he either didn't remember or likely just didn't want to talk about it. "That was some dream. Mine was not nearly as frightening. That is a good thing, as I can't remember it." Like me, he was sad to leave his tribe, and like me, he was excited to begin classes.

We wandered up and down the paths between sellers, said farewell to old friends, including the public scribe, who taught me to write my name. "So, young Jibutu, you have decided to continue your training. Very good. This old scribe is proud to have had, perhaps, some small part in your life."

"Scribe Kroob," I said, "you had a very great part in my small life. Had you not shown me great kindness and generosity and how to write my name, I might never have become enamored with the written word, or with the Healing Arts. I owe it all to you, and I thank you. May your basket *always* contain fresh melons."

"Come see me when you next come to Carnival. I look forward to hearing your stories, Jibutu. Safe Journey. And may *your* basket always contain sugared melons." We laughed as we hugged and parted. He was old, would he be here when I returned?

"What was that about?" Tems asked after we had left him. I told him the story of how I learned to write. We both laughed when I finished, as both of us had become squeamish at Kroob's blessing of sugared sweets.

By common agreement we avoided our respective tribes. We had already said our farewells there, and spent a bit of our coin

34

on sticks of spiced meats. Neither of us wanted sweets—the memory of the nectar being too fresh.

I bought a new brush and ink stone for Mother Roose, Tems bought a bright ribbon to tie back Mees's wild hair. "She loves bright ribbons, and is always giving them to some child. Maybe, this one she'll keep a bit longer, if only because it is a gift from me." At that, we both laughed. Healers are seldom attached to either people or things.

We were back at the Healer's Tent in time to help prepare and serve the afternoon meal and to clean afterwards. Leys prepared a drink for us, it was mildly bitter. He offered honey, which both Tems and I refused, to the laughter of the three healers. They remembered. I took a sip of mine and tasted a mild sedative. I looked at Mother Roose, who nodded that she knew about it, and to drink. Both Tems and I slept soundly until wakened a few hours later. We would travel in the cool of the night, so the extra sleep was greatly appreciated.

Chapter Five

One must open one's eyes to see the light.
One must open one's heart to know the truth.
One must open one's arms to hold a child.
— *First Healer of Yaylin*

THE SUN RESTED LOW ON THE HORIZON, painting the desert in vibrant reds and purples with hints of deep orange along the dune ridges. The moon rose to chase the sun to her night's bed, stars began to blink into the darkening sky. Papa supplied the escort, three of our bravest and most successful hunters, as well as a sliwa for each of us. No one would have to ride double, and we could make better time. Our sliwa were loaded, we mounted and, to the cheers of all the Tribes, we began our journey. We heard, "Safe Journey," over and over until the desert breeze carried away the blessings, only the sound of our breathing and that of our sliwa remained. As we moved farther south, the emptiness of the desert was total. It was silent except for low, moaning songs as the dunes as the sands cooled.

It is faster to travel at night in the desert. It is also cooler, and the sliwa enjoy the trip more, for like most desert animals, the giant lizards are nocturnal. They will travel during the day, but prefer to sleep in the sun and run at night. In large caravans, such as those moving a whole tribe, we often travel during the day at a slow pace. It is easier to herd the goats and the small children in daylight, but for this trip speed was of the essence. We needed to get to Yaylin, and the two healers needed to know if they would return with the escort to Carnival, or go on to a new assignment elsewhere. In either case, our escort must get back as quick as possible to help in moving the Tribe of Jib. This was not a sightseeing trip. Besides, there weren't too many sights to see on the desert that we hadn't seen almost every day of our lives.

At night the sand reflected moonlight in colors that ranged from light blue to deep purple shadows. At night, nothing looked the same. The colors were as cold as the stars above.

I like the desert night—the flowers bloom in the cool darkness, and, from a distance, they all appear to be pale blue. Their perfumes float in the night air. During the heat of the day, the flowers are closed and their perfumes burned away by the sun. I also like the warmth of the day, and the grays and browns of the sunlit desert.

Night and day—I thought of them as two different worlds and I loved them equally. The sliwa moved fast enough at night that we needed a cover to keep the chill from our skin. They kicked up sand, so we traveled abreast as often as possible.

The escort joined in our singing, and taught us songs they had learned from other riders. We laughed at stories and enjoyed the jokes Mees Healer and Tems shared. Tems did a good imitation of sliwa seeking mates—so good that the escort, between bouts of laughter, had to ask him to stop. Tems' mating call was too perfect, and the sliwa began to respond. We did not need two of our bull sliwa fighting! But it was funny.

When the cool of morning became the heat of day we stopped, circled the sliwa around us and ate a sparse trail meal of spiced meat and cold grains and drank our cool teas. The sliwa were fed before we left, and would not eat until we reached Yaylin. As soon as the last dish was cleaned we all fell asleep in the shade of our tired sliwa. Though Tems and I were excited, and a little apprehensive about school, we dropped to a deep sleep as soon as we were horizontal; there was no quiet conversation between us. Thankfully, my sleep was deep and dreamless.

Awakened before the sun slid over the highest dune, we ate a quick meal, packed, and were ready to leave before the moon had crawled over her dune in the west. We rode until after the sun exploded into our sky, filling our world with heat and light.

One of our escort, Dur, spoke to his partner as we began to set up camp, "I don't like the looks of the sky, Hart. Let's pull the shelter over us before we sleep. And be sure we're tied down."

One never argues when a desert dweller suggests shelter. The second day, when we again circled our sliwa, we dug some of the sand out of the center of the enclosure and tied a sliwa hide shelter flat between our sliwa before we crawled under it to sleep.

"Hsst, Jibutu? Are you asleep?"

"Hsst, yourself, Tems. If I slept, would you expect me to answer?"

"No," he paused long enough that I almost dropped off to sleep. "Are you frightened?"

"Frightened? You mean of the storm?"

"No. You're a desert dweller. No, I mean, are you afraid of school. Of Yaylin."

"I don't think so. Maybe a little, I guess, because it's unknown, but not really frightened. Are you?" He was, or he would never have asked. Now, would he be honest?

"Yes. A little," Tems replied. "Maybe not frightened so much as apprehensive. As you've noticed, I don't do very well around people I don't know."

"Tems, you will know them soon enough. And I noticed that once you're away from the healers, you certainly aren't shy." I smiled at the memory of our meeting.

"I, I guess I just don't want to say or do the wrong thing."

"You'll do fine, Tems. Pay attention, and you'll soon see what you can and cannot do."

This time, the pause was long enough I did fall into sleep. If he said anything else, I remained blissfully unaware of it.

I must have moved in my sleep, for I felt the comfort of my sliwa's belly against my back. Safe, I fell into a deeper sleep covered by the sliwa hide shelter which would keep the sand out—and the heat in.

My sliwa shifted, bringing his head and his tail into the enclosure; his hot breath added to my discomfort. I shifted in my sleep to accommodate his movement, and settled back into dreams.

I stood at the edge of a deep precipice, looking down into a pit. Only this pit held nothing but a dark void and a terrible roar. It held the roar of Boran, Storm God. The pit opened and the sand at the edges began to crumble, Boran roared louder and louder, the lips of his mouth began to crumble faster and faster. I could not outrun them. With a roar, the great Boran sucked me into his maw.

"Teh.... Teh.... Tih!" The word came into my dreams, insistent, loud, and changed. Sand filled my face. I could not breathe. Sand covered me, weighed me down. I could not fill my lungs. "Teh. Teh.... Teh. Tih." Boran called my name. He called it quickly, then slowly, then quickly, all with no pattern.

I woke, and still heard him call. Why did Boran call me? Why did he care about my name? A loose piece of the sliwa hide shelter slapped in the winds. I raised my head, wiped the sand away from my face. The wind howled, and the sliwa slept as the sands of the desert beat against them and began to weigh our shelter down in the center.

"Mother Roose? Mees? Anyone?" I called; the winds carried my voice to the desert with such ferocity I barely heard it, I doubted anyone else did either. I settled back against my sliwa and waited. And prayed to Boran it would be a small wind, not a long howler.

"Good call on the weather, Dur." I must have drifted back to sleep, for the next thing I heard was Hart's voice. "Is everyone all right?" At all our answers to the positive, he said, "Good. Now, come, help with the shelter."

The storm was a small one, but it carried a lot of sand. We gathered at the high end of the sliwa hide, and laughed at our inability to lift it. We scrambled out into the light of the setting sun, and began to shovel the sand off the shelter. By the time it could be lifted and folded, the sky had turned purple. When we stopped the next morning, the sky was clear and we did not need to stretch the sliwa hide.

The third night, we had barely mounted our sliwa when they started to run. "They smell the water of Yaylin," said Dur. "If we stopped guiding them, they would get us there, though at different times. So we must keep them under control and together."

"How far is Yaylin from here?" I asked.

Hart smiled as he answered, "About a five-hour ride. Perhaps four, the way they run. We'll be there before dawn."

Before dawn! I glanced at Tems, but he kept his face straight ahead, and from my view, he looked apprehensive. Did he know something I didn't? Or was he having a problem controlling his giant lizard? My face nearly split in two by my grin. My excitement far outweighed my apprehension. We would be there before dawn. I would not just see a real city, but I would live in one, for a while at least. I would receive the education of my dreams.

Both the wind and the sliwa kicked sand, so we all wrapped our faces, and rode in silence. I don't know about Tems, but I wrapped memories about me, too. Papa Jib was right—the memories kept me warm and happy. With that thought, I sat a little straighter and realized I truly did look forward to the

40

schooling. I also closed my mouth, for even the coverings could not keep all the sand out and I never learned to enjoy grit between my teeth.

The ride was monotonous—only dunes with occasional cacti and scrub plants, which, as we neared Yaylin became more plentiful. The moon waned, and the desert colors muddied. I smelled no water, but my nose is not as finely tuned as that of a sliwa. The escorts set a fast pace and we rode in silence. No trail songs this night. We each held our thoughts close. Tems and I rode with Mees Healer and Mother Roose between us.

We came over a dune and there, across the expanse of blue sand, was a walled city. I could barely control my excitement. "Look! There. Is that Yaylin?"

"Yes," Mother Roose said with a laugh. "That is Yaylin. We are about an hour out. And it will get much bigger as we approach."

The wall reached a height of at least eight tall men standing on each other's shoulders and circled the city—at least the desert side. It was a pale blue, paler than the sand. As we neared the wall, I saw men on top, walking, and looking out toward the desert. There were three gates on the desert side.

"The guards on top serve multiple purposes," one of our escorts said. "They alert the city if a rogue army attempts to invade, and they alert the gate keepers to the arrival of traders and travelers. But mostly, they raise the alarm in case of a sand storm. Yaylin gets a fair amount of such storms, which is why their wall is so high—it's a "ten-man wall," so-called because of its height. It keeps much of the sand in the desert out of the city, and with warning, the people have time to get all their windows and doors shuttered. Little of Yaylin is lost to the desert, thanks to the high walls."

"Armies?" I asked. "Is Yaylin at war?" A knot of apprehension tightened in my stomach only to relax at his response. My fear must have shown on my face, too.

41

"No, I was making a joke. Obviously, not a good one."

We stopped about 50 yards from the western gate and walked the sliwa in a circle, to calm them. One of our escort rode to the gate, to tell them who we were, and where we were headed. He soon returned, and we again mounted, this time we went in single file. As we approached the wall, the massive iron grate rose with a minimum of noise and the even more massive wooden door, hinged at the bottom and held by chains, dropped to the desert, again with very little noise, but a puff of sand and dust when it settled.

We rode over the door and under the grate into Yaylin. A guard questioned each of us; we were asked our names, destination, our business, and how long we thought we'd be in Yaylin. All the information was taken down in a large book. The escort was given permission and passes to stay a three-day. The Healers would to report to the guard when they had an expected departure date.

Students were exempt from passes, as the school would take care of them. For our duration at school, we would be considered citizens of Yaylin, but, the guard informed us, should we leave the school for any reason, we would need a pass or face the consequences of being arrested as illegal vagrants, and working out our sentence for the city of Yaylin.

Once through the gate and past the guard, we rode down a wide boulevard lined by shade trees. Between the desert and the mountains, water appeared plentiful. This area, a place of residences, remained quiet; however, down the street to the left, we could see lights and hear the sounds of the commercial stalls. Hawkers called their wares—everything from cloth to candy.

It made our carnival look small. I had expected the city to be quiet, and folks sleeping still, but shops were open and people milled about. The area was bright with lanterns, quite noisy, and filled with color.

My head swiveled as I looked up one street and down another. Never had I seen permanent dwellings, built of rock and wood. The streets, covered in cobbles, were smooth, and our sliwa did not like them. And the smells! Oh, the smells—cooking meats and grains and breads. To the right, where we turned, it was dark, and quiet but to the left, oh, the noise and the lights seemed to bounce off the stone fences and buildings. There was no openness. No room to breathe.

Tems and I looked at each other. Would we ever get used to this? Could we last to become healers? Fear began to cover my excitement.

"Yaylin never sleeps," Mees Healer said as if she read my very thoughts, "or at least not often. Fortunately, the school is walled off from the rest of the city so the noise will not be a distraction." We turned right at the second street; ahead of us stood another huge wall, with another huge gate, smaller than the one we just came through.

Mees Healer approached the gate and informed the guard who we were and why we sought admission. The massive door lowered on its chains and we rode over it, this time into a huge paved courtyard. In the courtyard grew several trees, each with two or three posts with metal rings attached.

"We'll stop here," said Mees Healer. "Escort, if you will kindly tie the sliwa to a ring, unload them, and take our boxes through that door" —again she pointed—someone will show you where to set them down. Then, if you will take the sliwa around that corner to the left, and follow the arrows, there is a large area for them to drink and eat and rest.

"Return to this door and you will be shown quarters here, or you may go into the city. Your passes are good for a three-day. But I warn you, if you harm a citizen of Yaylin, even in self-defense, it will go harshly against you. I am sad to say the law of the desert does not apply to Yaylin, and some of the citizens fancy themselves masters at picking pockets or more violent forms of robbery.

"I strongly urge you to wait until after you've rested, then allow yourselves to be escorted by a couple of healers. You will see everything—probably more due to our entrée—and you will not be harassed by the guard."

As our escort unloaded the beasts, I heard one—I couldn't tell which—tell the others, "That was damn fine advice. I've been to Yaylin before, and the healer knows what she's about." They all grunted agreement and set to the business of unloading the sliwa—which were very restless in their encouragement to speed up the process so they could get to water. Restless sliwa are not to be trifled with, especially these, who had been teased by Tems' mating calls. The men hurried, and we went to the main door of the larger building.

Tems stood behind Mees Healer and I stood behind Mother Roose. I had noticed that Tems always referred to Mees as Mees Healer, and never as Mother Mees. I wondered if that was manners or if it was due to a lack of closeness between them. They did not seem as close as Mother Roose and I, but I had seen enough couples to know that lack of public closeness did not mean lack of deep love.

Mother Roose lifted the heavy knocker and banged it three times, paused, then banged it once more. The door opened after a short wait, a young woman ushered us into a large hall. She wore a long robe, too fine to be of the desert, with a hood that covered her hair. Torches flickered in the sudden change of air caused by the opening of the great door. The dancing light brought to life the many tapestries and paintings hung along the walls. Benches or individual seats were placed outside each of several doors. The stone floor wore a high polish that reflected the torches as well as those who walked upon it. The walls were very high, and in the torchlight, seemed to disappear into the night's darkness.

"Enter, healers, and be welcome. May I call someone to be of service?"

"Thank you, Acolyte. Please notify Healer Authority Riam that Mees Healer and Roose Healer have arrived, each with an Apprentice Healer."

"I shall do so. Please, be seated, she will be with you shortly." The Acolyte bowed and indicated benches for us to rest upon. "May I offer you a refreshing drink while you wait?" Her voice was soft, but even so, the high stone walls of the hall whispered a hint of echo back to us. She looked at each of us but before we could answer, another voice rang clear and sharp in the hall. It came from the silently opened door at which we waited, "That won't be necessary, Acolyte. I will take care of their needs for the moment. Please, be seated and await further instructions."

The Acolyte bowed, said nothing, and sat on the small seat just outside the door.

"Come in, my sisters. It is so good to see you again." The woman, whom I assumed was Healer Riam, towered above us. Tall, fair of skin with light eye patches, and slender as a cactus spine, her carriage bespoke authority. Her face was also scarred by tats, but a serene beauty shone through. Perhaps it was her manner? Her eyes lit with humor, and her welcome felt genuine.

Tems and I hung back while hugs were exchanged by the healers, as they greeted one another as much-loved old friends. Once the hugs and general greetings finished, Riam Healer turned toward us, "And you are?"

"Riam Healer, Authority, I am Jibutu, Healer Apprentice, from the Tribe of Jib," I could hear Tems swallowing.

Finally, after she looked at him and raised an eyebrow, he stuttered his name and quit before giving his tribe.

"Well, Jibutu and Tems, I am, as you now know, the head of this School of Healing, and am addressed as Authority. Welcome. We will have plenty of time to get to know one another, but for

45

now, please accept my welcome to our conclave. You must be tired, as well as dusty, and would like to see your rooms and get a bit settled?"

"Yes, Authority," we answered. She clapped her hands twice, and the Acolyte who sat outside the door came in.

"Acolyte Elen, please take these two apprentice healers to their rooms. They are from the desert, so I have assigned them to the tower rooms. Tems may room with Renld, and Jibutu may room with Anka. Please escort them, help them get settled, and then bring them to the dining room."

As we started out of the room, Riam Healer spoke again, her voice soft, but not to be discounted. "Acolyte Elen, please take our new apprentices by the *direct* route to their rooms, and the *direct* way to the dining hall. You will have plenty of time for new-comer pranks later."

"Yes, Authority." Elen Acolyte bowed, but I could see a wicked little grin on her face. She turned to the door and motioned us to follow.

As soon as the door shut behind us, I had to ask, "What was that about?" Already, the closeness of the walls bothered me. I wanted to stay in the school, but I also wanted to run back to the wide-open spaces of the desert. My breathing grew labored at the idea of being locked in a small tower room filled with dark and evil seen only in my imagination.

Elen held her finger to her lips and motioned us be quiet. She led us down the hall and up the stairs, down another hall, up a different flight of stairs, and finally, up a very steep and curved stair. "These stone walls," she said, "have more ears, and eyes, than you can believe. Quiet is expected here, but of course, none of us is all that quiet, unless one of the healers is about. We like to have our fun, and one of the pranks of which I am guilty is to take a very devious route to show new students the way to their rooms. Next I take them on another long and tortuous route to the dining room. And then, of course, I leave them to flounder on their own.

"However, since Authority now knows my weakness, and since I like you,"—she paused and made eyes at Tems—"I shall show you the direct ways. That's not to mean you're off the hook, you understand."

"Off the hook?" asked Tems.

"You know. The hook on which we hang our robes, and other things. You're still on the hook, so to speak, to receive pranks, and jokes, and the like."

"Oh. We should still expect something from you?"

"Indeed. When you least expect it."

"Why are desert folks sent to the tower?" I asked. "Is it a measure of disrespect? Are we to be prisoners?" I had heard campfire stories of people locked in towers for crimes they may or may not have committed. It didn't sound like anyplace I wanted to be.

"Oh, no! Never!" Her shock at my question seemed genuine. I began to relax. A bit. "It is a matter of highest respect," Elen continued. "You see, most of the desert folk who come are used to open desert, and most of our spaces are small. By putting desert folk in the tower, though the spaces are small, the windows allow them to look out a long distance.

"Depending on which side of the tower the room is located one may have a long view of the desert, or a long view of Yaylin, or the mountains. It is entirely for your comfort. Once you've been here a while, you will have a say in where you choose to room. You do not have to stay in the tower, nor do you have to have a roommate. That, too, is done for your comfort."

"How so?" Now, I was curious, and my breathing began its slow return to normal.

Elen smiled at Tems, even though I had asked the question, "Have you ever slept alone? In a room with no other person?" At our nods to the negative, she smiled again. "I thought not. It

47

can be a bit off-putting when you are used to sleeping where you hear others sleep, to suddenly find yourself in a totally quiet room. Also, your roommates will help you find your way around the school, and act as your guides until you have settled in. Eventually, it will be your turn to help new arrivals." We stopped at the second landing, where Elen indicated a door.

"Here, Tems, is your room. Go on in. You live here now. You will find your things inside. I imagine Renld is awake by now, and he will help you get settled. If not, leave your door open and when I come back down, I'll help you." She paused and smiled at Tems. He blushed, but did not look away.

Odd, I thought. He blushed.

Elen turned to me, "Jibutu, your room is up one flight. I'll take you, and if Anka isn't available, I'll help you." I wondered how much help she would be as she turned and smiled at Tems one more time before the stairs curved and we were out of sight.

"Then," Elen said, "we'll come back down, get Tems, and go to the bathing chamber together. Afterward, we'll go to the dining hall to meet again with Riam Healer, Authority."

Chapter Six

Face your fears or they will sink their claws
into your back and use you as a sliwa!
— *Jib, Tribal Leader*

THE DOOR TO THE ROOM ABOVE TEMS' stood open. Inside, a young woman, with light skin and wavy brown hair much like Tems sat at the table reading. I noticed Elen did not knock or wait for acknowledgement; she spoke as she walked into the room. "Anka, meet your new roommate, Jibutu. She's one of the desert folks. Jibutu, this is your roommate and mentor, Anka." Turning to me Elen said, "Anka's from the mountains. Now, let's get your things put away, and get down to the dining room. I'm starved."

"Thank you, Acolyte Elen," Anka said quietly "I will see that Jibutu gets to the baths and dining hall in time." She spoke softly, but with authority, and Elen hastily retreated. Thus were Anka and I introduced—and immediately all but forgotten, I'm sure—by Acolyte Elen.

My box sat next to my sleeping roll. Anka's things were on one side of the room, mine on the other; the open space between us contained a table and two chairs under the window. Spare though it was, the room exuded a comfortable hominess that seemed the direct result of Anka's calm demeanor and welcoming smile.

"Please, Jibutu, pay Elen no mind. She thinks more of her stomach than anything else. I hope you don't mind that I assumed the privilege of arranging your things, and unrolling

49

your bedroll for you. Your brush, stone, and writing skins I placed on the table. We can get you settled after our time in the dining room. Shall we go?"

At the sight of my bedroll, my body suddenly wanted nothing more than sleep. I could barely nod my thanks at her thoughtfulness and to indicate that, indeed, I was ready to again traverse the myriad steps to the dining room.

Recognizing my exhaustion, Anka said, "I know you are tired. I understand your days and nights have been somewhat tumbled with desert travel. We have a couple of things to take care of and then you may sleep. First, we must meet again with Authority and then I will take you to the baths, where you may have a long bath and receive your apprentice robes. You will be given two robes, and it will be your responsibility to keep them clean and mended. Apprentices wear sand brown, Acolytes like Elen, wear light blue, and Hopefuls, like me, wear white."

And so began my schooling. I scarce remember what happened after that. There is a vague memory of going to a dining hall where Tems and I were introduced to everyone by Authority, saying good-bye to Mother Roose, soaking in a hot bath, climbing the stairs, and collapsing on my bed for what I thought would be a long sleep. When I woke, the shadows seemed to have barely moved. I heard a light grinding sound, and looked up to see Anka sitting at the table, grinding her ink stone. She must have seen my head move, for she looked at me and smiled.

"Good afternoon, Jibutu. Did you sleep well? Here is a plate of bread, cheese, and fruit as well as a bowl of juice, which I fear is now cool rather than cold, but it should still be refreshing. Please—come, sit." She indicated the chair opposite her.

"I don't know why I'm so hungry. From the shadows on the wall, it looks like I slept barely an hour."

"Oh, Jibutu, you slept around the clock! Most arrivals do, which is why there is a plate of food and a bowl of juice waiting for you. From now on you will be expected to dine with the rest of us in the dining room. So eat your fill now, and when the sun goes behind the far dune, we will go down to eat our evening meal with the rest of the students and staff.

"While you eat, please look out the window. We have the best view possible, I think: the edge of the desert and the beginnings of the mountains. Which is why I placed your bed and chair where I did, so you cam easily see the desert. However, should you desire to change sides, we can do that. I am equally used to both views and love them both, though I admit I hold a stronger attraction to the mountains, green and wet."

Anka had pulled the table away from the wall so we could stand in front of the window. I had not noticed the mountains as we approached Yaylin, so intent was I on the city. "Neh! Never have I seen such dark greens. The oases where we stay have, of course, much green, but it is light and airy, not as dark as your forested mountains. Is it dark to live in there? Does the sun penetrate, or is it always like night? Can the moon and the stars be seen?"

"No, it isn't dark. It is cool and alive with birds and animals. The sun is not as bright in the forests as in the desert, but it shines through the trees and warms us. And the meadows are full of grasses and flowers, and also sun, though not as hot as the desert. You will get several opportunities to go into the forest, so you will see first hand."

"I will? How so?"

"We go into the forests as well as the deserts to harvest medicines, treat the sick, and become more knowledgeable of— and therefore more comfortable in—our world."

I finished my bread and fruit, and the juice. Though I offered some to Anka, she declined to join me. I looked around for a bowl of sand with which to scrub my hands and found nothing.

51

"Come, we will go to the bathing chambers, and then we will take the grand tour of the school. You won't remember everything, but you will have an idea of what is here, and where. Your classes will begin in a three-day and until then we will just wander and allow you to become familiar with the school and what is here.

We were almost a small city. The frontcourt, where we entered, was paved with desert stone. There were two more slightly smaller courts for the growing of herbs and plants. One was the wet court, where fountains danced and plants grew in moist dirt. The other was the dry court, filled with sand and desert plants.

"This desert court, or the dry court as we call it, is probably familiar to you. What might not be familiar is we also have White Snakes in here." She pointed to a raised enclosure holding sand and cactus.

"White Snakes? You mean the Lily Snake? Here? Where?"

I had, of course, heard of these snakes, though I'd never seen one. They burrow deep in the sand and are highly poisonous. If one smells lilies in the desert, one prepares to die. It doesn't always happen, but the only time lilies are smelled is when White Snake is near the surface, looking for food or moisture, both of which humans offer. Instinctively I pulled away from the enclosure in which they were kept.

"We have small ones captive. You will learn to see them and be near them. We also use their venom in some of our medicines. Some students learn to handle them, but no one is forced to, and no one is forced to extract their venom. Most learn to see them, or sense where they are, and move away."

Mother Roose did not tell me about the captive White Snakes. I began to realize Mother Roose had not told me much about School. As classes began, I realized how much Mother Roose had taught me about healing, just not the classes. Perhaps she did not share about School because until I had undergone the

Nights of Nectar, as I called them, she did not know if I would come to School at all. As it happened, I was far ahead of the other desert students, and sorely lagged behind the mountain students. Fortunately, classes were small, and training was individual.

Apprentices spend most of their time reading texts, taking tests, and working in the gardens. Apprentices weed, plant, and under the strictest of supervision are sometimes allowed to harvest and dry the herbs and roots. Acolytes learn to prepare the various teas, unguents, and tinctures. Apprentices learn theory; Acolytes begin to learn practice. Hopefuls often work unsupervised with the sick and help in the classroom as teaching assistants.

As healers, we need to know our limitations, and the final months of the Hopeful's schooling are geared to that end, or so Anka told me. Anka often left the school—sometimes for a few hours, sometimes for a few days—in the company of a healer traveling to homes or villages to treat those in need.

When they returned, Anka wrote a report of what she had done and what she had learned then turned gave it to the healer she had accompanied. A few days later, her report was returned, with comments as to what she did that was correct, and where she needed to improve. Anka saved her skins in a box and frequently brought them out to study along with her regular lessons. One of the first things I learned from Anka was to write legibly, and to save everything. Fortunately, Mother Roose had also insisted I write legibly and to save everything. I had a special box with all the skins I had written while under her tutelage. And all of her comments.

"You will have no problems here, Jibutu," Anka said, looking over the contents of my box. "I see Roose Healer has marked your skins much as your instructors will. It's quite a shock to many when they arrive, to find themselves and their work subject to constructive criticism. These skins will give you a good reference for many of your classes. Your instructors will be pleased."

As the months went by, I began to suspect there was another reason I had been given a room in the tower. I noticed that most of the newcomers were given rooms below, and most of those who had rooms in the tower were better students, and in the tower by their request. The tower was a place of quiet.

Tems had long ago requested reassignment to a lower room. I think he liked being closer to Elen. While affairs among students are not forbidden, they are not encouraged. It will not do for two healers to bond, as rarely will they be assigned to the same Healer's Tent. I feared both Tems and Elen were in for some serious heartache. The fact of sterility caused by the nectar of the Death Cactus, and the unlikelihood of being assigned together is why healers are allowed casual lovers, but denied permanent mates.

I was relieved that Tems had different classes than mine. We seldom saw each other, and when we did, he almost always had Elen with him. I wondered how much studying they accomplished by 'helping' each other.

Not, mind you that we in the tower didn't socialize and laugh and sometimes gossip among ourselves. We even, now and then, had a bit of the forbidden fermented juice to sip and share. Mostly, though, our conversations were limited to our schoolwork, to seeking help for our studies, or giving help to others. It was a quiet, studious life and I thought primarily of my education.

Sometimes the laughter from rooms below reached our room; at those times thoughts—like the thrust of a hot knife—of Mother Roose, of Jib, of my tribe, intruded, and I would look at my box for comfort. As Papa told me, I would be sad but only for a moment, and then happy with all the warm memories placed in and about the box. My box was the last thing I looked upon at night and the first thing I saw when I wakened in the morning.

We in the tower were not sucked into the petty squabbles that went on below. Somehow we stayed away from them and they did not attach themselves to us. Although not a clique, we tower-dwellers did tend to stay together. We knew and respected each other, and got along well. Few but us cared to climb the steep, winding stairs to our rooms anyway.

For me, life was peaceful and regular. My days started with bathing, breakfast, then lecture, lunch, study, dinner, more study and, finally, sleep. I enjoyed my classes, and my classmates, and kept to the rules most of the time. I did love the now and then prank or slightly ribald joke, but seldom received reprimands, and never from Authority. I didn't think she even remembered who I was and that was fine with me, so I was a little surprised when I received a summons to her office.

"Well, Jibutu, you have been here almost a year now."

"Yes, Authority." I stood, facing her desk. I didn't know whether she asked me a question or stated a fact, but thought it best to respond. I didn't *think* I had broken any of the major rules, but I wasn't sure. She was far more intimidating than Papa Jib. But then, I knew Papa Jib. Authority was—is—my superior, not my friend. Why had I been summoned? Was she going to accuse me of something? Neh! My blood began to chill.

"Please," she smiled, "sit," she indicated a chair at the side of her desk. "Relax, Jibutu. You are not in trouble. We are very pleased with your work."

I breathed deeply, centered myself, and relaxed.

"As you know, Anka has almost completed her time as a hopeful. And you have almost completed your work as an apprentice. Normally, hopefuls may take only acolytes and beginning hopefuls on their final exam journeys; however, Anka has specifically requested you be permitted to join her group."

What's this? Anka mentioned nothing of it to me. But I have seen a secretive little smile on her face now and then, as she glanced my way.

"I talked to your instructors and they have agreed that you should be allowed to go. Their primary misgiving is that you will miss your final exams.

"If you desire to attend Anka on her journey, you will take your finals early. Then, if you pass, you will be allowed to attend, wearing the robe of an acolyte."

I stared at her. I could think of nothing to say. I knew Anka was preparing to go on the journey, her final exam. She would take acolytes and hopefuls into the mountains, show them where to find the herbs and roots in the wild. She would tend whatever sick came to her, and teach the cohort as she did so, all the while being evaluated by two accompanying healers who would evaluate her ministrations.

I knew most of the cohort who would make these journeys had been acolytes for some time, or had just become hopefuls. For an apprentice to be invited was, as far as I knew, unheard of. It was a singular honor to be requested. I don't know how long I sat, thinking over the invitation before I became aware Authority waited for an answer.

I *hope* I thought with my mouth closed.

When lost in thought, I often open my mouth and breathe through it, as the sliwa do when contemplating whatever they contemplate. If I am thinking hard, I also rub my head. My head hurt where I'd been rubbing it. "If it please, Authority," my voice came out a squeak, "I would very much like to takes my tests early, and go with Anka."

Authority smiled and nodded, "I thought you might. So did your instructors. I shall tell them to prepare your examinations which you will beginning next five-day. Congratulations, Jibutu. This is, indeed, an honor."

As I rose to leave, Authority gestured me to remain a moment longer. "Oh, one thing more. Please keep silent about this. Word will filter down soon enough. It is not a secret, but...." Her voice trailed off as she smiled and shrugged.

"I understand, Authority."

"I knew you would. I have heard it said you avoid gossip and its siblings which is good. Healers should not gossip, nor should they brag. I think you will be a good healer, Jibutu. You might also wish to consider whom you would like as a roommate, or if you would prefer being alone for a while."

"Thank you, Authority."

Gossip flowed like an unbound river in the school, especially among those on the lower floors. Sometimes, it became bitter and disruptive. At least two acolytes, who enjoyed gossiping, were said to have been threatened with expulsion from the school.

"Anka, what would happen to them? They can't marry because they can't have children. What would they do? How would they live? Has anyone ever been expelled?" What I really wanted to know, of course, is what *I* would do, if someone started rumors against me and people believed them?

Anka thought a few minutes, "I don't know. Perhaps they could enter one of the public houses. Or perhaps hire into a family to care for the children. I don't think we'll ever know, for the two who were reprimanded have quieted. One has even asked to move into our tower. I do not know of anyone who has been expelled. I can't even think such a thing. Imagine, going through the ordeal of the cactus, and not being serious enough about your studies...." Her voice trailed off. Expulsion was an unfathomable idea.

"Is that good?" I asked, "I mean, that one of the gossipers is moving into the tower?"

"It will be good for her. And I doubt she will interfere with our tower routine."

The acolyte moved into our tower and was a delight to have. She and the other one seemed to feed on each other, and separating them had the desired effect.

Now, I had to concentrate on my studies and final exams. I also had to tell Anka I would be part of her cohort and get ready for her journey. I could worry about a roommate later.

Chapter Seven

The tisane of the Healer is the poison of the Assassin.
— *Roose Healer*

IF ANKA WAS NERVOUS ABOUT HER JOURNEY, she didn't show it, but I could hardly contain my excitement. Until now, I hadn't realized how much I missed riding a sliwa. Now that I knew I would make the journey with Anka, I longed with a sudden pain for their musky smell, their sun-warmed bodies, their smooth scales. I realized, deep down, what it meant to be a nomad, and I missed that life. It was time for me to move again.

Anka had a great deal to do to prepare for the trip; I watched everything and even took notes, for eventually it would be my turn to lead a group. I greatly admired her poise as she chose her cohort. Ten of us would make this trek into the forestlands. Anka chose the seven acolytes or hopefuls, but not the two healers who would accompany us. I thought perhaps she would choose her friends from the tower, but most of her cohort came from the lower floors. "I chose them," she replied in response to my question, "for their quickness of mind, and their dedication. Most in the tower have been on a journey at least once, and I wanted to take new people who I thought would get along well and support one another, and learn. I know some choose only their friends, but that is not my style." Anka had no say as to who the two Healers who would accompany us would be. They would observe and only step in if required. This was Anka's final exam. Would I be so calm on mine?

Anka also chose the pack animals. And supervised the packing of their panniers. I had seen the yama about Yaylin, but had not realized they were used as pack animals in the forests. I assumed the sliwa were used everywhere as beasts of burden. My heart dropped to my ankles when I realized we would not get to ride the sliwa. "But, Anka, could I not ride a sliwa?" She laughed at the whine in my voice.

"The yama are smaller and eat vegetation," Anka explained. "It is easier for them to walk the forest trails and to eat on the trail than the great sliwa. If we took sliwa into the forest, we would need to take goats, too. Besides," she smiled as she continued, "the great sliwa would have a hard time negotiating the steep and rocky paths. They are perfect for the desert. Yama are perfect for the mountains. They also climb rocks should our trail take us there and are much more nimble than the great lizards. Perhaps as important, they do not mind the closeness of the forest or the narrowness of some trails. The yama are perfect for this kind of journey."

Anka paused, and a twinkle glinted in her eyes, "They are vegetarian, but if provoked, they will bite and their hooves are sharp."

"May I touch one?" They looked soft and docile, like something a child would like to own.

"Yes," said Anka as she handed me a piece of fruit. "Here, give him this, and you will have a friend forever. Hold your hand opened flat and put the fruit on your palm, so he won't accidentally bite your fingers instead."

I held the ball of fruit on my open hand and held it out to the yama. He looked at me, then at the fruit. After what seemed careful deliberation he stretched his neck and daintily took the fruit. He chewed it slowly and deliberately, savoring the fruit and its juice. And, I hoped, the giver. When he had swallowed, I held out my hand so he could smell me and then gently laid my hand on his back.

The hide of a sliwa is dry and smooth. The scales are small and there is an odor of musk about them. The yama was covered in soft wool. I reached between his eyes, and gently rubbed. Sliwa will all but swoon when rubbed there, so I thought maybe the yama would like it, too. He began making a noise deep in his throat. I stopped, thinking I had offended him and withdrew my hand. With grace and gentleness, he took my hand in his mouth and pulled it toward him.

I had been here a year and had never visited the yama stables. The call of the sliwa pens was too strong, and those giant lizards brought me comfort when I missed home so much. I realized my self-knowledge was being limited by not going through all doors available to me, only through those doors I knew and was comfortable with. I vowed to change.

"You truly have a way with animals." Anka said. "The noise he made just now is not a warning, but his way of telling you he liked you petting him, and he wants you to continue. You'll know when they warn you—a glint in their eye, a curled upper lip, and no sound at all. You must be careful, or he will follow you like a pet. They rumble like that when they are happy and content."

I petted my new yama friend a bit more, and then followed Anka as we slowly made our way to our room to pack my things. The yama did indeed follow me to the gate, and cried—a pitiful, abandoned soul—when I closed it between us, said goodbye, and walked away from him.

"Jibutu, I suggest you take your brush, ink, and skins. You will see much that you will want to record. You also need your heavy robe as your bedroll. And your bowls. It is mild enough that we will not need blankets if we have our heavy robes to wrap in at night. We want to take as little as possible to leave more room for the medicines we will harvest."

"And we leave tomorrow?" Of course, I knew we would leave tomorrow, but I had finished my exams and as yet had no idea how well I'd done. Or not done. It seemed I would make this journey in the robes of an apprentice. I smiled as I contemplated the color of my robe.

"Anka, do you know yet who your advocates will be?"

"No, we will meet them tomorrow as we leave." There wasn't even a hint of trepidation in her response. I think I would be nervous beyond measure. I was nervous now and it was not even my journey of examination.

"Well, you are well liked, and I'm sure there will be no problem. Your work is good, and...."

"Jibutu, I have probably never met them, nor they me."

"But, Anka, you know everyone here."

"Yes, I know everyone here, but they will be coming in from the surrounding areas, I think."

"So, *that's* where Mother Roose went every now and then. She came here to advocate. I wondered where she went, but she never talked about it and I never asked. Well, I may have, but she had her way of smiling and saying nothing. Oh, Anka, maybe she will be one of your advocates. Wouldn't that be wonderful? To see her again, and to talk with her and catch up on the news of my tribe."

"Jibutu, should your Mother Roose be one of my advocates, which I sincerely doubt, you would not be allowed to speak to her. They come as observers only and do not talk with the students unless to save someone from harm. Don't look so forlorn. Authority just wouldn't put her with us."

By the time this conversation ended, we had walked from the stables leaving the crying yama to his misery. The noon meal was almost ready, so we washed and walked into the dining hall. A quiet buzz emanated from those already there. The usual jokes and laughter were either missing or subdued.

"Look, Jibutu. Authority and more healers than usual have seated themselves at her table! The advocates are here, at least some of them. Come, let's eat, I'm starved."

62

Anka seemed as hungry as Elen always claimed to be. Never had I seen two people who ate as much as Anka and Elen, and yet both remained thin. "This should be our heavy meal of the day. Tonight we should eat light, and tomorrow break our fast with a light and sturdy meal in the morning. We will walk far tomorrow and won't wish to be slowed down by over-full bellies."

We were somewhat surprised Authority did not address us; Anka speculated all the advocates had not yet arrived. After the meal, we went back to our rooms to finish packing. Everything I needed fit into my heavy robe, which I could tie and wear over my shoulder. Anka prepared a trail kit for emergency wounds, and filled a healer's box with medicines we might need to treat the folk we would meet on our journey of harvest. We took the healer's box to the stable, where it would be inspected before we left. "I hope this robe lasts for the journey. I have been patching the patches!"

Anka looked at my worn robe and laughed before speaking, "Perhaps, when we return, you will get a newer one."

That afternoon, we spent time with those who would accompany us. Those from the forests were quite excited to be returning to familiar territory. Those of us from the desert were mostly just curious. We grew up in the wide-open spaces, and I think we shared a bit of trepidation about going into the dark and close area of trees. We longed for the desert.

"Anka, will you also have to make a trek into the desert, or will this be your final exam?" I don't know who asked, but I was interested by Anka's response.

"This trip is my final," she said. "I have gone into the desert, and possibly will again, once I wear the purple robe of a healer. If I am successful, on our return, I will receive my purple robe and tattoos—and get my first assignment."

"Do you want to go back home, to be healer for your village?" Someone asked.

63

"I dream of it, sometimes, but the world is large, and I welcome the opportunity to see more of it. All I have ever known is my village and Yaylin. My friend, Jibutu, tells me there is much more to see."

We all laughed at that. Most of us had known only our birth homes and the school in Yaylin. For some, that is enough. But Anka likes adventure. As, I think, do I.

We drank our teas and talked together of our hopes and dreams, and soon it was time for the evening meal. Authority's table was filled with hooded healers whose faces we could not see.

Authority rose to address us. "Healers, hopefuls, acolytes, and apprentices, this is a special time for us all. Tomorrow many of our hopefuls will begin their final exams. They will act as healer and leader. Those of you who accompany them will do so to support them and to learn. Each cohort will be accompanied by two experienced healers to accompany them as advocates. Please, do not engage in chitchat with the advocates. Their job is to observe, and while their primary focus will be on the hopeful leading the expedition, they will also observe each of you, and their reports will convey information on all of you, individually and collectively."

That last caused a murmur, at least among those who had not yet gone on a trek.

"Enjoy your meal," Authority continued, "and get a good night's sleep. Tomorrow and the next few days will be long and difficult, but I have faith all of you will do well."

Authority sat, and we finished our meal, somewhat subdued and thoughtful. That we would all be watched was something we first timers had not considered, though it made perfectly good sense. I wondered what the advocates would think of a brown robe in Anka's cohort. Although I was sure I passed all my exams, I had yet to receive my blue robes. I smiled as I thought how easy it would be to spot and report on me.

"Jibutu?" At my name and a gentle touch on my elbow, I turned. There stood Acolyte Elen, "Authority would like you to attend her this evening, an hour after meal is finished."

Had an order ever been more gently given? "Please reply to Authority I shall be honored, and will be there at the appointed time."

Now what? Was I not going to be allowed to go with Anka? Had I failed my exams? Why would she want me? She had already told me I would get my robes at a later date. I didn't care about the robes—at least that's what I tried to convince myself— I just wanted the education. I wanted them both. And I wanted to go on this trip. I looked at Anka. She had heard, I was sure, but her face was still and impassive. The old fear of expulsion tied my stomach in a knot.

"I suggest, my friend, that you have everything laid out and ready to pack as soon as you return from your summons."

"Then, you don't think I am being pulled?" I'm sure the fear in my voice was thick enough to spread on our breakfast bread.

"No." Anka hesitated before continuing, "I don't think so. I'm sure she would have told me first. Have you been bragging about going? Perhaps...."

"Anka! You know I have not bragged. It has been hard keeping my excitement in check, but I have done so. Several students know, or think they know, but not from me."

"Well, then, let us bathe and enjoy the water one last time before our trek. Then, you will be shiny clean to meet with Authority."

My hair was still damp when I approached Authority's office an hour after the end of dinner. I caught my reflection now and then in the highly polished stone of the walls, and could see sparkles where the light caught errant drops of water nestled in my curls. My curly black hair looked as if I wore a net of nighttime stars. I thought about my birth mother, and the net she placed upon me before she died, and wondered again who she

65

was, who *I* was. My robe was clean, though patched (almost all the apprentice robes were patched, as were most of the acolyte robes. The hopeful robes seemed to be in better shape. Perhaps they did less physical work? Or their families bought them new ones? I hadn't thought of it before. What a silly thing to think of now.

"Jibutu, Authority would like you to await her in this side office." Elen opened a door and I walked in to a small office that held a small desk and several lights. A carafe of tea stood next to a plate of light snacks. A healer stood with her back to me. When she heard the click of the shutting door she lowered her hood and turned to face me.

"Mother Roose!" I immediately stepped into her outstretched arms. "Oh, it is *so* good to see you." To my embarrassment, tears began to flow down my cheeks and great sobs racked my body. She held me until I regained control, and then we sat to talk. Until that moment, I had not realized how much I missed both her, and my tribe.

"Daughter, you are a coolness to these old and dry desert eyes. I have missed you, as has everyone in your tribe. Yes, I returned to the Tribe of Jib, and all your family sends their love.

"Authority tells me you are doing well, in fact, exceptionally well. I understand you are going out tomorrow. That is a singular honor, for an apprentice to accompany a harvest trek."

"I was requested, Mother Roose. By Anka, the hopeful—she is also my roommate. And I was allowed to take my final exams a week early, so though I will be attending as an acolyte, assuming I passed my exams, I will be wearing the sand robe of an apprentice." I grinned, "it will make it easier for the advocates to see and report on me." We both laughed.

"I won't keep you long, Daughter, but wanted to see you for a bit before we all leave tomorrow. I don't know if I will be able to see you when you return. If my cohort finishes early, I will leave immediately upon our return, and will not be able to await your returning."

"I understand, Mother." When I called her Mother, it hit me deep within my heart; part of the price we pay to become healers is that we can never be mothers. And though we can raise up apprentices, I think the bonding is seldom as strong as the bond between Mother Roose and me. We truly *were* mother and daughter. How many can say they have had three mothers, all of whom loved them?

"Authority will not be able to keep your appointment, and she requested I present this to you." Mother stood as she talked, and walked over to a box. She reached into it, and pulled out a blue robe. "Daughter, please remove your sand robe, and allow me to place the blue robe of acolyte upon your shoulders." Now, there were tears in her eyes. Tears of happiness and tears of pride in my accomplishments. When I saw her tears, mine began to flow as well. Never had two people been as happy as we.

We visited a few more minutes and as we were parting, a knock sounded at the door, and then Authority came in. "Aah, Roose, I see you found her. I hope you don't mind that I couldn't be here.

"You look good in the blue, Jibutu. Congratulations. Now, it will be more difficult for the Advocates to single you out." We stood about for a few more minutes, talking. Then Mother Roose handed me my heavy second robe, and I was dismissed to finish readying myself for the trek.

When I opened the door to our room, there stood Anka and the others who made up our cohort. They cheered when I came in, hugged me, and offered their congratulations. They brought a bit of fermented juice and some biscuits and we had a small party in my honor.

"You knew, didn't you?" I later queried Anka from bed.

"Yes. I knew. But I was sworn to secrecy. It has not been easy, Jibutu, keeping a secret from you. Again, I congratulate you. Now you get to wonder what your next assignment will be. Acolytes are used in various ways, as you know."

"Do you think I'll be assigned to Elen's duties?" I could think of nothing worse than being constantly at the beck and call of Authority. I wondered if Elen would ever finish her education and become a healer, or if she would forever be an acolyte, and at Authority's beck and call.

"No, I doubt that. You will more likely be assigned to help one of the healers in class, or perhaps in the gardens. That will be one of the things the advocates will report on, in your case. Who knows, maybe you will be assigned to the stables to muck stalls and work with the yama. I'm sure one yama in particular would be very pleased to see you."

My last thoughts as I drifted off to sleep were of my birth mother. She no longer seemed intent on stealing my name, or giving me a different one. Perhaps she knew I was happy? Perhaps she decided to leave me alone? I didn't know, but I felt she loved me, and was grateful I lived. I wondered if ever I would know her name or her people? Neh! Fate can be a cruel

Chapter Eight

Even the sliwa knows loyalty to a good master.
— Unknown Hunter of the Desert

THE MORNING AIR HELD A BIT OF CHILL as we latched the shutters to our window. Our little room grew dark, but would be safe against any sand storms that might blow in from the desert in our absence. Anka and I carried our packs downstairs to the dining hall for breakfast. This morning we ate with our cohort; the advocates ate with Authority. We would not know who our advocates were until we waited in the courtyard with our yama and panniers. Then they would arrive, introduce themselves, and go over everything Anka had prepared and packed. We would not leave until they gave permission.

The front courtyard held several knots of people, some with yama, some with sliwa. The yama danced their nervousness at the closeness of predators; however, the sliwa had spent the previous night gorging, and showed no interest in the yama. Anka led our cohort to an area where we put all the panniers on the yama. We left the medicine box and other supplies we would take with us on the ground, waiting for the Advocate's inspection.

"Good morning. I am Stietz Healer, and this is Ayres Healer. We will be your advocates for this journey. Please continue your conversations, we enjoy them."

I looked up, startled, as I had not heard their approach; nor had I considered they would also be listening to everything we said. The two advocates smiled.

69

"Stietz, don't tease so." Ayers was shorter than Stietz, round, and plump. Her cheeks glowed pink under her eye patches and tats, and her face showed many laugh lines. Stietz stood a head taller than Ayers, and didn't appear to have anything but her robe covering her bones. Never had I seen such a thin person, yet she appeared healthy, and her eyes glowed with humor. I hoped they would bring that humor with them on this journey.

Anka stood to acknowledge their arrival. "Good morning, Advocates. I am Anka, the leader of this cohort. This is Jibutu, new to the acolyte's robe," Anka smiled, and introduced the rest of us. "I believe I have everything we need; however, I would appreciate your verification and, if anything is not entirely correct, your instruction."

We had already strapped the panniers on the yama, and Anka had checked every one. She tightened straps here, loosened them there. And she saw to it that I had the yama who had earlier adopted me. "He will follow you anywhere," Anka reminded me, "and carry anything for you. Just give him a fruit every day, and a rub between his eyes."

Our advocates seemed pleased with their inspection of our cohort; we were among the first to leave. Because of my excitement, I was only vaguely aware that some of the cohorts had been held back. Later I discovered their advocates thought the medicine boxes had not been properly packed, or the amounts of medicine were wrong for where they were headed.

Anka led us out the main gate of the school, down the street, and then right at the second crossroad. Each of us held the halter to a yama, except for the advocates, who walked behind us. We each carried our belongings rolled in the heavy robes across our backs. Even the advocates carried their own robes and necessities. The panniers were for medicines and supplies—and only for medicines and supplies.

Though excited about the adventure, we remained somewhat subdued by having the advocates with us. We weren't sure of our role, of what we were expected to do or not do. Except for Anka, this was the first journey many of us had made and we just weren't sure how to act. Soon, the advocates began singing school and trail songs that helped to set the pace. We relaxed a bit and joined in.

The road was wide, this close to Yaylin, and we walked two abreast. We stopped by a stream at midday to water the yamas and to eat our noon meal.

"We will be leaving the road soon," Anka explained, "and when we do, the trails will be dusty. So no one remains in the back all the time, I ask that we rotate the leaders. I don't think it necessary to set a schedule, but when it is time, and you will know, the one in front may step aside to let the others pass. That way no one will always be in the back to breathe in all the dust."

We turned off the main road shortly after lunch. The dirt road we traveled was wide enough for us to continue two abreast, as long as no one came from the other direction. Fields flanked the road, with farmhouses scattered here and there, most set back from the road and surrounded by trees. Children ran to the road to stare and shyly wave. Some walked a bit with us, but never for long. If their mothers didn't call them back, we sent them home.

That night we slept in a farmer's field. He was delighted to allow us his field in return for the examination Anka gave his family. The rest of the family was fine, though one child had an infected toe. Anka treated the infection, gave some of the medicine to the mother, and explained and showed her how to apply it.

The next morning we were loaded and traveling before the sun cast first shadows. By noon we had entered the edge of the forest. The trees held moisture in the air, which seemed thick and made my breathing difficult. The farther into the forest we walked, the closer the trees grew to each other. Although the sun

71

now and then came through the trees, it was gloomy and damp. That night, we slept in a small meadow. I decided I did not particularly like the forest. I noticed the other desert dwellers in our cohort also seemed to have difficulty breathing, and we all hunched our shoulders as tightly as possible to make ourselves smaller as we walked through the trees. I wasn't at all sure some of those towering trees wouldn't fall on us. Anka and the rest seemed unafraid, and even seemed to enjoy the coolness and closeness of the trees. I did not share in their enjoyment.

"Good morning, my sisters," Anka greeted us. "Today we leave the road and follow the trail at the far end of this meadow into the mountains. We seek the following medicines and any others we might come across. If you see any, please sing out and let us know." Anka read off a list of medicinal plants. "We will go in single file now. Again, I ask that you take your turn in the back. If you see any other plants we can use, please, sing out. We are not limited to our list."

The trail was narrow; the trees banded together tight and dark, and seemed determined to squeeze the life from us. Shadows seemed to swallow the air. I soon found myself hunched like an old and crippled crone, to make myself as small as possible, and the air about me larger. It was comforting to see my sisters in front of me, and I soon ended up in the last spot, happy to be there. I did not mind eating the dust, or stepping around yama plops. What I minded was being in the forest. I walked with my mouth open, panting like a sliwa while I rubbed my head. Hard.

"Look! Cacia trees. A whole grove of them." I did not know when we left the tightness of the forest for the lightness of scrub brush and I don't know who saw them and sang out, but we all headed through the brush to get to them. The brush clawed at us and the cacia trees extended their thorns to impale us. As we had been taught in the school, we carefully cut away the rough bark, just so deep, so as not to harm the trees. Working helped relieve the tightness in my chest, though not much. My hands and arms shook as I plied my knife.

We carefully wrapped the pieces of bark we removed and placed them in a pannier. For our hours of labor, we seemed not to have acquired much. Anka led us back to the trail, and we ate our lunch in a small meadow. The sun felt good to my sun starved body.

"Jibutu, you do not like my forest, do you?" Anka sat beside me.

"No, Anka, I think not. It is so close and tight in here. I feel like I am stuffed back in my mother's womb and can't find my way out. It is even hard to breathe."

"I am sorry. Will you be able to continue?"

"If I do not face this fear, it will suffocate me. Yes, Anka sister, I can and will continue." Brave words, but words only. I questioned the wisdom of my intention to continue through several more days of this. Already, I did not want to continue. I wanted to stay in the meadow and never leave it.

"Good." Anka placed a bit of jer root in the palm of my hand. "Here, chew on this. It may help calm you, and will at the least calm your stomach."

Chewing raw jer root is like chewing a piece of solid flame. It burned and brought tears to my eyes, but my stomach calmed, and so did I. A little.

Anka rose and went to talk with the other desert dwellers in our cohort. There were three of us. I saw the advocates watch her, with approval in their eyes. They saw that Anka cared for her sisters and for our well-being.

We climbed through the forest until we were above it, on the meadow and shale side of a mountain. Here we found quine bushes, more jer plants with roots to harvest, and several bushes loaded with sil berry. Anka cautioned us not to take everything, but to leave some so the plants would grow and produce more for the next harvesters. Also, the sil berries were food for the

73

woodland beasts and we did not want to deprive them of their food. At least, she continued with a smile, not all of it.

I loved the mountaintop. It was like a green and gray desert open to the sky. I decided if I could get to the mountaintops, I could suffer the forests. But truly, I do not understand how anyone could choose to live in such a damp, dark, and dank place where the air is always thick and filled with flying motes. I swallowed hard as we began our descent from the open, sunny mountain back into the forest.

"The trek down will not be as long as the trek up." Anka called back to us. "Our panniers are full, so we will not stop to harvest. For those who love the forest, breathe deeply as we pass through. For those who are still deciding, well, we should be back on the road by day after tomorrow. Your ordeal is almost over." At that we all laughed, even the advocates.

We were gone a ten-day. It took us a seven-day to reach the mountain meadows and fill our panniers, and a three-day to get home. The weather held the entire time, until we entered Yaylin. Then the rains began. At first they were welcome, but when they turned cold, we were grateful for the shelter of our school.

The advocates watched as we unloaded the panniers, and then combed and fed our yama. We sorted the medicines and set them on the drying racks. Only after the medicines and the yama were taken care of did Anka dismiss us to bathe and wash our robes. I wondered about washing mine. I only had two, both filthy. However, on entering the bathing room, I saw fresh robes had been put out for all of us—lightweight and heavy.

Never had a bath felt so good. Each of us groaned as we sank into the hot water. Soon, we began to massage each other's feet and we all began talking at once. For the first time since we left, the advocates weren't with us. For the first time in a ten-day, there was no tension among us.

We scampered out of the bath when the evening meal bell rang. Suddenly, we were starved. Our excitement at making the journey, and being home, erupted from us as laughs and giggles. Even Anka. I don't know how the others slept that night, but I slept as if dead. If I dreamed, I do not remember.

⤛ ⋎ ⤜

"Jibutu, my sister. I passed. I passed!" Anka threw her composure to the sands and danced with joy. She grabbed me and we twirled and danced. "Now, I must decide on my tattoo designs. Will you help, my sister? With my tattooing? Oh, please, say yes."

So much for putting my notes and drawings from our trek into some semblance of order. I put everything in my box and joined in her merriment and excitement.

"Help with your tattooing? I have never seen it done. What would I do?"

"You will burn the cacia bark, pound it to powder and, as the artist cuts my skin, you will rub it in. Please my sister, do this for me?"

"I shall be honored to help with your tattoo ceremony." Honored, yes. Scared to death, most definitely.

"Jibutu?"

"Yes," I absently responded.

"Don't rub your head so much. On our journey, I feared you would come home bald." Anka smiled, but it was a serious sort of smile.

"Neh," was all I could think of to say.

All healers of school are tattooed with the school emblem, a healer's box, on their left cheeks. For their right cheeks, they may choose a design of their own. Many choose herbs or leaves, but that design is personal, and is registered in the Great Book. No two healers may have the same design. They may choose the same herb or medicine, just a different view of it.

Anka is such a pretty woman; it seemed a shame to deliberately disfigure her face. Healers are allowed beauty only in their hearts. Women must not be jealous of a healer when she

75

treats a husband or lover. Men must not lust after a healer. It is something we all know. But, still, it seems such a waste.

The day of Anka's tattooing dawned gray and miserable. It rather fit my mood, truth to tell. Anka would have her ceremony today, and in a three-day she would receive her assignment and leave. I would have our room to myself, at least for a while. I felt as if a part of me were being excised and tossed away—another great loss. I am very selfish. I loved Anka sister almost as much as I loved Mother Roose. And I was a little frightened. Never had I slept more than a few nights alone, and then only here at school, when Anka was gone.

Anka's ceremony would commence an hour after the morning meal. I was called to Authority's office after breakfast. She took me to the tattooing chamber and introduced me to the Tattoo Mistress, Healer Stietz, one of Anka's advocates.

The tattoo chamber was a small court on top of one of the school's many roofs. I had not been up there, indeed, had not known of its existence. A roof covered most of it, supported by columns. A stone bed stood in the center, with counters and various accouterments at the head of the bed. Why was the tattoo chamber outside, I wondered? Why so open to the elements with only a roof overhead?

"Welcome, Jibutu. Yes, you recognize me," Healer Stietz said. "It is tradition that the advocate who passes a hopeful also acts as Tattoo Mistress. I shall help you prepare the cacia bark, and Healer Ayres will do the actual cutting."

At the pharmacopia, I chose the bark under direction of Healer Stietz. We then returned to the chamber where I shredded the bark and placed it in a shallow cooking dish. A low fire burned under the dish and I stirred the bark until it had roasted a deep black purple. Now I understood why the tattoo chamber has no walls. Roasting cacia bark gives off a most unpleasant and pungent odor. It took most of the morning to get the bark to the desired color. I placed it in a stone bowl and with a stone pestle

ground it to a fine powder with no lumps. While I worked,
healers came and went. They attached curtains to the sides of the
roof, brought knives and needles, wines and medicinal teas and
juice drinks. They put a cover on the stone bed and a neck rest to
position Anka's head and hold it still.

They also brought Stietz and me something to eat so we
would not have to go back into the dining room.

"Jibutu, when Healer Ayres tells you she is ready, you must
take a small amount of the powder you have ground, on this
spoon, and sprinkle it where she directs. Then dip your hands
into the quine leaf tisane, here, to purify them, and gently use
your fingers to rub the powder into the cuts. This will hurt, but
you must ignore Anka's pain. You are learning to bear the pain of
hurting others, as she learns to bear the pain a healer must, at
times, inflict."

Anka chose a jer root as her personal tattoo. "Can you think
of anything uglier than a twisted, knotted jer root?" she asked. "If
that doesn't scare away lust, then nothing will." I helped her
draw the root so it twisted over her cheek and down her face.
The pigment of her eye patches would turn the scars white, the
color of the roasted bark would stay only on her lighter skin.

When our preparations were done, Anka was led into the
tattoo chamber, wearing a sheet wrapped about her. She bowed
to each of us and thanked us for our help and participation. She
lay on the bed and nestled her head into the rest. She closed her
eyes for a few moments, centered herself, then opened her eyes,
smiled up at us, and calmly announced, "Please, begin."

Scarring skin is not easy, even when done deliberately. Anka
had taken nothing to help with the pain, and she had to lie
perfectly still. Healer Ayers used a new glass blade to scrape the
skin of all hair, no matter how fine, before she began to make
many tiny cuts, each just deep enough to draw blood. Then, she
put the blade into a bowl of strong quine leaf tisane. Each time
she placed the knife in the bowl, I sprinkled the cacia powder on

77

the new cuts, then dipped my fingers into another bowl of strong quine leaf tisane, and gently rubbed the powder into the cuts on Anka's face. I rubbed in some of my tears, too.

When we finished, I was as exhausted as the Tattoo Mistresses. Anka's face was a horrid mess of scabs and powder and swelling. She would not be able to wash her face in water for a three-day, only in a milder tisane of quine leaf. It would burn, but would set the tattoos and stave off infection.

Anka stayed on the slab bed for a few minutes before she gingerly reached for my hand. "Sister, please help me sit." A moment later she stood. It was then I noticed the courtyard was full of healers.

Authority approached Anka, removed the sheet from around her and placed a new, purple Healer's Robe over her shoulders.

"Healer Anka, welcome. We have waited long for your arrival. A feast has been prepared for you." Only then did I notice the foods, wines and teas that had been placed on another table. "Please, Healer Anka, sit in this chair, and allow me to serve you." Authority escorted Anka to the chair of honor, then went to the buffet and brought a plate back for her. "Please, helpers, serve yourselves," she invited the advocates and me. As soon as our plates were filled and we moved away from the buffet, everyone else joined in.

The thin glass knife that Healer Ayers used to cut into Anka's skin had a small hole in its handle. Now Healer Ayers removed it from the quine tisane where it had been soaking since we finished. She dried it, and placed a leather cord through the hole in the handle. She turned to Anka, bowed, and placed it around Anka's neck. "Healer Anka, this blade that brought you pain is yours. As you have survived the pain, you now know others will survive whatever pain you may have to inflict in your duties as healer. Wear this knife with honor."

The three-day passed in a whirlwind of emotions and activity. My sister prepared to leave. She had her assignment; she would go through the forest, across the mountains, to a town on the southland border where she would be the Assistant Healer. I think there was a bit of disappointment in Anka's posture, but it was hard to tell. "Oh, Jibutu, I would have liked almost anyplace. I hear Michlin is almost as large as Yaylin, and like Yaylin, it, too, is a border town. I also hear there has been only one healer there for many years and that I will be her first assistant."

"Are you frightened? I mean of working with a healer you've never met?"

"A little. And a little frightened of the long journey. But more excited than anything. Oh, Jibutu, I'm a healer. And soon you will be one too!"

After arriving at Yaylin, I sought further instruction in the art of carving. I found a red rock, similar to my bowl, and worked on it in secret just for this occasion. I had carved and polished a drinking cup for Anka, waiting only for her to choose her personal design so I could finish it. Now, I carved a twisted jer root, the same design as on her cheek, onto the outside of the cup.

"That is beautiful, Jibutu. Anka will treasure it always." Healer Chelle watched as I finished the last of the polishing.

"Thank you, Healer Chelle."

"Have you shown your work to Authority? I think she would be most intrigued."

"No, I haven't. I never thought she'd be interested. I just do it for my pleasure."

"Authority is always interested in the ways in which healers deal with the stress of their jobs. Some of us compose music; some write poetry, a few carve. Your carving is exquisite."

"Thank you." I didn't know what else to say, and was glad when Healer Chelle smiled and left. I hurried to find Anka.

"Anka, sister. I found a red desert stone, nearly the same color as the one from which I carved my bowl of life. It was too small to make you a bowl, so I carved this cup for you." It shone like a red mirror, thin enough that it glowed red when light came to it from above. "Do not cry, Healer Anka, on the desert, red is the color of luck and life."

"Jibutu, sister, it is the most beautiful cup I have ever seen, or will ever own. Thank you so very, very much!" We embraced and held each other, until the tears stopped flowing.

In a single swift move, Anka dropped a necklace over my head. "Here. I made this for you from forest stones and woods I collected on your first journey with me." Before I could thank her, or speak, she was gone.

Someone asked if I would like to move to a lower room and smiled when I said I preferred to stay. I liked my tower room. It was quiet, and out of the maelstrom of petty arguments that seemed constantly to flow and swirl about the lower floors.

I began to understand the affair between Acolyte Elen and Apprentice Tems. It would be heart wrenching for them when they were finally separated, unless they did it of their own accord. Given the slow pace of their studies, it could take quite a while. Perhaps something would happen and they would break apart on their own. That would be better—Elen was still an acolyte, and Tems still an apprentice. Rumor had it that the time they spent together was not entirely used for studying the Medicinal Arts of Healing.

I was alone for the first time in my life. Surrounded by friends and family of choice, I was truly alone. The new experience needed savoring in solitude. I would trust the right person would come to be my new roommate.

Chapter Nine

Fight for your disabilities and they will become yours
forever.

—*First Healer of Yaylin*

ANKA'S DISAPPEARANCE FROM MY LIFE left a huge hole in my
heart. Her going away hurt as much as my going away must have
hurt my family; however, the luxury of mourning did not avail
itself. I had a two-day in which to sleep and prepare for my new
classes. As an acolyte, I would begin to put into practice what I
had learned in earlier classes. My favorites were in the
Pharmacopia and Surgery. I loved the smells of the medicines
and the intricacies of the surgeries. Of course, I would not be
allowed to operate until I became a Hopeful, and then only if I
wanted to, and had the "touch." But I would be allowed to
suture in the near future.

We did not have any new apprentices, so no one moved into
the room I had shared with Anka for so long. My room became
the gathering places for others. Anka and I had developed a
code, which I continued to use and my sisters and brothers
continued to follow. If the door stood open, all were welcome
to enter. If the door was closed, I preferred to be alone, but they
could knock and then enter. No one took advantage, and because
my room remained quiet—well most of the time—several of us
gathered there to study in peace.

I had not dreamed of my birth mother since my arrival at
the school. Indeed, I seldom thought of the fourth night dream,

or of her. By the time I fell into sleep at night, I was too tired to dream—or if I dreamed, I did not remember. My sleep was deep and restful. I knew of no way to find her, except through my dreams and I gave up trying; why expend the energy on such a useless worry, neh?

A hot wind blew from the north, "Breath of the Sliwa" we desert folk call it. The wind carried the smell of hot metals and desert dust. The Sand Drum sounded its low, rhythmic warning to shutter all homes and businesses. The dust still found its way into buildings. Not even the prison, or its infirmary, could keep the unwanted dust and sand out.

"Good morning Healer, Hopeful, and Acolyte." Lengo Ja, the healer at the prison greeted us as we hurried through the door. "I'm very grateful you came through this wind."

Healer Wicksing laughed as she removed her outer cloak to shake the sand onto the floor. "Why, Lengo Ja, you know it would take more than a little wind to keep us away, especially Acolyte Jibutu. She is from the desert and informs me that this is hardly worth the worry. Why, she says, it is barely a breeze. What do you have for us, this fine morning?"

"First, a bowl of tea to wash the dust out of your throats, and then the usual. I managed to treat the more serious wounds as they came in, but there are several lacerations, the usual stomach ailments, and what appears to be a broken bone or two."

Anyone caught fighting within the city walls was brought to the prison. There, the Healer would treat the more serious injuries, and the next day, a group of at least three would come from the school to treat the less serious injuries. Mostly, we treated the headaches caused by too much fermented drink. One time in prison was usually enough to deter repeat fights, but there were those who seemed to want to prove something to someone—if only themselves and soon after their release, would get drunk, get in another fight, and come back to the prison. Each time through the front doors meant a longer sentence out the back door and into the mines.

Healer Lengo Ja stood taller than any man I had ever seen. He was tall, and broad, and extremely strong. I am told his personal scar had once been recognizable as a cactus, but now his face also wore knife scars from some of his prison patients. Before he asked Authority for the position as permanent Healer to the Prison, several men died of their wounds before the healers arrived, for Authority would not allow healers or students to be there without armed guards. Lengo Ja's size alone seemed to bring the men to their senses. Although his strength was that of legends, I have never met a gentler, more compassionate person.

"So, Acolyte, how much practice have you had in stitching people?"

"None, Healer, I have practiced on fruits and tanned hides, but not on people." Was he going to let me help? My heart skipped a beat at the thought.

"How did you do?"

"I think I did all right. My stitches were small and neat and neither the fruits nor the hides complained."

At that, he laughed. His face crinkled into the oddest contortions due to the heavy scarring that looked like refracted sunlight, not something to frighten small children.

"Well, Acolyte Jibutu, I think today is your day to work on a person. We have a light load, and I understand several children are sick in the Flower Market area. If you would like to stay and help me, the others can go on down to the Market and get started."

I would get to do something other than watch! "Neh! I would like that, Healer Lengo Ja. Yes, I would like it very much."

"Good." At his nod the group I had come with turned and left. From remarks heard on the walk to the prison, none of my

83

fellow students wanted to go there. Most of the prisoners were dirty, smelly, and crude. In many cases, they were also violent. However, I had never had a problem working with them. I thought most seemed ashamed to be seen by healers in such a setting. Especially, I think, they were shamed at being seen by women healers.

"There are three men waiting. One was in a knife fight with another man, one came home too late and his wife cut him, and one, well, we don't know what his crime was. He was found on the street, with a gash on his head. Was he robbed, or what? At any rate, they all need stitching, and will be good practice for you."

On entering the surgery, I saw two men sitting on their cots, with their backs propped against the wall, and the other man stretched out, flat on his back. That one held his head and moaned, but was not conscious. The two who were cut seemed in distress, but nothing like the other man.

"Healer, Mem, please, fix 'im first. His cries is bad." The dark-haired man spoke; the other man nodded in agreement. I said nothing, but walked to the smaller, lighter man and checked his wounds; they could wait a bit, as could the wounds of the dark haired man. As soon as I touched the third man, 30,000 bees seemed to swarm from his head up my arm. I swayed but did not fall.

"Jibutu? Are you all right?" Healer Lengo Ja stood next to me, a steadying hand on my arm. At his voice, the bees vanished.

"Yes. But this man is not at all well. He has a serious head wound and his brain is swelling. We must get his head raised, and see what we can find. He doesn't know what happened. His last memory was walking to his home, and then the pain."

Lengo Ja looked at me, not quite trusting, "How do you know this?"

"Because of my fourth night dream. Something happened, and I changed. All I know is that sometimes I can touch a person and it feels like 30,000 bees race up my arm, and I know things about that person."

The two wounded men looked at me with big eyes, then they looked at Lengo Ja. "I don't want 'er stitchin' on me!" They both spoke at once and pulled away.

"Not to worry. I have already touched you, when I looked at your wounds, and no bees raced up my arm." I smiled at them, hoping to reassure them. I really did want to stitch their wounds.

"She's going to stitch you. I have my work cut out for me with this man. So do as she says."

"Would you like me to help you prop him up?"

The Healer laughed. I had forgotten he was so large and strong. "Thanks, but I think I can manage. However, when I lift him, you could put some pillows under his head and shoulders, if you would."

Once propped, we could more easily see his wound. Carefully, I cut his hair away from it, and gently washed the blood off. "Healer, it doesn't look like the skull has been damaged. Perhaps we could put ice on his head to help with the swelling? And keep him sedated?"

"Good choices, Jibutu. What shall we sedate him with?"

I mentally ran through a list of sedations, with their side effects and finally had to admit I didn't know.

"Excellent. You know your limits. You will do the purple robe proud. Here, make a solution of this powder in quine leaf tea, one dip of powder to one bowl of the tea. We'll try spooning it down him, but if he can't drink it, we'll make a wet poultice for the wound."

When I finished mixing the powder with the tea, we applied the poultice. Whatever the powder was, it quickly entered his blood through the open wound, and he became noticeably quieter. I found out later the powder was dried venom of the lily snake. The drying of the venom released much of the poison, but what remained could be used as a sedative and painkiller.

"Now, gentlemen, it is your turn." I smiled at them, and approached the first with a bowl of clean water, and a bowl of strong quine leaf tisane. In the second bowl rested my needle and the thread. I reached for the first arm, and just as I grabbed it, he jerked and screeched. I couldn't tell if it he yelled from pain or from fear.

"Ser. I assure you, I cannot, and will not, read your mind. I am here to stitch your wound and nothing else."

"But, Mem, you read 'is."

"Yes. No. I didn't read his mind; I read his injury—unlike you, he couldn't speak to tell us what was wrong. Now, this is just plain water I am going to wash your wound with. Healer Lengo Ja will stand right here and watch me. Should I do anything incorrectly, he will step in, so you have nothing to fear." While I talked to him in as soothing a manner as I could, I also held his wrist, and washed his wound. It didn't look serious, it was not deep, and I saw no foreign matter in the wound. "Will you hold your arm still, or do you want me to strap it down?"

His eyes widened, "It gonna hurt?"

"Yes. Some. It will sting more than hurt, but you cannot move."

"Strap it."

Not only did I strap his arm, I gave him a rolled, clean rag to bite on. He fainted at the first prick of the needle.

"You did a good job, Acolyte. Both on handling the men and on stitching the wounds."

"Thank you."

"Now, let us have a tea in my office, and then—"

Before he finished his sentence, high-pitched bells started their clamor. At first they were far away, then closer and closer. I had never heard them before, but from the look on Lengo Ja's face, I could tell it was serious.

86

"Fire! We must hurry!" He placed his hand on my shoulder and turned me toward the door. He picked up his medical box as we left his office. Outside, people ran and screamed.

"Holy Boran!" I looked in the direction Lengo Ja faced, where the sky had turned black with smoke. "The Flower Market! Hurry!" We ran into the mayhem of a flaming, smoking hell.

The Flower Market was the poor section of town. The few buildings were made of old, dry wood. Most dwellings were barely shelters made of felts, hides, or palm fronds. It was a warren of alleys, a stew of disease, poverty, open flames and cooking pots. It was where my sister Healers and students treated the poor in return for payments of flowers, ribbons, or a smile and a hug. Anyone who needs treatment gets it, and everyone receiving treatment pays what he or she can.

"Jibutu, here. Tie this over your face." Lengo Ja handed me a rag he had wet in a fountain. "Breathe as little of the smoke as you can." I looked, and his face was hidden behind a rag. "Come." His hand on my shoulder guided me through the throng of people running in the opposite direction.

"The Market." I gasped. "We must get to the Market. That's where our clinic is. That is where people will gather."

"Make way! Make way!" No one argued with Lengo Ja as he walked against the tide of frightened, fleeing people. "What makes you think any will be there?" His voice was choked with the smoke.

"Because," I said, "the poor have nowhere else to go but to the healers. These people who are leaving do not live in the Market area. Look at their clothing. They are not abandoning their homes, they are going *to* their homes to make sure they remain safe."

We reached the Market area, and found the clinic. "You were correct, Jibutu. I have spent far too much time in the prison."

When we reached the open market, we found the acolytes separating the serious from the minor injuries, with the healers and hopefuls doing the treating. There weren't too many burns, mostly just fear, and several bruises and scrapes where people fell in their panic to get to the clinic.

The smoke became noticeably thicker as we worked, and light pieces of ash began to drop on us. Also some small embers that floated down had to be put out before they could start another fire. Because of my late arrival, I was on the outside edge of the clinic. Lengo Ja quickly moved to the center of the group, where his presence was welcome. Some of the acolytes held children, trying to calm them.

"Come!" I felt someone tug at my robe and looked down. "Come," he demanded, "Mama not get up." A thin, dirty child pulled at my robe. Tears puddled on the lids of his eyes. "Come. *Now.*" He pulled harder and I followed thinking wherever he led, it would be near. We went closer to the conflagration. "Come. Close. Hurry."

He led me to a shelter, just beginning to burn. "Mama *there*," he pointed to a corner where a woman lay on a pallet.

"I'll go. You wait here. Better, you go back to the clinic."

"I stay."

There was no time to argue, I ran into the shelter, which quickly filled with smoke. She tried to crawl, but couldn't. "Help me. My legs won't work. I can't move."

A board had fallen on her legs. I reached to move it, "You must crawl when I lift the board. You must!" I barely got the board lifted and she managed to pull herself out from under it. "Can you stand?"

"No. Maybe. Help me," and then she screamed. The whole shelter seemed to explode in fire and noise. The force threw me on top of her. My right arm flung out as I fell, burned. Never had I felt such pain. I lost consciousness in the roar of the red and deafening silence.

The desert oasis. Hot sands. Burning sands. Cool water-fed date palms. Peaceful.

"Aaiiiyaaaahhhh!!!!" A woman screamed. Alone. No, she gave birth. A baby girl. Me. I know it's me. My birth mother was alone, as Papa Jib had said.

"Oh, my baby, I have no milk." I suckled, and whimpered.

Her head. It was bald, and tattooed with stars and strings.

I floated above my mother and me. The heat of the sun was unbearable. Who was this woman?

The sun rested on the crest of the dune. There was no shade.

The woman dozed, and woke to find men about her, one was Papa Jib. Nearly dead, my birth mother handed me to Jib. As she did so, she placed a star-filled net over my head. Her throat dry, she tried to speak, even as the sun rolled down the dune to take her.

"Her name! Her name is....

"Teh...!

"Teh...?

"Tiiiiiii......" The name changed, and then burned away with the flames of the fiery sun as it rolled down the dune, covered my mother and burned away her life.

"No!" I screamed, and struggled to reach her. "No. Mama. Come back. What is my name? Who am I?"

"Jibutu? You're all right now. You're safe." A known voice drifted through the dream.

"Where am I?" I struggled to move, and couldn't. "Where am I?" I screamed louder? "I can't see. Who are you? Where am I?"

"Jibutu. Shhhh. You are in the Infirmary. It's me, Elen. You're safe now."

"Elen? Why can't I see? Why can't I move? Why am I *here*?"

89

"There was a fire, and you were injured. You are safe, now. Here, I'm going to give you a bit of tea in a spoon. It will help. There. Rest. I am here."

I felt a cool hand grasp my left hand and hold it. Soft murmurings of reassurance found my ears.

I slept. Safe, free of pain, free of dreams and fear, then I woke. As sudden as the dawn on my beloved desert, I woke to the fear and pain of fire. My eyes were held shut, my right hand and arm burned with living fire. My legs were bound, my right arm was bound, and someone held my left hand.

"Where...?" My voice sounded like the croak of a water thumper.

"Jibutu, you're awake? You're safe, relax. I'm Healer Chelle. Be still, now, and I'll get you some water."

I relaxed, a little. I felt her arm go behind my head and lift it, and then I felt a cup next to my lips. I drank.

"Slowly, Acolyte, or you'll spit it back."

I sipped. But I drank it all.

"Why am I here? Why does my right hand hurt so?"

"Do you remember the fire?"

At her question it all came back to me. "The woman?"

"She is fine. She is just down the hall. Her wounds were slight, thanks to you. She has asked about you every day."

"Her son?" I remembered the boy, pulling my robe, urging me to hurry to his mother.

"Jibutu, there was no child. She said nothing about a child."

"Ask her. He came to me at the clinic and pulled me to his mother. He was about four. He did not come in? Oh, surely, he survived. Please, tell me he survived." Panic began to cover me, an unwanted blanket on a hot night.

"I will ask."

"Why am I bound? Why can't I see?" Questions tumbled out of me so fast Healer Chelle could not get a word in.

"Jibutu! Hush a moment, please. And listen."

90

I closed my mouth.

"If you will not fight, or grab for your bandages, I will remove the ties. You struggled so, we feared you would cause yourself more hurt; that is why you were bound." As she spoke, I felt her hands at my legs, and then the bindings fell away. "Your head is bandaged because of the explosion. The pharmacope did not know how badly your eyes were damaged, if at all, so she bandaged them until you wake, when she can do a proper examination. She will be in later, so be patient. Your right hand was severely burned, it must remain as it is until, until it is examined."

"How severely burned? I want to do surgery. Will I be able to?"

"Jibutu, do not start with the questions now. You are safe, and need to rest. Here, drink a bit more water and sleep again."

This water held a sedative, but I drank. I was too thirsty to refuse, and I wanted back into that pain-free darkness.

Chapter Ten

If you tell yourself you are limited—you are!
— *Jib, Desert Leader*

WHEN NEXT I WOKE, my hand still burned, but not as badly. On top of the burning I now had to contend with the itching. And they would not allow me to scratch it. My eyes were still bandaged, but I was no longer tied down. Having given my word to not disturb my right hand or my bandages, I almost asked to have my hands retied, as the itch seemed to increase in ferocity by the minute.

"Hello? Is anyone here?"

With no answer to my call, I carefully searched the table by my bed with my left hand until I found the cup. This time, it contained a sweetened tea. I still held the empty cup when a cacophony of herb smells assaulted my nose.

"Pharmacope! You've come to remove my bandages!"

"Ah, I should have known I couldn't sneak in. How are you feeling this evening? Here, let me take the cup."

"This evening? How long have I been here? I think I'm better, but my hand still burns, and now it itches. And these bandages on my head also itch."

"How long? It's been a few days since the fire, let me think...oh, the fire was...yes, you've been here a four-day."

"Four days? I've been in bed for four days? Neh!"

"Ah, well, yes. Yes, you have. But you're healing now, so, well, let's see about removing the bandages over your eyes. But, first, I need to get Authority. She asked to be here. Don't go anywhere, I'll be right back."

Don't go anywhere? I'm blind, don't know where I am, where did she think I'd go?

Not two minutes passed, and the pharmacope returned. "Jibutu, Authority is here."

"Acolyte Jibutu, I am delighted you are feeling better. I need to tell you something before we take the bandages off. Here, hold my hand." Authority stood next to me, and took my left hand into hers. "Let's get you sitting. Hopeful Elen, will you gently move her right arm, so she can sit with her legs over the side of the bed? Thank you."

So, Elen was here, too. And she was now a Hopeful. "Hello, Jibutu. I'll try not to hurt you as we sit you up, and move your arm. It is on a board, so I will move the board, and not touch you."

When I sat, I smelled the pharmacope behind me. Authority held my hand a little tighter. "Jibutu, I must tell you, your right hand was damaged beyond saving. Actually, it had been burned off."

Before I could react, pharmacope began to remove the bandages over my eyes. "Jibutu, I don't think your eyes were seriously damaged—if at all—but as I remove the bandages, if the light hurts you or you feel any pain, please let me know, and I'll stop."

I could not speak. My hand was gone, and maybe my sight? My brain whirled. Bandages dropped.

"Jibutu, can you see light?"

"Yes."

"Does it hurt?"

"No."

More bandages were unwound. Again, the question; again, the answer. At last, I looked upon the face of Authority as she stood, still holding my hand. My left hand. My only hand. I blinked, several times.

"Acolyte, can you see?"

"Yes, Authority. I can see. I see you, and the concern on your face." I turned my head, "And I see acolyte, I mean Hopeful Elen and the concern on her face." I turned a bit, "And I see you, Pharmacope, with the big smile on your face."

"Very good. Would you like to sit in the chair for a bit?" Authority's face lost some of the concern. "Here, let me tie this sling on for you." She then helped me to the chair.

"Elen, will you get Jibutu a meal from the dining hall? I imagine she is starved. We'll stay with her until you return." Authority turned from Elen back to me.

"I am truly sorry about your hand. We had to remove it above the wrist. When the explosion came, it knocked you on top of Mali, and a burning timber crashed onto your hand, breaking the bones, and searing the wound."

"Mali?"

"The woman you saved."

"Her son. Is he all right? Has he been found?"

Authority and pharmacope looked at each other, then pharmacope spoke. "Jibutu, Mali's son was four when he died two years ago. She has no other children."

"But," I stammered, "I saw him. He spoke. He pulled my robe and told me to hurry. That his mama was trapped and needed help."

"Mali has no idea who pulled you to her, but she is most grateful you came. And most saddened by your loss."

Elen returned with a meal and broke the silence.

"I told the cook the food was for you, Jibutu. She fixed a special bowl of stew, and two sweets for dessert." Elen smiled as she placed a tray with a bowl of spicy stew, two huge sweets, a carafe of my favorite fruit tea and a flower blossom on a long stem on the table by my chair.

"Jibutu, Pharmacope and I must leave. Elen may stay if you would like company. If you need anything, ring this bell." The two healers walked to the door of my room, stopped as if on the same stick, and turned to me. "You will be fine, Jibutu. It will take time, but you will be fine." They smiled and left.

"Oh, Jibutu. I'm so sorry. You don't know it, but Tems has been here every day, and, well, almost everyone has been by to see you. Now that you're awake, you'll see."

"Elen, congratulations on becoming a Hopeful. When did that happen?"

"The day after the fire."

I looked at the bowl of stew. It smelled of home. I picked up the spoon with my left hand and realized I had no idea how to eat. "Elen, if you don't mind, I think I'd like to be alone while I eat. I'll ring the bell when I'm finished." Elen understood and left me to make a mess eating with the wrong hand. Tears of grief and anger and frustration streamed down my cheeks as more stew went *on* me than *in* me. Exhausted, I rang the bell. Stew seasoned by tears is not good.

"Please, tell the cook her stew was perfect, and thank her for the sweets. If you don't mind, I'd like to go back to bed. I'll keep the sweets for later." Elen cleaned me, helped me into a new gown, and into bed. At my request, she propped me with pillows, so I wasn't lying completely flat. "Elen, do you know how long I'll be here, in the infirmary?"

"No. But now that you're awake, and can see all right, I imagine it won't be more than a few days."

"Thank you."

"Jibutu, if you need anything...."

"I know," I sounded petulant, even to me. "Ring the bell. I need my hand back. If I ring the bell enough, will it grow again? Neh! It won't." She didn't know what to say, looked at me with pity and left.

95

I have no idea how long I lay there, staring at nothing. If anyone stopped at my door, I closed my eyes, and they kept going. I did not want company. I wanted my hand back.

Would I still be allowed to become a healer? Would I be sent home? If I went home, what would I do? No one gets by for nothing in the desert. Doubts and questions and fear raced through my mind in an unending circle, faster and faster. I drank more tea. I picked up a sweet, but couldn't eat it. And then the stew came back before I could reach a bowl. Covered in my hot and now stinking dinner, I had no choice but to ring the bell and put up with the ministrations of my well-meaning caregivers. Again. *I* was supposed to be the caregiver; *I* would be the healer. Somewhere in the back of my mind, I knew I would learn some lessons from this, but right now my anger bubbled at the edge of my being.

✙

"I'm sorry, Jibutu. I know you prefer being on this side of the bed. But, look at it this way—you will now have more empathy for those *in* the bed." Elen smiled as she finished getting me into another clean gown and back into bed. I'm afraid I was not a good patient. I glared back at her.

"I'll bring you something else to eat. Something not as spicy as cook's stew."

"Don't bother. I'm not hungry. Just go away, and leave me alone." I knew when I said it that I was being petty, but I didn't care. My world continued to turn and heave and roll around me.

"I'm here, all night, if you want company." Elen smiled as she patted my shoulder. Where had she learned such caring? When had she learned it? It couldn't have been while at the beck and call of Authority, could it? At that thought, I added one more fear to the miasma that swirled about me. Would I be consigned to Elen's old job?

I wore my petulance like a prized robe. I indulged in self-pity. I snapped at anyone who came into my room, anyone who dared offer me sympathy. I did not understand the difference between sympathy and pity. People soon left me alone with my anger, my frustration, and my fears.

Chapter Eleven

When one path is lost, another will appear.
—*Grandin, Caravan Master*

I HAD TO FACE REALITY, though not a reality I wanted to face. My right hand was gone. The good news was the fire cauterized my wound. The bad news was the fire caused my wound.

The hand that no longer existed burned and itched and nearly drove me mad. I continued to be sullen and angry, and when a shadow so much as crossed the door to my room, I closed my eyes and feigned sleep. I wanted to see no one. I wanted to return to my desert and die.

Alone, I would look at the place where my hand had been and will it to grow back. I imagined it growing. My wrist ached, and I was sure the ache was proof the bones were beginning to regenerate. That's all I wanted—for my hand to grow back, though I knew it wouldn't. I wallowed in self-pity. Why? Why me?

"Do not pretend to sleep, Acolyte Jibutu. I know the difference between those who truly sleep, and those who pretend. I will tell you the secret, if you would like to know."

Caught. I opened my eyes at the strange voice, and saw a short woman, almost as wide as she was tall, smiling at me. Her purple robe seemed as big as a healer's tent pitched next to my bed. "Who are you?" I demanded, with no manners at all. "What do you want? Go away."

"Ah, I am Hakka Healer, from Michlin."

"I don't recall ever seeing you."

"That's because you haven't. I don't get over here very often. Michlin is on the other side of the mountains, almost the other side of the world, actually, and until a second healer came, I never thought it prudent to come such a distance, and be gone for such a time, leaving my people without a healer."

"Michlin? That's one of the larger cities, isn't it?" Something besides pain and anger tugged at my drugged mind. Michlin? I knew it, somehow.

"Yes, it is second in size only to Yaylin, and on the other side of the mountains. Like Yaylin, it is a border city. Where Yaylin borders the desert, Michlin borders the Grasslands—and the Great Lake. Also, as in Yaylin, we have mines."

"Good. You have a place to go back to." I shut my eyes.

"We have a tree in our area—"

"Good!" I snapped. "I hope you guard it well." I turned over, and groaned with the sudden pain. Boran! Would this chatterbox never leave me in peace?

"Acolyte Jibutu, your manners are terrible. However, as a healer, I'm used to pain bringing out the worst in people. Now, you may do your best to anger me or ignore me, but I'm not leaving until I'm ready." I could hear the smile even as she scolded me.

"As I was saying, we have a tree, we call it Yellow Bark, for the color of its bark. I have brought cuttings, from some of those same trees for our gardens here at the school, but more important, I have brought the bark from some mature trees." She paused. I continued to ignore her. "The bark makes a healing tisane that can be applied, or even drunk. It is most efficacious when applied to burns and wounds, hurries the healing and lessens the pain."

"Will it make a hand grow back? Can it do that?" I shamed myself with the petulance in my voice.

"No, Acolyte. It cannot cause a limb to regrow. Not even the Shamans of the Grass can accomplish that."

Groaning with pain, I rolled back to face her. "Shamans? You know shamans?"

"Why yes, of course. Why?"

"What are they like? I've been told they are, well, that we are not to associate with them. Why?" My fourth night dream came back, and I wanted to know about these shamans.

"So, I have your interest, eh? And you are more interested in shamans than in the tisane. Well, I'll make a bargain with you. If you will allow me to unwrap your stump and place it in this bowl, I will tell you what I know of shamans." She did not wait for my answer, but had my stump quickly unwrapped, and soaking in a bowl of deep purple liquid.

"I thought the bark was yellow?"

"Oh, it is. But when heated, the liquid becomes purple. The deeper the purple, the stronger, more effective, the tisane."

"I admit it feels good. My hand, the one that isn't there, doesn't hurt so much."

"Good. If you will leave it there for a while, I'll tell you what little I know about shamans. My good friend, Lu Shahnnah, is one," she paused, as if collecting her thoughts. "The shamans are People of the Grass, and in their own way, are also healers, though most of them take drugs to walk the God Paths, as they call them. They claim to see hidden roads and forgotten secrets."

"Why do healers dislike them?"

"Ignorance. Generations ago, healers thought shamans were frauds; shamans thought healers were ignorant. Why this interest in shamans?"

I paused. I didn't know this woman, and yet, felt I could trust her. "After my fourth night dream, I was sure I told Healer Roose I was to be a shaman-healer. She claimed I never said the word shaman. If not, it was certainly in my mind. When I asked about them, she told me they were charlatans, and not to think of them again."

"I see," Hakka chuckled. "I suspect Roose has never met one. Come to think of it, I doubt if anyone but the healers in Michlin have ever met a shaman."

"Michlin! Now I remember! That is where Anka went, as healer. She is *your* assistant!"

"Oh, yes. You're right. Here, hold your stump in the liquid, while I get your letter." She reached around and pulled a pouch from her belt and began to go through it. "Aah, here it is." She pulled out a piece of red leather. "Anka bought this leather in the market, and made this envelope for you. Her letter is inside."

"The leather is beautiful." I ran my hand over it. It was smooth, polished, and not sliwa. The sides were neatly stitched, and the flap that folded over to close it was cut in an asymmetrical design. A sliwa had been tooled into the leather, and in his mouth was the clasp.

"She did the tooling, too."

I held it, and tried to figure out how to open it with one hand. I refused to ask for help. Hakka Healer continued to study my stump. I placed the corner of the envelope under my rump, and used my hand to slip the thong off the button the tooled sliwa held in its mouth. Inside was a piece of skin, with Anka's writing on it.

Dear Sister Jibutu,

I was so excited when I heard Healer Hakka was going to travel to the school, leaving me here alone. My first thought was to write you a letter, and when I asked, she said she would deliver it to you. Now I am at my desk, after a long day, and not sure what to write.

The trip over took forever, or at least it seemed to. We took the low roads, through the deep and dark valleys, but the guides say there is a high road that is slower, more in the open, with wonderful views. I think you would like the high roads.

101

Michlin is on a mountainside riddled with mines. The Healer's House looks out over a vast and wonderful panorama. Below and to the right is grassland as far as one can see. It is like the desert, only covered with grass instead of sand. Instead of sliwa, they have giant beasts, called buflo, that eat the grass and give milk to drink and use for cheeses, meat to eat, and hides for leather. I found the leather for the envelope in the market, and thought of you and life and red.

Looking down and to the left from Healer's House is the Great Lake. Again, it is so large I can see no opposite shore. People live on boats on the lake, and travel all over. They even have gardens on their boats! Sometimes they travel alone, sometimes families and even villages will tie their boats together to form a bright floating island. (Hakka does not like going on the boats as they move up and down, which her stomach does not like. I love the boats and the people, so I treat them whenever they need it.)

Oh, Jibutu, how I wish you could be here. While you might not like the trip over, I think you would love the town and the people and the lake and the wide, open spaces.

Please, write a letter back to me and give it to Hakka. Tell me all the news and the gossip. Are Tems and Elen still together? How many newbies are there? Are you enjoying surgery as much as you thought you would? Oh, I miss you so much.

Love, Anka Healer, your faraway sister"

➤⠂⠄⠶⠷⠶⠂⠄◄

"Sad news, Jibutu?" I looked up, and Healer Hakka looked at me with such love and sympathy that my tears fought to gain their freedom, and I fought to hold them in.

"No. Yes. Did you read her letter?"

102

"Of course not. It was not addressed to me." The shock in her voice would have knocked me off my feet, except I was already off my feet. Shame flooded through me.

"I'm sorry. I'm being quite the yama plop, neh? She asked if I'm enjoying surgery as much as I thought I would. Of course, she has no knowledge of, of...." And that was when I finally began to cry.

Hakka Healer smeared purple salve I assumed was made from the Yellow Bark, over my stump and wrapped it in soft cloths. She then held me in her ample arms until my tears were reduced to sobs, my sobs to sniffles, and my sniffles that finally lost themselves in the first real and natural sleep I'd had since the fire.

⤞⟶ ᐁ ⟵⤝

The fire of my burning stump reduced itself to an ache, with only now and then bites of the fire ants, or what felt like bites of the fire ants: quick, sharp pains that ended almost before I registered their pain. They came less and less frequently, and the pain began to lessen in intensity. I slept, ate, and let Hakka Healer change my bandages. Elen and Tems were frequent visitors, as were the students from the tower. My hospital room soon became the study room of choice for many of my friends.

"Tomorrow, I think you will be discharged, and after a three-day of rest in your room, you may begin your classes again."

"Thank you, Hakka Healer. I look forward to the classes. At least, I think I do."

"Oh," said a new and deep voice, "I'm sure you will." I looked up to see Lengo Ja at my door.

"Lengo Ja Healer, come in. This is—"

"Hakka! My goodness, it's been years. How are you? Why didn't I know you were here?" Lengo Ja stooped in the door to my room.

103

"Why, Lengo Ja, for heavens sake, look at you. I thought you were a healer, not a fighter. Gracious, look at those scars!" Hakka Healer fairly ran to meet him.

They embraced, obviously old friends. I managed to keep my chuckles quiet—Lengo Ja, tall and muscular, and Hakka, at least as wide as she was tall. Standing next to Lengo Ja, she barely came to his waist.

"Well. Well. I will leave you to visit our patient, but I will wait for you in the dining room. We have much to discuss, Lengo Ja. Yes, much."

Never had I seen anyone as flustered as Hakka seemed. Both she and Lengo Ja blushed. Had they, like Elen and Tems, been lovers? I sighed, I would never know, and it wasn't my business. Still, for the second time since the fire, my curiosity was piqued.

"Acolyte, I have brought a friend, Weets Nier. Perhaps you remember him." Lengo Ja came into my room, followed by a man of average height, his head shaved, a red scar along one side, with neat stitches marking it at intervals. I did not remember him.

"Greetings, Acolyte Jibutu. I understand I owe my life to you and your...ah...*touch*. And I thank you too, for your neat stitching of my scalp. When the healer told me of your, ah, accident, I asked to see you in person."

"I'm sorry Weets Nier, I didn't recognize you. How is your head?"

"Very well, thank you."

"Jibutu, Weets is a metal worker. He was on his way to an appointment when someone saw fit to rob him of his tools and money. That is why we had him in the prison clinic that day. And, that is why he wishes to speak with you."

"I don't understand."

Weets passed his hand over his scarred head. "Acolyte Jibutu, I believe I can make you a new hand. It won't be a hand with thumb and fingers, but I think we can design something you can use—just a two-part hook, at first, one you can learn to use to grasp and hold things. Then, perhaps, we can work to design and make more, ah, intricate and useable tools. Healer Lengo Ja says your, ah, heart is in surgery, and I see no reason why, with some extra work and lots of extra practice, you can't fulfill that dream."

Chapter Twelve

The desert sings of sorrow, if one will only listen.
The desert sings of joy, if one will only listen.
The desert sings of life, if one will only listen.
—*Children's Song from the Desert*

LIFE AT THE HEALER'S SCHOOL CONTINUED. Weets Nier worked with the healers to devise a hook to replace my hand. For me, the hardest part was getting used to the cable system I had to put on every morning I wore the hook. Plus, I had to retrain my muscles, so I could pull and contract the cables to open and close the hook. It would take a while, but I could see that once I had it mastered I would be able to once again study surgery—or at least stitch lacerations.

I was assigned to the pharmacope, and helped the healer in charge prepare the medicines.

Crash! The bowl slipped from my grasp, shattered on the floor. I left the mess and slammed out of the room. My stump, too tender yet to apply pressure while wearing the hook, could not get a firm grip on the mortar while I tried to train my left hand to use the pestle.

I stomped to the gardens—two hands are not needed to pull weeds and in pulling them, I learned to use the hook to gently hold the plants while I cut them. Weets was working on a scissor hook, and I looked forward to trying it. He has spent many hours following me around, watching how I used the hook, seeing what modifications he might make. Soon, I would have a chest full of specialized hooks. He had wanted to tool intricate designs in the hooks, but I convinced him the designs might catch and hold diseases, so he made them plain and lightly polished. However, the boxes he made for each one—there his artistry shone.

As I pulled weeds, and thought about my new hooks and hands, my frustration died. I returned to the pharmacopia to clean my mess and began, again, to grind the herbs. I ignored the quiet smiles of those who watched me.

Once I became proficient with the tools of Weets Nier, my time was once more divided between the pharmacopia and the surgery, and my days remained full and busy. I went each seven-day to the prison, where the mornings were spent helping Lengo Ja and training his assistant, Mali, the woman whose life I saved when I lost my hand.

Mali could not read, and though Lengo Ja tried to teach her, she said she too old to learn. Still, she had a memory like the jaws of a sliwa closed around its dinner. Tell her something once, and it was hers. She couldn't be left alone with the prisoners, but her presence seemed to calm many of them, and she performed whatever tasks we asked with dispatch and professionalism. And, I think, she loved Lengo Ja.

My instructors allowed me to experiment now and then. I had to think out the problem, write it in either my right hand scrawl as I learned to hold the pen, or my increasingly proficient left-handed scribble, state my reasons for the attempt and the results I expected. Many times my experiment failed, but sometimes one worked, and we would have a new medicine, or a new procedure. My instructors remained patient with me, they encouraged me, and they were there to ensure I harmed no one, including myself.

By now, the fire ants only came once in a great while, usually in the middle of the night as I slept after a particularly long and grueling day.

"Jibutu. You need to learn *gentle* firmness." Pharmacope smiled as she anticipated my reaction to my next project.

107

"Practice picking up the eggs from this basket and moving them to that one."

I reached for the first one, expecting a hard and brittle shell, "They are soft, neh?"

"Yes," said Pharmacope, "these are the unfertilized eggs of the white snake. The shell is more like leather than like the brittle eggs of birds."

"Unfertilized?" At my question, she finally laughed. "If I break one, no snake will come out?"

"No. No snake."

As I reached for the last egg, my shoulder itched, then twitched, and I clamped too hard. The egg burst, making a mess on my arm, my robe, and my hook.

"Relax, Jibutu. I'll get a rag and help clean you." Pharmacope always had clean rags at hand. I relaxed and let the cables fall from my shoulders. Pharmacope removed the hook to clean it. I took another clean cloth and began to clean my arm.

"Pharmacope? Look!" the white of the egg soaked into my skin. "It is poison, neh?" I feared the snakes so much I now fought hysteria.

"No, we use it in some medicines. Look, Jibutu, where it has gone in. Your skin looks different. Why, it's growing scales. You're turning into a—"

"Neh!" I shrieked, grabbed the cloth and scrubbed as hard as I could as I ran to get sand for a decent washing. It was then that I looked and realized she joked. I looked back at her, doubled with laughter, and stormed to my room. It was, of course, a joke I would have pulled on someone, given the chance. Elen would have loved it.

That night, Pharmacope came to the table where I ate with friends. She had my hook and cables with her.

"I must apologize, Jibutu," she began, loud enough for everyone at the table to hear, "My attempt at humor this afternoon was both thoughtless and cruel. I have cleaned your hook and cables. Please accept them, and my sincere apology."

I looked from Pharmacope to my tablemates then back to Pharmacope. She was almost in tears. I stood. "Pharmacope, it is I who should apologize for my tantrum and for running away as I did. I am truly sorry. Please, accept my sincere apologies."

"Why, then, I'll forgive you, if you'll forgive me."

We laughed and hugged and she walked away to eat with her friends, as I continued with mine.

"Jibutu, what happened?"

"Tell us."

"Please?"

"Why, you just heard. No need for more. Besides, it is time for dessert."

That night, my wrist didn't hurt. No twinges, and not a single fire ant of pain.

"Pharmacope, I would like to practice with the eggs again, neh?" This time, I was more careful and moved them from basket to basket and back again without mishap. "Please, may I rub some more egg into my stump? Last night, for the first time since the fire, it didn't hurt at all."

Pharmacope massaged the egg into my stump daily, for a ten-day at least. As she did so, she noticed the muscles were developing, regaining tone.

"After dinner, Authority would like to see you in her office."

"Please, Apprentice, tell her I will be there." The young man inclined his head and left me. Now what, I wondered.

On entrance to her office, I found Authority, Weets Nier, Lengo Ja, and Pharmacope, all seated. There was one empty chair.

"Please, Jibutu, the chair is for you." Authority smiled, then continued, "Weets Nier, would you like to explain?"

"Ah, me?" He seemed somewhat surprised, and a little embarrassed.

"Yes."

"Ah, well, Jibutu, I heard about how the egg white soaks into your skin. It reminded me, ah, of something I heard or read a long time ago. And, ah—" Weets Nier paused, took a sip of tea, and began again.

"Years ago, the man who taught me told of someone who, like you, lost a hand. That man, in desperation for relief, smeared snake egg on the stump. He figured it would either, ah, cure him or kill him. Either was fine by him. But, ah, it soaked in." He paused again.

"Then he asked a friend to make him a cuff of untanned white snake skin, thinking it would dry and shrink to his stump and keep the sand and dust out." Weets Nier stopped talking.

"Well, man," Lengo Ja spoke, impatience in his voice. "Tell her. Go on, now."

"Oh. Ah, yes. In fact, the cuff did grow to him, and his friend made another cuff, an outer cuff, of tanned snake skin to hold his hooks."

"Neh! It *grew* to him? It became part of him? Part of his skin?" I had never heard of such a thing. But then, I'd never heard of the unfertilized eggs making muscles grow, either.

"Yes."

I whispered my next question, "Did he need the cables?" I didn't breathe until Weets told me the answer.

"Ah," Weets Nier stopped and smiled at me, "No."

"Sand didn't get under the cuff and cause sores?"

"Ah, no."

I looked about me as the information sank into all of us, but mostly me. I could barely speak, my voice squeaked, "Me? You want me to do this, neh?"

They all nodded yes, then everyone spoke at once.

"Only if you want to."

"No guarantee—"

"It's your choice."

"Think it over."

A two-day later, Pharmacope massaged my stump with another egg. Weets Nier fashioned a cuff from the skin of a young and fresh-killed white snake and fitted it around and over my stump. He then wrapped it in a clean cloth soaked in more egg

Again, my wrist itched. I could feel the skin growing to me. It wasn't painful, but certainly not pleasant, either. A five-day later, Weets Nier declared it a success and fitted me with a new outer cuff of tanned snakeskin and a collection of changeable hooks.

It took time to master the new hooks, but not much. Truly, it was almost like having my hand again. No longer did every move require careful and conscious thought. I could move my hook as easily and unconsciously as I had moved my hand.

Days became weeks became months and somewhere in that time I gained my hopeful's robe and regained my sense of humor. The time arrived for me to choose and lead my own cohort to harvest medicines and treat those who requested it. Of course, I had led others, but this time it was my final exam. With great joy, I received my assignment to the desert, though I wasn't sure how much of the desert I still remembered.

"Tems? May I have a minute of your time?"

"Of course, Jibutu. Congratulations, on your forthcoming journey." Tems did not seem all that happy. As I looked at him, I realized he has not appeared happy for some time. Where I had been in my white robe for a year, he still remained in blue of an Acolyte.

"Thank you, Tems. It is my journey I wish to discuss with you. I am being sent into the desert, and would appreciate your

111

company. I hadn't realized it, but the cohort I chose are all mountain people, and I could use a desert-wise hand to help as needed."

"Will...will Elen be coming, too?" I couldn't tell if he was excited at the prospect of showing her the desert, or excited to be finally away from her. They had been a couple for so long that Authority confided in me that if this journey didn't break them apart, she did not know what she would have to do. Never, in all the time she had been a Healer had two Healers bonded like Tems and Elen, and it worried many, including her.

"No, Tems. I'm sorry, but I did not invite her to my journey."

He let his breath out and only then did I realize he'd been holding it.

"Yes. Yes, Jibutu, I would be honored to come. I hope I can be of help to you."

""Wonderful. We will leave with the caravan that is going to Bel Harq, travel with it to the Caravan's Oasis, get some sleep, and leave for the desert at midnight. My cohort will meet in my room tonight, two hours after finish of dinner. Please be there." I smiled, turned, and hurried off to the pharmacopia.

The day of our departure came, and when my cohort entered the courtyard and saw the size of the sliwa some were not sure they wanted to go. From the mountains, they were used to yama. Only Tems and I were truly comfortable with the sliwa.

"Will they let us ride them? Or do we have to walk?"

"They will let us ride them. They have been fed, so we do not need to bring food for them. However, because we are going into the desert, we need to bring our food and our water. So each sliwa will carry food and water and empty boxes for our harvest. Because at first we will travel with a caravan, our pace will be slow, which will give you all a chance to walk and to ride—and become familiar with the sliwa. At the oasis we will camp away from the others so we will not disturb them when we leave at midnight."

"We will go at night? In the dark?"

"How will we see to harvest?"

Tems laughed. A laugh of camaraderie, not derision, "There will be plenty of light, the moon will be nearly full, and it is during the full moon that many of the flowers we need bloom. It will also be cooler for our sliwa and us. We will camp and sleep during the heat of the day."

"If you have any questions about the desert, please ask. Tems is also from the desert and, if I'm busy, he can answer your question."

My advocates looked over the sliwa and our packs. I could tell by the way they checked the saddles and bridles that they, too, were of the desert. I demonstrated how to mount and ride a sliwa. "I will show you again, when we reach the caravan. It is better to walk the sliwa through the town as they are easier to control."

The advocates gave the go-ahead, and we walked through the main gate, to the same second crossroad Anka had led us so long ago. Where she turned to the right, we turned to the left, and I led the group down the road to the gate, signed us out, and we went down to the desert and the waiting caravan.

"Good morning, healers. I am Caravan Master Zaga Gon. While you are with my caravan, my word is law. If I say jump, you jump. You may ask me how high you should jump while you are in the air. Do you understand?"

"Yes, Caravan Master, we understand." I answered for all of us.

"Good. We will reach the first Oasis tomorrow. I understand you will leave from there?"

"Yes, Caravan Master. We will leave in the middle of the night; we will camp away from your caravan so as not to disturb you when we leave. Or at least, disturb you as little as possible."

"Thank you. All right, everyone. We're ready to go. Walk or ride at your pleasure."

The caravan leader laughed often, and led the whole group in singing as we headed out to the desert. He made sure we understood he was honored to have us with his caravan, at least for the short time we'd be with him. His riders enjoyed flirting with my cohort, and kept a watchful eye on the sliwa. I believe they were disappointed that there were no problems, and they were denied the opportunity to become heroes.

When we reached the oasis, the leader showed us where to camp and invited us to share his meal. Before we turned in, we held an open clinic for those who had need. Mostly, we treated blisters and the sore feet of people not used to walking on the sand. This close to Yaylin, we saw no one with serious illness or injury.

It felt good to again have a sliwa between my legs, to be back on the desert, to feel the heat, to be able to see for miles and miles. The perfume of the desert came straight from the gods to bless me. The sliwa seemed happy to be free of Yaylin. Once away from the caravan, we had a bit of play, and let them race across the sands. There was nothing here we needed and, if they were a bit tired, the sliwa would be more tractable and easier to manage.

For the most part, our trek was a success. The forest folk were amazed, almost frightened, of the wide openness of the desert. Tems was a big help with them. On the ninth day, as we returned to Yaylin, our boxes loaded with cactus flowers, cactus roots, drying snakes, and whatever else we found along the way, we came upon a small camp.

I called out, but no one answered. Their sliwa stood, and looked at us. "Tems?" I asked. This didn't look good to me.

"I don't know, Jibutu."

"Stay here. I don't like the looks of this. You stay with the cohort while I investigate."

114

"I'll come with you," Advocate Sohns rode his sliwa next to mine. He, too, called out. Again, we received no answer.

Healers do not carry weapons, nor do we carry money, however I had my cactus knife in hand. If this were an ambush, I would go down fighting to protect my cohort. Advocate Sohns smiled, and pulled his own cactus knife. "Be slow to use it, Hopeful. Remember, we heal, we do not injure."

And then the wind shifted. We put away our knives. The dead do not ambush. It appeared they had run out of water, but we couldn't tell for sure. It was the first time many of the cohort had seen this much death this close—three adults and one child. It was the child, still embraced by his mother's arms, who was the hardest to see and leave. We stripped the bodies as we laid them out on the sand, folded their clothes, and stacked them next to the bodies. We left them entwined as we placed them on the sand and slit their throats so any blood they still contained could drip back to Mother Earth. We could find nothing to identify this family other than a pendant the woman wore around her neck. I placed it in my robe. This small group was so close to Yaylin; so close to the Caravan Oasis, and yet not close enough.

Once the bodies were stripped and laid out, and everything had been folded and neatly stacked, the advocates, Tems and I, stood at the head of the small family and sang our Desert Song of Death. The mountain folk formed a circle about the people. We released the sliwa to the desert to find their way.

> Great Boran,
> welcome the breath of their lives
> upon your winds.
> Allow them to sing to their people.
>
> Great Mother,
> welcome the lives of these people
> of your desert.

Allow them to find joy and peace
in their sacrifice.

Great Desert,
welcome these, your dwellers.
Allow their sacrifice
to feed and nourish those who have need.

Nameless Ones,
you may free to go
where you are now needed,
free of pain and want.

Your sacrifice has been noted, and received.

Bless.

Those of our cohort who came from the mountains found our desert ways of caring for the dead interesting. They bury their dead. We leave them out for the nourishment of others.

We were a subdued lot as we returned to the school, all of us lost in our own thoughts. Singing did not seem appropriate. Once the sliwa were unloaded and cared for and the harvest distributed, the cohort were released to write their reports and return to their lives. By the time I got to the baths, I had forgotten the pendant, until I removed my robe and it fell to the floor. I took it into the bath with me, and washed the grime from it. Carved into the circle of green stone was a sliwa protecting its egg. I would give it to Authority, who would use it to try to identify the people, and notify their tribe.

With a clean body and a clean robe, I went to the dining hall for a bowl of juice and quiet, for now I had to write my own report. Mother Roose and Anka taught me well and I kept a nightly report while on the journey, so all I had to do was finish it, and give it and the pendant, to Authority.

And then came the hardest part of all. The waiting. Did I pass? I was a nervous wreck. I don't know how Anka had stayed so calm. Or had she only appeared calm? I tried to maintain an outward semblance of calm, but beneath that surface, I paced with anxiety. What if I failed? What would happen then? My early conversation with Healer Hakka came to mind and I suddenly wondered if I could train in the shaman school—if I could find it? Or would I be outcast in both?

The forced separation of Tems and Elen had the desired effect. While Tems was away with my cohort, Elen moved to the tower. Tems seemed relieved when he returned to find he had a new roommate, a young man from the forest. The whole school seemed to breathe easier once the affair ended. Fortunately, they were able to remain friendly, just no longer a couple.

When called, I entered Authority's office to find Authority—and Mother Roose! I wanted to run to Mother, but held back, my heart a cold stone in my chest. Their faces were formal and cold. I had failed. I was to be rejected. What would I do? Where would I go?

But then, Authority's face beamed like the desert sun. "Jibutu, it is with pleasure I tell you that you passed. Your tattooing ceremony will take place in a three-day."

"Daughter," Mother Roose said, "I am so *very* pleased. Welcome to the Family of Healers." I had passed my test. I was now a healer, though the ceremony would not be for three more days.

Chapter Thirteen

To be alive is to know pain.
To embrace pain is to receive fuel to live.
To avoid the pain is to quit.
To quit is to die.
—*Wisdom of Yaylin School of Healing*

I HAD LONG AGO DECIDED on my personal design, a sliwa. My sliwa wound from the center of my eye patch down a bit, and then up, his tail surrounding my eye. I kept it simple, as if I drew a design to carve. Simple, I thought, but striking. Most healers had their designs curve around their cheeks, so mine would be quite different and possibly more painful, as there is less flesh over the eye. But, after the loss of my hand, I thought I could survive a few small cuts.

In anticipation of my assignment, I packed most of my belongings into the sliwa box Papa Jib and my tribe had so long ago given me. I did not want to have to pack with a sore face. I fairly danced through the days until my tattooing and assignment. My heart soared to greet the desert hawks with the hope I would leave school and return to the desert with Mother Roose.

"Jibutu, come. It is time." Authority knocked on my door. "We will go to the healer's bath today."

Blue and purple paints covered the walls of the healer's bath, which I had never seen. The colors were meant to soothe. Light came from holes in the ceilings, plugged with glass points that reflected the light throughout the room. Plants grew in pots placed about the room. "It's beautiful."

"Yes," said Authority, "after a day with patients or students, we need the peace and quiet. There will be few giggles in this room, though, of course, there will be some. And laughter."

The student bath was a noisy place. The only time I could find a quiet time there was when everyone else was in the dining hall, or in bed. As a healer, I would now come here, to the healer's bath. A place of quiet and calm. A place of renewal.

"Use this soap on your head and face. It is quine soap, and will help disinfect." Authority handed me a bar of green soap. "Use this on your body. It smells good." She smiled as she handed me a bar of yellow soap. "And leave your robe here."

I dropped my robe and stepped into the bath. It was warm and scented like the yellow soap. I lathered my body and watched as the suds quickly disappeared through a hole in the side of the bath. Like the student baths, the water here was constantly replenished from the hot springs beneath the school.

Authority dropped her robe, and stepped into the bath. "Allow me to wash your back. Your muscles are tight, Jibutu. Try to relax. It will make the tatting process easier." She kneaded my muscles until I felt boneless. "Good. It is time for breakfast. We will have a light meal in the tattoo court."

Authority wrapped me in a clean, white sheet, and escorted me to the rooftop where I would receive my tattoos.

I ate something; fruit, I think. Nothing heavy and, to be honest, I don't remember a great deal of that meal. I drank a juice and then Authority led me to the stone bed where my tats would be carved.

I crinkled my nose at the smell of the roasted cacia bark. There was no breeze and though someone stood with a large fan to move the air, it wasn't enough.

"You'll get used to it," Mother Roose said, with a smile on her face.

I remembered Anka and, like her, I settled, took a couple of deep breaths, and said, "I am ready. Please begin." The tattooing

119

was like going through the fire all over again. The pain of the cuts, the burn of the cacia bark being rubbed in. But this pain meant I was a healer. I smiled, a weak smile, but a smile.

I would accept this pain. I would embrace this pain. I would study this pain. I would pull this pain into me, and it would fuel the fire of my life. I was a healer! This is pain I would inflict on others, in order to heal them.

The tears of Mother Roose softened the pain. I would cry when I healed.

I would accept this pain....

"It is finished," Mother Roose smiled down at me.

"Already?" My question brought chuckles from people I could not see.

"Yes, already," said Healer Sohns.

I reached for the hand of Mother Roose, "Please, help me sit." I sat up slowly, with the support of both Roose and Sohns. After looking around at the people on the roof, I stood. I smiled. They clapped. Authority draped the purple robe of a healer about me.

"Please, Healer Jibutu, sit here, and allow me to serve you." Then, I smelled the food and was ravenous. Authority served me a plate of spiced stew; Mother Roose filled her plate and sat next to me.

Sohns Healer placed the cleaned knife on its thong about my neck. When I was through eating, Mother Roose led me back to my room, where she sat with me as I slept.

✣

"Healer, your face is healing beautifully. I am pleased the scabs have fallen, and the tissue is a healthy pink."

"Thank you, Authority."

"Sit. Please."

I sat.

"Jibutu, I know you would love nothing better than to be assigned to a desert tribe, preferably yours. However, after

120

several discussions with Roose Healer and others, and reading the letters from Hakka Healer, we all think your talents are most needed in Michlin." Before I could speak, she raised her hand for silence. "I know you hate the mountains, and I am assured you will be taken there via the high road, which has fewer, if any, trees." At that she smiled.

"Michlin is growing, and Hakka and Anka both need help. They have specifically requested you. They are sure you will be able to work with the People of the Grass, as well as the miners. They aren't sure about the Boat people, but Anka is comfortable with them."

I said nothing. My dreams fell in shards and pieces all around me.

"Jibutu, I know you wanted the desert. We all want our home country, to show our tribe or clan what we have learned and to return to them our love. However, even Roose Healer agrees, your path is over the mountains." She held the papers out to me. I had to stand to accept them.

"Thank you, Authority. I," I refused to cry, but my voice cracked. "I will be ready to leave tomorrow."

"The caravan that will take you is not leaving for a three-day. You have time to relax and visit with friends."

"Thank you." I turned and left her office, making it back to my room before the tears rolled. I allowed myself the time it took the shadow crawling up my wall to cover an inch to wallow in self-pity. When the shadow had crawled the inch, I stopped sniveling, washed my face in the quine tisane, and left my room, and the school.

"Healer? Lengo Ja? Are you here?" I stood in the dispensary of the prison. It was empty, and quiet. "Hello? Mali?"

"Oh, Jibutu. How good of you to come." Mali stood in the door leading to Lengo Ja's small garden and quarters. "He is not well, and would not allow me to call a healer. Please, come." Mali led me to the quarters where Lengo Ja lived. As I looked around

121

it was obvious Mali lived there, too. The breeze caught her dress, and wrapped it around her body. Even more became puzzlingly obvious.

"Lengo Ja? Friend, I have come to say good-bye. I leave in a three-day to go across the mountains to Michlin." As I spoke the words, excitement began to fill me, then consternation as I looked at my friend. "Please, what is wrong?"

Lengo Ja looked at me for a long time, dropped his feet over the side of his bed, and sat. Finally, he stood. He looked a beaten man. "Jibutu, let's go for a walk. Mali, please stay, I'll be back soon."

We left the prison, and walked to the weapons market, where we would be left alone. Lengo paused at a table in front of a food vendor, "I'll get us a tea and a sweet." I sat and waited for his return. I looked at the knives, and other weapons, and wondered if they would ever cease to be made and used.

"Jibutu, something strange has happened. I need to talk to Authority about it, but...." His voice dropped off. I waited as long as I could.

"But, what?"

"Huh? Oh." Clearly something bothered Lengo Ja so much so that he found it difficult to talk about. I became quiet. In time he would tell me. "Jibutu, Mali is pregnant."

"Yes, I noticed."

"She is pregnant with *my* child."

"But you drank the fermented cactus juice. You *can't* be the father." Now, I understood his confusion. Everyone knows healers are sterile.

"I am the father," he said. "After the fire, I took Mali in— she had no place to go, and one thing led to another, and, well.... The other thing is, we love each other. She has been with no man since her child died. And she has been with no man but me since she moved in."

"By the Great Boran! This has implication for all healers. Yes, my friend, you *must* talk to Authority."

"All I can think of is that I drank the juice many, many years ago. Perhaps it wears off? Perhaps we need to drink it periodically? Perhaps by the time it wears off, women are past the age to bear children, and by then, most men don't care? I don't know. I truly don't."

"I hope we don't have to drink it again. I never, ever, want to go through that ritual again. Why, it was months before I could even think about eating sweets!"

"I know." Lengo Ja rubbed his forehead at memory of the headache, and laughed.

"How is Mali taking it?"

"She alternates between fear that I'll be sent away, and joy that we, of all people, are having a baby."

"Why would you be sent away?"

"We are not allowed mates. You know that. I had not realized how desperately lonely I was, until Mali entered my life."

I thought of Elen and Tems, and all the other little affairs of school. "Perhaps it is time to change the rules, neh?" I paused before repeating myself, "Yes, perhaps it is time for change."

Lengo Ja sighed. Then straightened his back and smiled. "Yes, I think you are right, it is time for change. She is a great help in the dispensary. Even if I have to give up my purple robe, I'm sure the prison will let us stay."

Give up his purple robe? After all he'd been through? Impossible!

"Do you want to raise a child in prison?"

"Hmmm, hadn't thought that far ahead. No, but I'm sure we can get a small house just outside the walls. Someplace close enough that I can be here almost as fast as I can now. Jibutu, I can understand the rules, the traditions, and I respect them. But I'm an old man, Mali loves me, I love her, and...."

His back slumped again. His eyes stared into a place I could not see.

"Would you like me to come with you to speak to Authority?"

"What? No. Thank you, my friend, but I got myself into this mess, and I guess I just have to get myself out of it." Lengo Ja stood, looked at me and said, "Thank you, Jibutu. I appreciate your friendship. I will take Mali with me when I see Authority. I would appreciate you not speaking to anyone until you hear it from another source."

Our walk had circled back to the beginning. My excitement remained somewhat tempered by Lengo Ja's news.

"Friend, as you well know, whatever a healer hears is never spoken without permission. I will be gone to Michlin in a three-day, so when this is resolved, if you would care to tell me, write. Letters go between the school and the clinic in Michlin every so often."

"I shall."

I hugged both Lengo Ja and Mali good-bye, and began to hum a mountain song Anka taught me as I walked toward my own adventure.

Chapter Fourteen

A river runs through the center of the world.
It carries all the tears ever cried so they cannot be cried again.

A river runs through the center of the world.
It holds all the hurts and sorrows so they cannot be felt again.

A river runs through the center of the world.
It carries life for those will drink of it.
— *Lu Shahnnah, Shaman of the Grass*

THE ROAD WE FOLLOWED meandered along the edge of a river. Trees grew close to both sides of the road, and the caravan master joked with me as I hunched tighter and tighter into myself. At least, I hoped he joked.

"Healer, if you would ride, we could make better time, at least to the high road."

"Thank you, Caravan Master Ject Zon, but my yama carries full panniers. They are heavy and I do not care to add to his burden." He muttered something I couldn't hear, nor could I read his face. His back was to me, but it seemed to move as if he laughed.

"Healer?" A quiet voice spoke at my side, once the caravan master left.

"Yes, Ter."

"Don't let him bother you none. We ain't in no hurry, we gets paid whether we be fast or slow. We be out of the trees after our noon eats. And the high road is better walked than rode no how. He be tormentin'."

"Thank you, Ter." I walked on in silence. Now and then I wondered about Lengo Ja and Mali, but mostly I looked forward to ending this trip, and to being with Hakka and Anka.

It was about an hour after our noon meal, when the caravan master called out, "High road to the right. Be sure your canteens are full." He stopped, went to the river, and filled his canteen. We all did likewise, allowed the yama to drink their fill, then returned to the road, turned to the right, and started going up a fairly wide path. I would not call it a road. It was wide enough for two yama, loaded with panniers, to pass, but that was about it. The trees began to close in even more. Perhaps it was my imagination, but it seemed we slowed down until we barely walked. Perhaps it was the steepness of the trail.

"Dat mans, he be mean to you, Mem Healer. Fix his drink tonight."

"Ter, what do you mean?"

"He go through trees slow. He know you not like. You wait. We get out, he go fast. Watch him, Mem Healer. No trust him."

Ter had barely whispered to tell me this, and as soon as he finished, he dropped back. So, it wasn't my imagination that we seemed to go more and more slowly. And, sure enough, when we broke through the tree line our speed picked up. Did the man not know a healer could choose the caravans, and a bad report from me would be bad for his business?

"It will be lighter longer up here. We'll go farther than usual before we stop for the night. If you see dry sticks, pick them up. The more dry wood, the larger and warmer, our fire. Right, Healer?" Caravan Master Ject Zon looked at me with an expression that dared me to disagree with him.

"Caravan Master, your word is law. If you say more wood means a larger and warmer fire, I see no reason to disagree." I smiled with as much sweetness as I could muster.

I had noticed earlier, and again at our first break, the men gravitated a slight distance away from Ject Zon. They all

126

contributed to the stew, and cooperated in getting the chores done, but there was no camaraderie between the Master and the workers. And the men were always quiet. Tonight would be interesting, as we were now in my element of open skies, and I had a feeling Ject Zon had controlled his temper about as long as he could.

"Ject Zon, I notice your caravanieri do not sing as do other caravans. Is this a mountain tradition? When I traveled in desert caravans, whether my tribe's or a commercial one, we had much singing to while the miles away. Why is it you and your men don't sing?"

"Healer, we've nothing to sing about. We're happier in our own thoughts, and not talking. Sing? Hah! We'll be too high tomorrow to have extra breath for singing. Ter won't even have enough breath to come whisper in your ear." His laugh was not one of humor.

"Your scars look new. You just get your robe?"

"Yes, I did."

"I suppose you'll want to stop at any villages we come to?"

"Only if asked."

"By the Great Ris, but you healers are ugly damn people!" At that outburst, Ject Zon tossed his drink to the ground and stomped off. He slept in a small tent, on a pad. The rest of us swept the rocks away, as best we could, and rolled in our blankets.

"Mem Healer?" Ter whispered close to my head. "Mem Healer, don't be thinkin' too harsh thoughts 'bout Ser Zon. His wife and son died. Healers couldn't help. It ain't personal, Mem." Ter moved back, rolled in his blanket, and remained quiet.

Ter was the only caravanieri who seemed to show any respect for Ject Zon. The others all did their jobs, but remained separate. Ter would see something and do it, whether to fill Zon's drink bowl or set up his tent. Like a devoted servant, he was never seen or acknowledged.

127

Sunrise came early at this height. A bowl of warm tea, a bowl of warm stew and within the hour, we were ready to go on. I started to pour water onto my bowl to clean it, but Ter stopped me, "No water, Mem Healer. Use grass. Wash when we back in trees. Water scarce up here."

"Thank you, Ter." He gave me a handful of grass, which I used to wipe out my bowls. I noticed the others put their grass in a sack, so I added mine.

"Good to start fires with." Ject Zon nodded his approval at my action.

When the sun stood overhead, Ject Zon called out. "A five minute rest. Trail food. Drink. Then we go." He looked at me, and added with a snide derisiveness, "If our Mem Healer agrees, of course."

I smiled and sweetly replied, "Caravan Master, you are law unto this caravan." I drank a bit, took a handful of the nuts Ter offered, and said, "I'm ready."

The view was spectacular. We could look down into the deep valleys, many of which only had sunshine at their floors for a few minutes at midday, when the sun shone straight down. The valleys were black with trees, and spent far more of their day in shadow and darkness than we on the high road.

The high road wove around, up and down, but did not dip into the trees. Ject Zon continued to bait me, and I continued to be sweet. The men smiled when their boss couldn't see them. The morning of our fifth day on top of the world, Ject Zon approached me as we packed to leave. "Mem Healer, we will be back in the trees tonight. And, if we don't slow too much, we should be in Michlin by nightfall tomorrow."

"Ser Zon, I shall do my best not to slow you down. I assure you."

"Well, the hard part of the trip is ahead. We should be past it by noon break, but we need to hurry, and to be careful."

"I don't understand."

"The Shales. The whole side of the mountain is loose shale. There is no path across it so we let the yama decide how to go. The shale, it slips easily, and rocks from the cliffs above fall now and then. I will tell you when we get there, and when we do, no talking until we're across. That means you, Ter. No talking until across The Shales."

"Yes, ser." Ter muttered.

"I understand," I replied.

We walked, each in our own thoughts, and suddenly Zon stopped. "We're here. Tie the leads up, and follow your yama. I'll go first. Mem Healer, when I'm at that pointy rock, you start. Then the men, and you, Ter, you bring up the end."

"Caravan Master, as healer, I ask for the last position. That way, if anyone is hurt, I can help. It is a healer tradition to be last in rough areas."

He looked at me, spat, and walked away. I watched. He let his yama go, and where the yama stepped, he stepped. When he reached the pointy rock, the next started out. "Mem, please, let me follow you."

"No, Ter. I will go last. You may follow the men if you wish when it is your turn. You and the men go. I'll be along shortly."

"Yes, Mem. I send the mens, then go last but you. Don't fall! It be your death. You come carefully when I gets to the pointy rock." Ter followed his yama, and when he had reached the pointy rock, I set out, following my yama. It was a long way down and steep. I concentrated on the yama and where to place my feet. Until Ter began to roll and tumble down the shale. He rolled like a log, more than tumbling end over end. I remember thinking he might survive but then the ground moved under me. I heard yells, but when I looked, I only saw sky and gray rock and sky and gray rock. I, too, rolled and tumbled down the shale. Perhaps I wouldn't die. Perhaps I would wish otherwise. My world disappeared into blackness.

129

When I opened my eyes, I saw the stars. I moved my head to sit, and the stars began to whirl. I lay back down. "Ter? Ter? Can you hear me?"

He heard me, and moaned.

"Ter, be still. I'm here, and I think I'm all right. Just be still, I'll find you."

I sat, using great care. My body hurt, but nothing seemed broken. It didn't seem to matter what part of me I touched; I hurt. I was one solid bruise.

"Ter. Can you talk?"

"No, Mem," he moaned. I couldn't even think a chuckle at his response; I hurt so badly. I crawled until I found him.

"Ter, I'm here. I'm going to run my hand over you to see if I can feel anything. If I hurt you, tell me. Or just scream."

"Yes, Mem. I scream loud," his whisper hid the pain.

"Ter, I think you have a broken leg, and maybe a broken arm. There is nothing I can do in the dark. We have no water, I don't know where my box is, but I have some quine leaves. They are bitter, but will help with the pain." I reached into my robe, and miracle of miracles, the small jar of leaves had neither fallen out nor been smashed. It must have been cushioned by the folds of my robe.

"Here, I'm going to put some in your hand. They taste awful, but just hold them in your mouth as long as you can, then swallow. Don't swallow the leaves, just your spit."

"Yes, Mem."

The stars gave enough light that I could see Ter's outline, and the rocks, so I moved what rocks I could, and lay down next to him, covering both of us with my robe. Ter moaned softly. I must have dozed because I jerked awake when a cold, wet nose poked at my face.

The sky began to lighten, and standing over me was my yama. Mine being the one with my medicine box. And my extra canteen.

130

"Good girl! You found us! Ter, we have water, and I have supplies." I propped his head in my lap, and poured water down his throat.

"That be good, Mem."

"Yes, and it's getting light enough I that can see. Ter, we're almost at tree line! You stay here, I'll be back in a bit." I slid down the few feet of shale until it ran out, and I was in the forest. "Boran, can you hurry some light into this place?" I searched for two long and two short sticks. When I found them, I dragged them back to Ter. I chattered to him as I went through my panniers.

"Ter, I'm going to find some bandages, then check and set your arm if need be, and then set your leg. Here, chew some more quine leaf. Ah, I found them. Now, I want you to bite down on this. It's just a piece of bandage I rolled, it has a little more of the quine leaf in it. The arm is sore, but not broken. I wish I could say the same for your leg. I'm going to straighten it and tie these two shorter straight sticks to it to hold it in place. It's going to hurt like fire, but there's nothing else to do. When the bone ends meet, it won't hurt near so much. Then, I'll make us a healing tea."

I sat on the ground, opened the pinching hook I normally wore, propped a stick to keep it open, and wrapped it in a cloth and then using my hand and hook I grasped his ankle. I placed one foot in his crotch, and said, "On the count of three—one, two," and I pulled. Slow and steady. Ter called out, bit the rag, moaned, and then was quiet. "Three." I wrapped his leg in the splint as tightly as I could then built a small fire, and when he returned to consciousness, had a bowl of tea ready for him, and a bit of trail food.

"Thanks be to you, Mem. It don't hurt so much, now."

"Well, I'm glad to hear that! Do you think Zon or anyone will come for us?"

"No, Mem. He figures we be dead, and they go on."

131

"Well, won't he be surprised!"

My yama bared her teeth and called, and we heard an answering call. Soon, Ter's yama joined us.

"The yama, they come down all stiff legged, slide with rocks. They almost always make it."

"Good. Which of the two is the nicest?"

"What, Mem?"

"Which yama is the nicest? The most tractable? Which one would take an extra burden?"

"Oh. That be mine, Mem. But I can't ride."

"You won't have to. I have an idea." I pulled my other robe out of the pannier, and pushed the two long poles through the body and neck of the robe. I tied the sleeves tight, then folded the hem of my robe over the poles, and tied them at that width. Taking the long ends of the poles, at the wide end I tied them to the outside of the yama harness.

"You, friend Ter, will ride in style. I've filled my large canteen with quine leaf tisane, and whenever you want some, we'll stop. Now I'm going to bring your yama around and then help you into the sling."

"Mem, I ain't never seen nuthin' like this. Will it work?"

"Of course it will." I hoped I didn't lie. It wouldn't be all that comfortable, but it would be better than leaving him alone while I went for help. It took a bit of maneuvering, but together, we finally got Ter into the yama sling. His broken leg cushioned by a couple of packs from his panniers rode on top of his good leg. I led the yama and tried to keep the end sticks that dragged on the ground from hitting too many roots or rocks. My yama followed, but just in case he had other ideas, Ter held her lead.

We were in the forest, now, but this time, I could not indulge my phobia. It was imperative I get Ter to the clinic at Michlin as soon as possible. He needed a bed, and proper food and medicines. He moaned when he went over a root or was jarred by a rock, but he never complained. I stopped now and then to give him some more quine leaf tisane, and noticed he had begun to develop a slight fever. Bone fever. How far were we? How far had we yet to go? We had already gone down the mountain; surely, if I just kept us going down and to the right, we would find the low road soon.

Darkness was almost upon us. I remembered Anka's bough bed, and laid several boughs on the ground and shoved them under Ter. I then untied the poles, and settled him on the bed. I did not take him out of the sling, but found his blanket and covered him. Then I built a small fire and made a tea of jer root.

"Ter, drink this. It will help your stomach. We're almost there. We should be in Michlin tomorrow." I curled on the boughs, next to him, and hoped we'd find the road soon. Ter shivered and moaned softly as I dropped into the darkness of sleep.

Ter's moans woke me. I kept hearing my mother calling my name, and would wake to answer, only to realize it had been a night bird. I never heard the whole name, only "Ti." Why did my birth mother continue to haunt my sleep, and never tell me how to find her? Neh! Dreams!

Chapter Fifteen

Oweeee! Oweeeee! Owwwwweeeeeee.
Oweeee! Oweeeee! Owwwwweeeeeee.
—*Song of the Hurt Child*

IT TOOK A FEW HEARTBEATS for me to realize the moans that wakened me were not Ter's but mine. I think not a space of my body was free of ache. It hurt to wiggle my toes, it hurt to wiggle the fingers of my hand, it hurt to think. I lay still for a few more minutes, and then all but screamed as I forced myself to stand. "By Boran! Even my hook hurts! Neh!"

Ter slept through my moans and expletives. I poured some of last night's tea over a cloth, and mopped his face. In the light of dawn, I couldn't tell if he was gray from shock, or gray from lack of light. He did not wake, and would not drink any of the tea. I decided on shock.

It took several tries before my fingers and muscles would move enough to tie the sticks back on the yama's harness. Eventually, we wove our way between the trees, at an oblique angle down the mountain. Surely, I thought, we were near the road. An hour or so later, nearly blinded by my swollen face and eyelids, I stumbled on a bit of level ground.

"Ter, we're on the road. At least I think we are. There should be no more tree roots to joggle you." He said nothing, but his breathing seemed to relax a bit.

Mustering all the strength and ability I could, I heard only Ter's low moans and ragged breaths, and the steady clops of the

134

yama as they stepped along the road. The exercise warmed me, and loosened my muscles a bit; still, I walked far too slowly. The hospital was too far away, and every moment Ter slid farther and farther along his lifeline, in the wrong direction. Anger at the caravan master for leaving us as if we were dead began to burn in my heart, feeding me with a bit more strength. With each step I ground the name of Ject Zon into the dirt of the road. Left Ject, right Zon. How *dare* he leave a member of his crew for dead without proof? How *dare* he leave a healer for dead?

"Ter, the sun is overhead. Please, try to drink." I held the bowl of tea to his lips; he opened them and swallowed a few sips.

"Mem. Leave me. Go."

"I shall not leave you, Ter. We should be in Michlin soon."

"Mem, we no close. No traffic." He closed his eyes and slept.

No traffic? He spoke the truth. There was no traffic. Surely, if Michlin were close at hand, there would be traffic. I drank a bit of tea, ate a few nuts from the trail mix, and continued to place one aching foot in front of the other. And quietly, I sang the song all hurt children sing as I walked along, grinding the name Ject Zon into dust.

"Mem? Need you help?"

I stopped, focused, and realized the voice was right next to me. I looked to my left, then up. Atop a beast of burden sat a man.

"How far to Michlin? I need to get this man to the healers."

"Excuse me, mem, I think you could use a healer yourself."

"I am a healer, ser. But, yes, I too, can use their ministrations."

"What happened?"

"We were on the high road, and this man and I were the last two to cross The Shales. The ground shook, we fell. He has a broken leg. I am one bruise."

135

"Where is your Caravan Master? Did he not come to your aid?"

"No, ser, he did not. Ter tells me he assumes all who fall to the bottom die."

The man turned, and began barking orders to those behind him. It began to dawn on me that I had not heard a rather large caravan of carts coming behind us. While he barked his orders, I again began to walk.

"Mem. Wait. Please."

"Ser, I cannot wait." Impatience began to grow. "I need to get this man—"

"Yes, healer. And you will walk but few steps before the wagon is ready. Better you just wait."

"Wagon?"

"Healer, were you not listening? We prepare a wagon for you. In fact, it is empty now. How best to raise this man to the bed of a wagon?"

I looked out of the slits I used for eyes, and saw several men waiting for orders.

"Do you have a board? If he could be placed on a board, it would be easiest on him to move him from the sling to the board, then lift the board to the wagon, and then at the hospital, lift the board to the bed."

"Jole, get a board out of the supply cart. You and Unta take orders from the healer. Braht, put some blankets in the wagon, and arrange them as the she tells you."

Ter cried out as they moved him and his broken leg to the board, but was quiet after that. The men gently placed rolled blankets along his side, to help hold him from moving as the cart traveled. Without ceremony, they lifted me to the bed of the wagon, and propped me in the corner where I could watch Ter and talk to Braht, who would be our driver.

"Healer, I am Semp Istan, Master of this Caravan. I trust Braht to get you to the hospital. I will bring your yamas. Now,

136

this is a fermented juice, it is sweet, and I strongly suggest you get a bit down your patient if possible, and have a bit yourself." Semp Istan handed me a small bottle. The spirits warmed me from the inside out, and I'm sure did the same for Ter, as he managed to drink a bit, too. "Good. Safe Journey. Braht, all due speed." The wagon began to move, and then it moved faster.

"We go at good, steady pace. Not tire animals, get us there before dark." The wagon rolled forward, with a slight sideways movement. Perhaps the wheels were not even?

⟶⟍𝒲⟋⟵

"Sister? Jibutu?" A voice came to me through my dreams. "Sister?"

"Anka, let her sleep." Another voice. Anka?

"Yes, Hakka Healer." Hakka?

"Shhh, you're safe." I felt something cool on my face. Cool, wet, and smelling of quine leaf.

I opened one eye.

"Ah hah! You played. You weren't asleep. When did you get to be so lazy, sister? Was it after I left?" I looked into the smiling face of Anka. I was at Michlin.

"When?" My voice was barely a croak.

"Night before last."

"I've slept two days?" I struggled to sit, but I hurt too much.

"Yes. You are terribly bruised, and your patient is also. However, we cleaned him, and wrapped his broken leg. He's much better, thanks to you."

"Did he tell you what happened?" My words came out slowly, with long pauses between each one. My mouth was dry. "Drink. Please," was all I could mumble.

"Oh, I'm sorry. Here. Just sip." Anka held my head up, and placed a bowl of tea to my lips. I sipped until the bowl was dry.

"Ter, the man with the broken leg. How is he?" Ah, my voice was back. I could talk, though slowly, but I no longer croaked.

137

"He's resting. We sedated him, and he still sleeps, but the fever is gone, and the moans have stopped. Whatever happened to you two?"

"We took the high road. At least we took it to The Shales. Then as Ter and I, the last two, walked across them, the ground moved, and we fell. All the way to the bottom."

"Yes, that's what Ject Zon told the authorities, that you had gone to the bottom and died."

"Well, we went to the bottom. That much is true." I closed my eyes for a few minutes, and woke to bright sunlight in my room. My eyes opened easily, and I could actually move without wanting to scream. I turned my head, and across the room, on another bed, slept Anka.

With great care and deliberation, I began the process of sitting. The room began to spin as I sat, so I placed my head between my knees until it stopped. When I raised my head, this time, the room did not spin, and I took stock of my body. I was purple-yellow-green-blue—every part I could see—but no longer swollen. I stood and walked to the chair at the foot of my bed, put on the robe draped over it, and sat. Exhausted. And hungry. No, starved. It had been days since I'd eaten and weeks since I'd had anything but a trail meal. My stomach growled. Anka woke.

Anka and Hakka accompanied both Ter and me to the Court of Inquiry. Ter and I were invited to sit at one of the two tables in the front of the room, facing a table on a platform, at which sat three stern-looking men. Both the front tables were empty, and when we sat at one, two men came forward. Ject Zon sat at the other table and Semp Istan sat next to me, blocking my view of Ject Zon. Ter, still recovering from his injury, shook from fear of this proceeding.

"Are all parties to this Inquiry present?"

"We are, Ser Inquisitor." Semp Istan spoke, apparently, for all of us.

"Although this Inquiry is informal, it will determine whether or not a Formal Inquisition will be held. You will each be given the chance to tell your side of the story, and to answer all questions put to you with honesty. Anyone caught lying, especially to curry favor, will immediately surrender to the constable. Do you understand?" He looked at each of us in turn, and we all responded that we did.

"Ser Istan, please begin by telling us how you met the two people next to you, and why you requested this Inquiry."

So, it was Istan who called us together. I glanced back at Anka, and she and Hakka were as blank as I. They had no idea, either.

"...and, if it please, I make claim to the two yama, the panniers, and the trade contents of the one. The other panniers held belongings and equipment of the healers, and have been turned over to them. I claim all but the healer's supplies and personal items of the two injured under the Rule of Finders."

"Ser Zon? What say you?"

"They wasn't abandoned, and they wasn't found. Mem healer was with them, as was Ter. They be mine." Although I could not see him, I could hear the anger in his voice.

"Ser Zon, when they slid down The Shales, did you not tell your remaining men that the two who fell were surely dead, and to leave them?"

"I done told Ged to go see. He lied. He went and came back, and said they was dead."

"Mem," whispered Ter, "That can't be."

"Ser Ter. You will have your chance to speak."

"Sorry, ser." Ter sat.

"And, Ser Zon, after, ah, Ged, told you, did you make any effort to recover the bodies?"

"No, ser. I didn't want to put my other mens at danger."

"Did you plan on returning for them, once you reached Michlin?"

139

"Uh, yes ser. But, well, one thing led to another, and we ain't got there. Yet."

"So I see. And is Ser Ged here?"

"Uh, no. He be at work."

"Ser Zon, you will tell the Bailiff how to locate him, and he will be brought within the hour."

"Now, Ser Ter, if you would care to tell the Inquiry what you whispered to the healer a few minutes ago..."

"Ser, I told Mem healer that Ser Zon lied. You see, all the mens who work for him, 'cept me, be deaf and can't talk. Ser Zon, he never learned to use the finger talk, and I did all the talking. If he told Ged to go and look, Ged wouldn't know what he meant. And if he did go, and come back, he couldn't tell Ser Zon nuthin'."

That explained the quiet of the men on the trail, why there was no singing or joking. And it explained the hand signals. I thought it some kind of code between the men so Ject Zon wouldn't hear them. I did not realize it was an actual language. The School needs to know about this.

"Ser Istan, you claim the two yama and the panniers and the contents of same?"

"Yes, Ser Inquisitor."

"Ser Ter, are any of the contents of the panniers your personal property?"

"I has two blankets, two bowls, and a carving knife"

"Ser Istan, you will see any personal belongings be returned to Ser Ter, the rest is yours under Right of Finders.

"Ser Zon, you will forfeit."

"What about him? He still works for me. He still owes!"

"No, his indenture ended when you abandoned him as dead. Are your other men indentured?"

"Yes. And they be staying that way!"

"Constable, will you please escort Ser Zon to the cells. And bring in all his men. I wish to interview them. Ser Ter, the Inquiry will pay you to translate for them, are you willing?"

Ter looked from the Inquisitor to me, then back to the Inquisitor, "Yes, Ser Inquisitor. I be willing."

"Very good. When a wagon is ready, I will send someone to get you. I think it will be easier on the men if you go and can explain what we want." He banged the Rock of Justice on his table, the three inquisitors stood and filed out of the room.

Semp Istan spoke, "Come. We'll go back to the hospital in my wagon. Ter, what do you carve?" Ter spent the few minutes of the ride back telling Ser Istan about his carving, and how he sold each piece he made to earn a bit of money. Ser Zon set the price and kept the money to pay off his debt. Or so Ser Zon said.

Chapter Sixteen

The Great Loss is not dying,
the Great Loss is not trying.
—*Lu Ahnah, the Lost Shaman*

THE ROOM ANKA AND I SHARED resembled our tiny tower room inasmuch as this room, too, was round, but this one was much larger, and built out over the edge of the mountain. We each had our own window, with almost the same view. Anka's looked out primarily on the Great Lake, and mine primarily on the Sea of Grass. The grass fascinated me, it stretched as far as I could see, and where the waters of the lake changed color with the sky, the grass changed colors with the season. Both moved with the wind in much the same way.

Built on the side of the mountain, Michlin gave the impression it would slide downward at any time. I was assured it would not. The buildings were made of the very stone of the mountain, most coming from the mines, but several of the wealthier homes had been carved into the mountain itself. The main street of Michlin sloped gently, and looped back and forth to the bottom. The mines were located above the hospital, the people lived below. The markets were all on the plain below, where the poor lived, and the farms were located.

If the wind blew from the south and west, we smelled grass. If it blew from the south and east, we smelled the Great Lake. Usually, it blew down the mountain, and we smelled dust and the dark green trees that made the forest.

142

"Sister, look! A village is coming. I don't think I've seen this one before. At least I don't recognize their pennant." Anka pointed to the Great Lake; when I looked, I saw perhaps a hundred boats lashed together coming from the horizon to our harbor.

"They've come at a good time. Harvest this year was above average. There will be much bartering, I'm sure. Market will be very interesting."

"And many fights and accusations of thievery, I'm sure. We'd better tell Hakka it comes. I doubt she's seen it."

"She won't see it until it's settled in the harbor, and even then it's doubtful, the way her eyes are fading."

"At least she can still see close things. Anka, what happens when she goes blind? Can we keep her here, where she is familiar with where things are?"

"I don't know. She has talked about going back to the school. However, that is a path we cannot walk until we are upon it."

Our room nice and tidy, we headed for the dispensary and our patients, and I gave the floating village no more thought. It would be many hours before it arrived, if it did not veer to another harbor, or anchor in deep water for some reason.

"Jibutu, I have to go out to one of the homes in the Grass. Would you like to come?" Whenever Anka made a trip to the grass, she always asked if I'd like to go with her. I had gone a few times, shortly after I arrived, but the grass was as bad, if not worse, than my memory of the dark forest. Perhaps worse, because the grass grew thick and tall and closed in on me like water in the bath. Along the edge of the mountains, farmers plowed it under, and grew grains and other crops. They used the buflo to pull their plows, and to ride while they herded the buson, a cousin to the buflo. The buson was shorter, stockier, and humped at the front shoulder. Where the buflo had long, horizontal horns that went out to either side of its head, the

143

buson had short, curved horns that went forward. The buflo supplied labor and milk used to make a variety of drinks and cheeses. The buson supplied meat and hides. The giant herds of buson also helped keep the grass down, so I've been told. There were no giant herds near Michlin.

"If you need me, I'll come, but I'd rather not."

Anka laughed. "No, that's all right. I just wanted to give you an opportunity."

"Thank you. And I'll extend the offer to you when the village arrives." I much preferred the gentle rocking of the boats to the closeness of the grass. We had long ago agreed on the division of labor to our mutual satisfaction. I got the surgery and the boats; Anka took the Grass. And Hakka hovered wherever she thought she could be of use. Fortunately, our Chief Healer liked all the administrative details, and we gladly let her deal with the paperwork. We preferred dealing with people.

When there were prisoners needing help, I usually went. They usually required stitching—either from fights or from accidents in the mines. The Warder at the prison stood taller than Lengo Ja, was broader in the shoulder, and had a scar that ran diagonally from above his right eye down through his eye patch. Fortunately, he could still see from the eye, only the lid had been sliced, but he looked three times meaner than Lengo Ja. And I think he was, at least to the prisoners. With healers, he was deferential almost to the point of worship.

"Good morning, Warder Mall Kam. I understand you have some men who require my ministrations."

"Yes, Jibutu Healer. I'm not sure what it is. The super thought they malingered, but finally even he could see they was sick. I put them in the other, smaller room, away from anyone else. I've prepared your tisanes, and have clean rags for you."

I thanked Mall Kam and walked back to the smaller room. The four men shivered in their fever, and all had used the

144

buckets by their beds. By now, there remained nothing in their stomachs, but still they heaved.

"Can you describe your ailment, please?"

"Mem, we ache. We shiver. We lose our food. Our heads, they hurt."

"You all feel the same?"

"Yes, Mem."

"Are you drinking anything?"

"No, Mem. Nothing stay down."

"Well, gentlemen, I think you ate something you shouldn't have. I'll make you a jer root tea, and I want you to sip as much as you can. And rest. You should be fine in a couple of days."

I turned and left the room. Eight eyes closed, and four men moaned in their agony.

"Mall Kam, I think they ate something spoiled up in the mines. Maybe they saved some meat for later? I don't know. But if you have a trusted one remove the buckets, empty and wash them, and let the men sip a jer root tea I'll make, I think they'll be fine in a couple of days. Anything else?"

"No, Jibutu Healer. There is nothing else."

"Then, I'll go back to the Dispensary. I believe I'll be there all day, so if you need me...." I washed my hands, and returned to the dispensary, where I changed my outer robe before seeing any more patients. Not for the first time was I grateful for the staff of our dispensary who did our cooking and our laundry, and other than our rooms, the cleaning.

That night, as we sat at the evening meal, Hakka spoke, "I talked with the Mayor today, and he tells me the harvest this year is the greatest in his memory. The people have reaped an exceptionally high yield of grains and vegetables. Oh, and the orchards were so full, the branches were beginning to break due to the fruit. What a blessing."

"Well, that explains the family I saw yesterday," said Anka. "They must have tried to make their own beer, using some of the excess grain. They'll be all right in a couple of days."

"I bet that's what the prisoners, did, too. They're always trying to make beer or spirits from their food. After what they went through, I'm sure those four won't try that again."

Two days later, the wails of mourning began to fill Michlin.

"Healers, I need to know whether to close the gates?" The Inquisitors asked the question. Around our conference table sat the Constable, along with the Mayor, Warder Mall Kam, and a representative from the mines.

Healer Hakka, as Chief Healer, spoke for us, unless we were directly asked a question. "Gentlemen, I do not know. Never have I seen such an outbreak." She paused for what seemed hours, but probably only lasted a few seconds before continuing, "I see your concern. My concern is that if the gates are closed, people will have no access to the dispensary."

"Yes, Mem. But what can you do? They get sick, they get better, and then their lungs fill with body water and they die. How many have actually survived?"

"That we know of, fewer than two people out of five."

"Fewer? One in five?"

"Inquisitor, my records indicate more than one, less than two."

"Ser Istan, I am going to close the Mountain Gate. Please tell your brother I have no choice. Healers, what can they do if their miners take sick?"

"Make them comfortable, and bury the bodies deep. If you have an old shaft, bury them there, but cover them each time you add to it."

"Warder, how many are in your dispensary?"

"Five, Inquisitor. Unless more arrived since I've come here."

"Healer, same advice?"

146

"Yes, Inquisitor."

The Inquisitor thought, and then with a heavy voice, said, "I am sealing the prison. Warder, take whatever you need with you, and when you get inside, receive no more until this is over."

"Inquisitor, please. We often use the prison dispensary as an overflow for ours. We cannot be sealed. It would serve no good."

The Inquisitor looked from Mall Kam to Hakka, to Anka, to me. We all nodded in agreement.

"Very well. I am sealing the gates of Michlin until this outbreak ends, one way or the other."

"Ser Inquisitor?" Mall Kam addressed the gray haired man. "We will need a large pit for the bodies. Where shall it be dug?"

"Mall Kam," sighed the Constable, "you are right. Body bearers must be allowed access to the town to collect the bodies and then outside to the graveyard to bury them. I suggest we use the farther edges of the cemetery. We shall need the names of each of the deceased, but they will be buried together. Have you trusted ones who can dig the holes? They will need to be deep, wide, and long."

"Yes, I have several, and if their sentences are commuted so they can go home to be with their families...?"

"Done!" The Inquisitor made the decision.

"I shall issue the orders, and prepare the passes for the burial detail and for the healers. No one else may enter or exit the gates."

"Perhaps I should set a tent in the Market area for those who come and require the services of a healer? Anka and Jibutu can handle the cases within the gates, but someone should be outside."

This time, the Inquisitor did not decide so quickly before he answered. "No, not now. You will all have passes to go forth and back, so it will not be necessary for you to give up the comfort of your bed, or your fellow healers. If the time comes when I must revoke your passes, then we will readdress the issue."

147

It was official. Michlin stood under siege of plague. Besides offering comfort, there remained little we could do. We offered what comfort we could, and taught family members to care for their own. Soon, the staff began not coming to work. Either they, or someone in their family, were sick. Still, people came to the dispensary. Most had the plague; many had wounds that needed caring. Several had pulled muscles from moving loved ones.

And then, one morning, Hakka did not come for breakfast. Anka and I raced to her room.

"Hakka, what's wrong?" Anka and I asked together.

"C-c-cold. F-f-feverish. Stay out. I have it." But, of course, we would not stay out. We washed, changed robes, and cared for her. She began to feel better, and we hoped it was a real feeling better, but soon, her lungs began to fill. We propped her in a large chair, and she breathed somewhat easier.

Exhausted, Anka and I dropped into our beds. I slept, and dreamed. The dreams were frightening, and when I woke, I could not remember them. The temperature outside had dropped, and I shivered with the cold, pulled up my other blanket, and dropped back to a fitful sleep, and dreamed of winter storms.

First came the winter storms with their winds that chilled my bones, and then the sun began to fall on me, and burned my skin. It was one or the other, but never did they balance. And all the while I could hear my birth mother calling, *"Tiiiiii.... Tiiiiii.... Staaaaaay.... Staaaaaay...."*

Chapter Seventeen

If you can find the Cauldron of the Gods,
If you can submerge yourself in the boiling contents,
If you can climb out whole and unscathed,
Life is yours.
—*Kack Dor, Historian*

VOICES. THE WINDS WARMED, and now carried voices I could hear. Blue wind spoke, full of humor and compassion.

"How is Mother Hakka?"

Hakka is a mother? When did that happen? Who is the father?

The yellow wind, tired to the point of collapse, answered, "Much better. She's eating a bit." Hakka is sick? No, she was sick. She's better now. Good.

"I think our little one is also better. Her fever has broken." Someone else is sick? Shouldn't I help? I struggled to wake, to sit, to help. I failed.

"Here. I brought you something to eat. It isn't much, but the gates are now open, and food should start coming into the city. It's been three days since anyone else got sick." The yellow wind began to turn brown.

"Anka, I think you need to rest a bit. I'll sit with Jibutu while you eat and then rest. There is nothing else you can do." Anka! The yellow wind is called Anka. Who is Jibutu? Why does the blue wind want to sit with that person? The words rode the winds as they swirled around me.

"So you wake, after all?" I opened my eyes and looked into the face of the most beautiful woman I had ever seen. Her face a perfect oval, even her head, shaped like a perfect sliwa egg, was as bald as a sliwa egg. Her eyes were brown with amber flecks, her smile one of warmth and compassion. The voice of the Blue Wind.

"Who?" My voice cracked. My mouth was as dry as that of a desert mummy.

"I'm Lu Shahnnah. Don't talk yet. Let me get you a bit of juice. Sip. Here, I'll hold your head." When I had sipped about half the bowl of juice I closed my eyes and she lowered my head back to its pillow.

"Thank you. Who are you? Where am I? Where is—?"

"I'm an old friend of your Chief Healer, Hakka. I've been gone for a couple of years, and returned to find the city locked down with plague. I immediately came to offer my help and support."

"How did you get in?"

She smiled, "I have my ways. You should know them."

"I should? Why?"

"Because you're a Lu, one of the family of Nah."

"I'm a what? Of the family Who?"

"A Lu. A shaman. Of the family of Nah."

"I'm sorry, but I'm a healer from the Tribe of Jib."

"Yes, so Anka has told me. Now, you are tired, and must rest, and when your strength returns, we'll talk. I am eager to hear your story, and to find out just who your mother is. We are of the same Family. You know that, don't you?"

"I know no such thing. If you were of the Tribe of Jib, I would know you. You are not of the tribe, so therefore...."

"Anka told me a bit of your fourth night dream. Rest a bit, now. We'll talk later."

I had slept for days, but needed no further coaxing. How could I still be tired? And yet, this little bit of conversation exhausted me. I slept.

"Mother Hakka, we need your help."

"Why, child, in my condition, I don't know what kind of help I can be."

"See?" I said, "now drop the subject." But Shahnnah would not drop the subject. Like a baby sliwa with a goatskin, she would not let go.

"Ah, I think I know. You, Shahnnah, want to take Jibutu back to the Nah family compound, and you, Jibutu, do not want to go."

Shahnnah smiled. I glowered.

"Yes. I thought so."

"I need to stay here, Hakka Healer, where I can be of help to you and Anka, and the people of this city."

"Village, I should think. Oh, Jibutu, we've buried more than half our people. No one was spared, as you know."

My voice softened. It was still hard to comprehend, but of ten people, seven died. Sometimes whole families. Sometimes all the elderly of a house died, sometimes all but the babies. And then, as fast as it was upon us, it left us. "I know, Healer Hakka. You lost many good friends."

"Yes. I did. As did you and Anka." That, too, was true. Unbidden pictures of people I knew and loved came to my mind. People, like my Tribe, I would never see again.

"But," I began to argue, "Hakka Healer, all I've ever wanted to be was a healer, and then a surgeon. I have worked hard to be good at both. Besides, I am the only surgeon here. I can't leave."

"You, my child, do not *want* to leave. Both Anka and I can operate if need be. True, our stitching is not as neat as yours, but it holds. No, child, I think you must go."

I sulked. "I don't want to." Hakka Healer smiled.

151

"Cousin," began Shahnnah. She still insisted we were related, "Although I'm sure your company, and your help would be welcome if you stayed, nevertheless, your training is required. Once trained, you may return."

"How long will the training take?" I sighed, resigned to going, and equally sure I would hate it.

"I don't know. We normally start when we are children and it becomes our lives. I will have to think on your training, once I have you at the compound, and see what your strong points are. You have received much of your training already, through the healer's school and through your natural curiosity. I would say, at the most, two years."

"But, how do you know, I mean, really *know*, I am, or am to be, a shaman?"

"I didn't tell you?"

"No, you've always taken it for granted that I would know."

"Jibutu, have you looked in a mirror since you've awakened?"

At that, I laughed. "No. Healers do not look in mirrors—at least not often. We are so ugly we frighten even ourselves."

She took a deep breath, and sighed. "So I understand. When you were sick, your hair fell out."

"I know. That's why I wear a cap, until it grows back. My head is cold."

"Jibutu, I'm sorry, but it won't grow back."

"What?"

"I was here when your hair fell out. I'm sorry, Jibutu, but I was so shocked at what I saw, I rubbed a salve in your scalp to keep the hair from coming back."

"What did you see?"

"The Net of Star paths"

"The what?"

"Look at my head, Jibutu. What do you see?" Shahnnah put her head down so I could see the top of it.

152

"I see a star, and what looks like several lines tattooed in with colored inks, and smaller stars and circles, in blacks, blues, and purples. That must have hurt, getting all those tats on the top of your head."

"They are not tats."

"Neh?"

"When our girl-children are born, their mothers place a hand-made net on their heads. The net is made with special threads and beads. If the net is accepted, it goes into the scalp, and that person will be a shaman. If the net falls off, the person will not be a shaman."

The breath left me as if I'd been hit in the stomach. I collapsed into a chair, trying to breathe.

"My dream." I saw Papa Jib in my mind, telling about finding me, and the net the woman, my birth mother, placed on me. "When Papa Jib found me in the desert all I had on was a net. He never thought about it again, and rode to get me to my Mama. My hair must have grown in over it, because no one remembered seeing it. Papa figured it dropped off on the ride, to be lost in the desert."

"It did not drop off, and because the salve was not applied immediately after acceptance, your hair grew thick and fast."

"And my fourth night dream. When Mother Roose asked me who I was, I thought I replied that I was Shaman-Healer Apprentice Jibutu. When I asked about the Shaman part later, she denied I'd said it. She told me to forget such thoughts."

"Yes, child. Many healers fear the shamans. Truly, though, they are but another form of healer, aren't they, Shahnnah?"

"Yes, we are." She turned back to me, "Did your birth mother give her name? Or yours?"

"Papa said she tried to say something, but he couldn't understand it, and forgot it. She was weak, and dying. His sole thought, when he knew she had died, was to save me. People say he rode his sliwa so hard and so fast the feet wore off."

153

"I doubt that, but it makes a good story."

"I know it isn't true, but it is the desert way of saying he rode in a single-minded hurry." Anka joined us and the conversation.

"But, how do you know I'm a...a Nah?"

"All nets are different, but all nets have similarities. The Family Nah has one large star, the Family Dil has two, the...well, you'll learn all the families and how to recognize them later. Anyway, you have one large star."

"What if someone made a mistake?"

"There was no mistake. You can't see, but I can. There is an aura about your head that is filled with love. I can't quite read it, but your mother and someone who loved you made the net. And I can tell from the design, that person was a perfectionist. The Nah star is purple. The others are blue and green, and the god lines between them vibrate with color and strength. Yes, we are related."

"Jibutu Healer, I handled this city alone for many years before Anka came. I have welcomed her, and you, as sister healers and as daughters." Hakka held up her hand to keep me quiet. "However, I think I have no choice but to release you, for a while at least, and allow you to receive your additional training. I shall write Authority and tell her of your work, and of my decision to release you."

And so it came to pass I walked through the streets of Michlin, saying goodbye to those of my friends who still lived, and to the city of my first assignment. Well, I didn't walk. Shahnnah didn't think I was well enough to walk, so she hired a wagon and loaded my things into it. And then we were out the gate and heading toward the grass.

The road through the grass was wide enough for two large wagons to pass, but as the farms faded behind us, the grass grew higher and higher, and closer and closer. I said nothing, but Shahnnah saw.

Seeing my distress at being unable to see beyond the grass, Shahnnah stopped the wagon. "You will be sore tonight, and for a few days, but we'll ride and you will be higher and able to see over the grass. I will show you how." She stopped the two buflo that pulled the wagon, pulled a couple of thick pads from under the seat, and placed them on the shoulders of the buflo, close to their horns. "I'll help you up."

"You want me to ride?" I'd rather ride a sliwa—they are closer to the ground, and not as bony.

"Yes, I want you to ride. You'll be higher. Now put your left foot in my hands, and when I raise you, grab his horns, and swing your right leg over." I did as she spoke, and suddenly, I sat atop this mighty creature. His shoulders were the highest part of his body, and I could now see over the grass. "There. Put your feet on his horns, next to his head, and that way you won't slide. Their movement, as you have noticed, is slow and even, and other than having one hip go up and the other down, then reverse, you'll be quite comfortable. Until we stop for a break." Her knowing grin flashed slightly wicked. I didn't care. I could see!

She pulled on the horns of her buflo, and threw her leg and body up. "You'll be doing this in no time."

"Does the grass go on forever?"

"No," she laughed, and then said, "It just seems that way. Look, there toward the left, on the horizon. See that hump? That's the oasis where we'll stop for a rest. That hump is trees. The oases are well spaced so travelers can have a place to stop for midday meal, and then to camp for the night. There are trees, a well, and usually lean-tos that can be shared."

We rode in silence until I had the rhythm of my buflo and no longer felt I had to concentrate quite so much to stay on its back.

"Lu Shahnnah, does the grass ever burn?"

"Sometimes."

155

I shivered at her answer. I saw flames dancing about me, racing on the grass.

"Not at this time of the year, don't worry. You will learn the ways of the grass." She smiled. I changed the subject.

"Riding a buflo is nothing like riding a sliwa."

"I've never ridden a sliwa. Actually, I've never seen one. Truth, I'm not even sure what they are."

"They are giant lizards. We of the desert use them as beasts of burden, we ride them, and in times of great need, we eat them. Papa Jib, headman of the Tribe of Jib, always kills the older ones. Their meat is stringy and tough, and needs to be stewed a long time. The young ones are tender and juicy, and once in a while, we slaughter a young one, but only if there are plenty."

"What does sliwa taste like?"

"Oh," I laughed, "like sliwa. It is a white meat, and tastes like nothing but sliwa. At least, I've never tasted anything else like it."

<hr />

"We're coming to the oasis. If there are people, they will possibly offer us part of their food, if they are still eating. It is polite to accept, as well as to offer some of ours either to the same pot, or for them to take with them."

"The desert has the same manners."

"They will address us as 'Lu', let me reply, and then repeat my response."

And then, we were there. The oasis was a delightful circular area with three lean-to shelters surrounding a central plaza area with a well, and a built-up area for a fire. All around the circle grew trees full of lacy leaves that offered shade. The trees were a gray-green color, and I saw no fruit on them. From the smell of the fire, they used dried buflo dung, as we used dried sliwa plops.

Around the oasis, the grass had been cleared to bare earth.

Two adults and a child turned as we entered the circle. I noticed they immediately looked at our heads, uncovered in the hot sun.

"Lu. Lu. Please alight and be welcome at our meal. It is almost ready. I am Pan Nadir and this is my wife, Shahn and our son, Panli."

"Peace upon you and your family, Pan Nadir. We appreciate your hospitality."

"Peace," I followed, "upon you and your family, Pan Nadir. We appreciate your hospitality." I saw a slight movement of Shahnnah's hand, and continued, "We would be honored if you would accept some of our food for your pot." Shahnnah circled her thumb and finger so only I could see.

"Are you not worried about sparks from the fire setting the grass alight?" I whispered, but am sure Pan Nadir and his family heard.

"No. See, there is a grate over the coals, and on the other side of the pit is a lid. When we finish cooking, we place the lid on top, and the fire goes out. Also, that bucket, there, holds water if we need it. And, as you noticed, there is only dirt for quite some way all around the oasis."

The Family Nadir looked at me and then at Shahnnah. I could read it in their faces. I was a Lu. Why did I not have this most basic knowledge?

We slid off our beasts, took them to one of the lean-tos, and then returned with our share of the food. Shahnnah walked normally. I hobbled. Never had my hips hurt so badly. I don't think they hurt this badly when Ter and I took our tumble down The Shales. I took a few herbs to make myself a tea. Again, I was watched, but nothing was said, until Shahnnah offered the food, and we all sat. A groan escaped as I sat. All eyes turned to me.

"My cousin, as you have rightly noticed, is a Lu. However, a Lu with a strange story, which we will tell as we eat."

Our bowls were quickly filled with stew, and we were each given a piece of flat bread to scoop the contents to our mouths.

"This is delicious, thank you for a wonderful meal. It reminds me of stews my mother cooked."

157

"And, if you don't mind my asking, who is your mother? Perhaps my wife and she know each other?"

I smiled before replying, "I doubt it. My tribe, the Tribe of Jib, is from the desert."

"The desert? But, you are of the Family Nah."

"That's what my cousin tells me. You see, my father Jib, and several of his friends, rode their sliwa to an oasis to be sure it was cleaned before bringing the Tribe."

"What's a sliwa?" The young boy, Panli, asked

"A giant lizard. We of the desert use them as beasts of burden, as well as, sometimes, food."

"What's a desert?" The quiet of an active child could no longer be held. He had questions, and must ask them. His mother started to shush him, but I held up my hand.

"A desert is a vast expanse of sand. It lies on the other side of those mountains."

He turned to his father, "Will you take me? I want to see, and to ride a...a sliwa!"

"Perhaps, some day. Now let the Lu finish her story."

"Did a sliwa eat your hand? Is that why—?"

"Panli! Mind your manners. And be quiet." Panli's parents both spoke at once, and the boy lowered his head in contriteness. When he looked up again, and made eye contact with me, I winked.

"It is normal to ask about my hook. Children do not have the filters adults do. Allow me, please, to explain. You see, Panli, I was in a fire, and my hand was in the way of a burning timber, and I lost it. Now I have a hook." I moved it and showed him how I could open and close it. Then I began my story.

"My father Jib, and his men came to the oasis. There, they found a woman who had just given birth to me, and was close to death. She spoke, but they could not understand her, for she was weak from her ordeal. As she died, she handed me to Jib. I had only a net upon my head. Jib left the others to deal with the woman, placed me under his cloak, and raced his sliwa back to his tribe and a wet nurse. The only thought he had about the net was that it was a useless thing for a baby offering no protection from the sun or the winds at all. By the time we arrived at the Tribe, and he handed me to the woman who would become my mother, I had hair, and the net was neither seen, nor thought of again. Not until I became very sick, lost my hair, and Lu Shahnnah saw it."

"Lu?" Panli looked me straight in the eyes, "Why do you have tattoos on your face? They are ugly."

"Panli! That was most impolite. Apologize at once."

"But, Mama, they are. Lu's are beautiful, this one is ugly."

"Panli—"

I couldn't help but smile. "Please. It is an honest question. Perhaps not tactful, but children value honesty above tact, neh? Besides, he's right. Our tats and scars are not meant to be beautiful, but to be ugly so when, as a healer, we need to treat someone for a time in our healer's tent, their spouse will not think wrong thoughts and be jealous. Healers may not marry." I told Panli and his parents about my training, and receiving my tattoos. "I think this is a question I will hear often while here. If not aloud from children, then silently from the eyes of the more, uh, tactful adults, neh?"

Chapter Eighteen

The hearts of men may be discerned
by one who sees with eyes
and follows where the cards will lead.
—*Joy Moon, Blind Artist of Chusett*

"COUSIN. JIBUTU. WAKE. We are home. We are almost into Chusett." Shahnnah sat on the bench of the cart; I rode in back, crammed between boxes. Riding the great beast that first day had not only tired my body and made it sore, it also was a bit of a setback in my recovery. Shahnnah decided I would ride in the back where I could watch the sky, and nap as I needed. The excitement in her voice was contagious. At least a little.

"I'm awake." I stretched and wiggled myself into a sitting position. It had been a long three-day, but I slept most of it, warmed by the sun.

"Good. Can you climb to the bench while we move, or should I stop? I want you next to me as we go through town." She slowed the cart, and I scrambled over the seat back onto the bench. "The Nah Family Compound is on the far side of Chusett." She began pointing out compounds, and telling me the families associated with each.

All I could see were high walls with trees growing behind, and closed gates. The grass receded to the background. Fortunately, the streets were wide, and laid out with thought to animals, carts, and people.

"We will go straight to the Family Compound, but come back into town later. I want to show you the market, and introduce you to friends. Family comes first, though.

A whisper seemed to ride the air. I noticed people on top of the walls. They watched us, and excitedly pointed and called to the next wall, and soon people were at their gates calling as we rode by, "Shahnnah, Lu Shahnnah. Welcome home. Lu, we welcome you." And then we were through the town, and almost in the grass, before Shahnnah slowed at a gate. She did not stop the beasts, merely slowed them. Then the gates swung open on silent hinges and we rode into a huge courtyard.

All of the Tribe of Jib could have camped in this courtyard and not be crowded. A well stood off to the side. A pump brought water up from the bowels of earth, and poured it in a trough. Lace-leaf trees grew around the edges; their slender limbs looked barely strong enough to support the leaves. Behind the courtyard was a huge house. Shahnnah watched me as I took it all in.

"It's huge. The front building is primarily barn for the animals, and quarters for the servants. Behind are the homes of the family. Come."

Before I could get down, people swarmed about us, lifted us down, and then lifted our belongings out of the back. They swarmed about Shahnnah and hugged her, and their joy at her return spread to me, a stranger. I, too, was hugged as a long-lost relative, new to their arms.

We were ushered through a hall and into another courtyard, smaller, though still large. In the center was a large bath and around the edges were several buildings, some joined, some had small gardens between. The bath was oblong, and tiled, with lace-leaf trees to shade it and the buildings. Those who carried our belongings took them into a small building; the rest stopped, removed their robes, and jumped into the bath.

"Come, Jibutu, it is time for a swim!" It wasn't a bath at all, but a swimming pool. I removed my robe and my cuff and hook and jumped in as I saw them do, and kept going down. Water

161

covered me. I sank even further. Push, I seemed to hear, and when my feet touched the hard bottom, my legs collapsed, and then I pushed. My head exploded from the water, I gasped for air. Someone grabbed me and pulled me to the side.

"Jibutu, you do not swim? I am so sorry. Come, hold to the edge and 'walk' to the other end. I will come, too." I stared into the faces of those in the pool, who looked at me as if I somehow wasn't quite normal in their eyes. "Come, everyone, I know you all wonder about this strange Lu I brought home. She is of the Family Nah, and she has an interesting tale to tell. We will swim a bit, then sit in the shade, have food and drink, and she will tell her story, and answer your questions, for surely they are many."

Laughter again resounded, and once my feet were on the bottom, and my face in the air, I could join in. "Lu?" a hesitant voice next me, I looked down and saw a child who spoke.

"Yes."

"You do not swim?"

"No. I was raised in the desert. We had no water for swimming."

"I will teach you to swim. When everyone is gone, and the water is quiet, I will come get you. It's quite easy. I am the best swimmer here, and the best teacher." Before I could say a word, he dove under the water and like a fish swam between legs of people and popped up at the other end of the pool, grinned and waved.

⋙ ॐ ⋘

One by one, people exited the pool, dried and dressed, and wandered into one of the buildings. I, too, got out of the water, dried, and dressed, and looked for Shahnnah. "Lu, where are my things? I would like to change into something cleaner."

"Come. I will show you your room, and the dining room, which is where everyone is headed. This is, or was, my room. Now that my mother has gone, I have her quarters. I thought you would like this room, it has a window for breezes, and you

162

can watch the grass, if you want. It is also private, which you will probably want for your studies. If you prefer another room, we will move you tomorrow."

The room indeed had a window open to a small garden. And shutters. The window was tall enough, and low enough to the floor to also be a door. It reminded me of my tower room at school, though this room was not round, and the rocks had been painted to look like grass, with animals and children playing. It was a child's room but, I thought, am I not a child again? A bed stood against one wall, there was a table, two chairs, shelves holding books, and shelves holding my clothes, which had been unpacked and neatly put away. My surgery accouterments and Bowl of Life, and other belongings had been placed on separate shelves. I had nothing to do but change clothes and join the others.

I would have preferred sand on the walls, and sliwa. For some reason I didn't quite understand, these people had shown only love and acceptance, but I felt petulant. I did not want to be a shaman; I wanted to be a healer. I had trained, and trained hard, to heal, and that's what I wanted to do. I changed into a clean robe, plastered a smile on my face, squared my shoulders and went to the dining room, determined not to let them see my petulance.

I was not sure it should have been called a dining room. Used to the quiet ebb and flow of talk between fellow students in the school dining room, I was totally unprepared for the noise that assaulted me as I entered. Laughter and conversations yelled from one table to another. I started to back out, but I had been seen, and a chant erupted, "Jibutu! Jibutu! Come. Sit here. Sit with us." Several people made room for me at their tables, and I had to make a decision. I did not see Shahnnah, but the little boy who offered to teach me to swim stood on his stool and waved. My smile was no longer forced, and I sat with my new friend.

"See? I told you. She's my friend and I am going to teach her to swim." His little chest puffed out like a male sliwa to impress the females.

"Well, little friend, before you explode with pride, perhaps you should introduce yourself to me, and then introduce your friends, neh?"

"If she's such a good friend, how come she doesn't know your name? Huh?" One of the boys at the table jabbed my friend good naturedly, and the table erupted in taunts and laughs.

"I, I am called Fish, Lu. And this is Jornal, and Beldan, and Rayli, and Radsa. We are the best swimmers in the Family Nah. But I am, of course, best of the best." At this last, all the boys laughed. It was obvious they were good friends.

"You may be the best swimmer, Fish, but I, Jornal have the best manners." Before he could be stopped, he rose, and went to the serving board to get me a plate of food. Only when he was there did he realize he had no idea what I liked, or what to put on my plate. He turned, looked at me and raised an eyebrow.

"Anything," I mouthed.

Dinner proceeded with great merriment at my table and the others, but when my plate was empty, I excused myself from 'my boys' as I had begun to think of them, and returned to my room. I was sure I would sleep for a week. And the boys would have great bragging rights within their universe. Not one of those well-mannered boys asked about my hook. Had Shahnnah told someone and word spread? Or were they, truly, well mannered?

A day bed stood in the garden. I went to it, lay down, and looked at the stars. Gorgeous and glittery on the black of night, they were not the stars of my desert. A tear soon followed by a second, then a third, and more fell down my cheeks. I rolled over and let the sobs of self-pity claim me. I wanted to go home.

"Why do you cry, Lu?"

Chapter Nineteen

The minds of God can be seen in a drop of water.
You must only look with your heart.
—*Lu Thonyyar, First Shaman*

"DO YOU FEEL UP TO WALKING into Chusett this morning?" Shahnnah sat at the breakfast table with me.

"Yes, that would be good. When do we leave?"

"As soon as we put our plates in to be washed. Hurry." Shahnnah's grin, contagious as always, beamed at my answer. It did not take long before we were on the road walking back the way we had come.

"You have made friends here, Cousin. Jornal tells me you share the same garden and love of looking at the stars."

"He told you?"

"Yes. He said he went into the garden last night to look at the skies, and you were there, and that you talked about your home. He is very interested in the desert. And your sliwa. He is a good boy, not prone to talking to the elders. He trusts you. You can trust him."

"Thank you. And yes, he is a good boy."

"Now, we come to the market. Tell me, how is it different from your markets?"

I looked around the area, suddenly aware of the sights and smells of hot metal and cooking meat, of baking bread and flowers with heady perfumes. "Well, our markets are mobile. We meet once a year, and have no permanent shelters like you. Space is on a first come, first choose basis. Whoever gets to the area first, spreads his blanket and lays out his wares. There is no logic to who goes where. I see here you have flower sellers in one area, foods in another—each product seems to have its own place."

"And at night? How do the sellers protect their wares from theft?"

"Theft? In the desert? Oh, that's easy. It doesn't exist. To steal in the desert and be caught means to die. If the seller isn't around and you wish to buy something, you move the item you wish to buy to the back of the blanket it sits on, and then when the seller comes back, he knows that item is spoken for and waits for whoever moved it to return to buy it. Or by noon, it goes back in the front."

"Come, we will begin your training today. First, you must get your god cards."

"God cards?"

Shahnnah smiled, "Yes. Come, right over there, in the corner, is Joy Moon's stall." As we walked to the stall, several people stopped us, spoke to Shahnnah, smiled at me. Word had spread that a new Lu, an untrained Lu, had arrived. "The market seems a bit more crowded than usual."

"It's me. They all want to see the new Lu."

"Do you think so?"

I laughed, "Yes."

We were at the stall. An old woman, with sightless silver eyes sat on a three-legged stool. As we approached, she stood and came to meet us. She reminded me of Hakka only her robes were brightly colored and she wore many light and flowing scarves in equally bright and varied colors. I do believe she was as wide as she was tall. "Ah, Lu Shahnnah, you have come to see me. And who is this Lu who isn't a Lu that came with you?"

"Peace be with you, Joy Moon. This is Lu Jibutunah, from the desert far away. She has come for training."

"Peace be with you, Joy Moon," I repeated.

166

"And with you, Lu Jibutunah of the Desert."

"Joy, I think she needs to start with her god cards. What do you think?"

"Place your hands in mine, please, Lu Jibutunah." She put her hands, palms up, over the counter.

I placed my hand and my hook in her hands, and was enveloped with a peace that flooded through me, and flowed around me. Her hands were smooth, but strong. The feeling of peace was so strong, my knees almost buckled before she released me. Even my hook warmed, and she seemed not at all surprised that she held a hand and a hook rather than two hands.

"Yes. I shall lay out six decks and we shall see which one chooses her." Joy Moon cleared a place on the counter, and then spread a scarf of grass-green woven fabric upon the space. She then placed a second scarf of woven deep purple on top, with the top scarf hanging over the edge of the counter nearer her. She reached under the counter, and placed decks of cards under the purple scarf so I could not see them. "Now, Lu Jibutunah, hold your hands above the cloth, and slowly move them over the decks, until one speaks to you."

"Just do it, Cousin. You will know." Shahnnah replied to my look of puzzlement.

Slowly I moved my hook and my hand over the cards. "Neh!" A surge of power went from one deck up my arms. "Oh. It didn't hurt, but startled me."

Joy Moon and Shahnnah both laughed. "Don't move your hands."

"Well, let's see which deck." Joy Moon removed the purple cloth, and I saw the decks. They were all basically the same, except mine. It had a painting of a sliwa on the top card. Joy Moon laughed, "I wondered who these cards were for. I felt very strongly to paint them, and could not understand the reason. No one here has been to, or come from, the desert. Until now. And now I understand why I painted them." She wrapped them in the

167

top cloth and told me, "Keep them wrapped in this cloth and carry them in this pouch. You may also get a box, if you'd like, but keep them in the pouch inside the box. Lu Shahnnah will explain them to you. I am always here if you have questions and she is not available."

"Thank you, Joy Moon."

"Your training will not be as hard as you think. It is not like the school you went to. The hardest part, for you, will be the opening of yourself. The trust you must learn in yourself, not just your abilities. And, yes, you are a Nah."

"Joy, could you see who her mother was?"

"No, I could not. She is closed. When you learn to open, come back, and maybe then. But, please, Lu Jibutunah, do not wait until then to come visit an old and blind artist. I would enjoy your company, and the stories I'm sure you can tell."

"Thank you, Joy Moon. I look forward to many visits with you."

"There are 80 cards in your deck, four families if you will, plus some that are alone. You must spend time with them, and see what each card tells you. You must learn what the cards tell *you*, not what they tell someone else. Then, when you begin to read the cards for others, you can learn what the cards mean for that person."

"What do you mean? I'm not sure I understand."

"Well, say you are reading the cards for me, and the Death card comes up. Now, to one not trained, they might think I am going to die, but a travel card has also come up, and a working card. The Death card, in this case, might mean the end of living in the same house and moving to another place for a better job. Death does not always mean dying in the traditional sense. Death can mean the end of something, the end of a place, a time, a situation. You will learn."

"And how do I learn?"

"Go to your room, shuffle the cards, look at them, shuffle them again; what do they tell you? What do they tell you today, what will they tell you tomorrow? Just learn them today. Tomorrow I'll show you ways to lay them out."

I held the cards, studied each one, and cried. How Joy Moon, with her sightless silver eyes, could see to paint them I could not fathom and to paint my desert with such accuracy, with all the scenes of my memories. As I looked at them, they did, indeed, seem to speak to me.

"Jibutunah, come, sit at my table and show me your cards," became a frequent request. Everyone wanted to help me learn. Everyone wanted to know me a bit better. Mostly, as they said, everyone wanted to look at the cards and see what my beloved desert looked like.

"Lu, come. It is time you learn to swim." Fish knocked on my door, and called. "Come. Now. No more excuses. You must learn to swim, and this is a good time. Almost everyone has gone to the fields."

I sighed, stood, and opened the door. "I will be right there." Fish fairly wiggled with excitement as he escorted me to the pool, though he tried to contain it, and be serious. What had I agreed to?

"Come into the water at this end, where it is shallow. Just stand and splash. Now squat down. Get your face wet. Hold onto the edge, bend at your waist, and put your face in the water, turn your face to the air and breathe in, face in water and breathe out. Relax. Move. Relax. Breathe. Relax." The orders came over and over, with the patient Fish standing next to me. His hands always touched, always reassured.

"Good. Now you aren't so afraid. Tomorrow, we will have lesson two. Now, we play." And suddenly, a wall of water kicked up by his hand, was in my face. He dove, and came up behind me, laughing. "Here, I'll show you how. Hold your hand like this, and then move it fast, shoving the water."

Fish had as much fun showing me how to raise the water as he did in trying to teach me to swim.

"Now, you must pay me."

"What? You said nothing about payment." Whatever could this child want in payment? "Besides, I have no money."

"Lu, I don't want money. I want you to read your cards for me. Bring them after lunch." Before I could form a response, he was off, running and laughing.

I returned to my room, picked up a change of clothes, and went to the baths. The pool was for swimming and playing, not for bathing. The pool water was cool and refreshing, but I wanted a warm bath, a long soak.

Few were at lunch when I went into the dining room. The serving board held only cold meats, cheeses, and breads. There would be a hearty supper once everyone returned for the evening meal.

I shuffled the cards for Fish to cut, "Fish, you do know I've never done this before? And that whatever I say may not be correct?"

"Yes," he grinned, "you just read. You gotta start somewhere, sometime."

Chapter Twenty

Water is Life
—*Desert Proverb*

IN THE TWO YEARS I had been at the Nah family compound, I had been welcomed and treated as a cousin by everyone in the family, and everyone in the village. Though not the Tribe of Jib, they were family and they loved me. I loved them.

"Joy Moon, what a surprise!" I heard the genuine pleasure in Shahnnah's voice. "Please, come in. Jibutu and I were just talking about—"

"You were just talking about your future, which is why I've come. Aren't you going to offer an old lady an iced beverage? A small glass of something, uh, adult, in it would be nice too, if you get my meaning." Joy Moon smiled, and sat in the most comfortable chair in Shahnnah's quarters. I hurried to get the requested drink, a berry tea with some red wine added. I knew from past visits she fancied this drink.

"Aaaah, thank you Lu Jibutunah. Very nice." She took a couple of swallows, and the silence was broken. "You wonder, I'm sure, why I'm here."

"Well, I know you don't come often enough. And that I'm delighted you are here, now."

"Shahnnah, you are right. But I have my business, and...." Her voice trailed off, leaving us to imagine what else she might have said. I found it hard to imagine Joy Moon anyplace other than her stall and apartment in back.

171

"I have dreamed."

Shahnnah raised her face to me, "Joy Moon is a dreamer. When she uses that tone of voice, it means something important."

"Joy Moon," I asked, "are you also a Lu?"

"No, child. I am an orphan. I was abandoned at an oasis sometime after I was born. It is assumed I was loved, as my body was wrapped in an expensive cloth, but for whatever reason my parents could not keep me. They probably knew I was blind even at that early stage, and they could not deal with it. We don't know."

"I'm sorry, Joy Moon."

"Don't be. Larl Moon found me, and brought me home to his wife Celu, who remained childless. She found a wet nurse, and as you can see, I thrived." Joy Moon placed her hands on her ample girth and laughed. "By the time anyone thought to test me, or even train me, I had become an artist of some note, and frankly, wasn't interested."

"But," I continued, "you dream."

"Yes, Jibutunah, I dream. And when I have certain dreams, especially when they repeat, I pay attention. Now you and Shahnnah must pay attention, as well."

"Speak and we shall hear. What do you wish to tell us?" Shahnnah wore a serious, almost worried look as she asked the question.

"It is time for you and Lu Jibutunah to leave. For Lu Jibutunah, it will be forever, for you, Lu Shahnnah, I don't know.

"Your mother and her new mate left many years ago, taking Achennah with them. They went across the mountains, then across the desert, to Bel Harq. Your mother, Lu Ahnah, knew she would never return, and therefore transferred the Family to you."

"Yes. I know."

"Lu Jibutunah, do you know of the caravan road between Yaylin and Bel Harq?"

"Yes. I have been on parts of it often."

"Were you found anywhere near that road?"

I looked at Shahnnah. Could we be sisters? "No, Joy Moon. I was found several days ride to the west."

"I just wondered. It is not like Lu Ahnah not to have written, still what with the wedding of Achennah, the new family, well, I can understand." Joy Moon smiled, "She never was good at letting people know what was going on. She knew, therefore, it was fine."

Shahnnah smiled at the memories of her mother.

"However, it is time, Lu Shahnnah, for you to turn the Family over to someone else. Lu Jibutunah has been here almost two years, and it is time for the two of you to leave, and make the same trek as your mother. You must find your mother in Bel Harq. She knows who is the birth mother of Jibutu."

"But, why do I need to turn the Family over to someone? I am not my mother, you know. I do write."

"I know. But I dreamed you going into the desert with Jibutu, and not coming back. Perhaps, when you get to Bel Harq, you will meet a mate, and stay with your mother."

"I come out of the desert? Do I go back to Yaylin? Or here?"

"I don't know. I see you on many long journeys. I can't tell if it's one long journey, or several shorter ones. But you will not return to the Land of Grass. When you leave us, it will be forever.

"Now, the rainy season is near. I think you need to be on the road before the rains come and make travel miserable. Especially in the mountains." With that last, she emptied her glass, stood in a cloud of silken veils of grays and greens and yellows, and appeared to float her way to the door. "Fish!" She yelled, "Fish, come. It is time to walk me home." Joy Moon turned as she

173

reached the gate. "Lu Jibutunah, you will find your birth family. And when you do, if you think of it, please, send a letter. Someone will read it to me." Then she was gone. I looked at Shahnnah, no longer perplexed at her abrupt departures.

"That was quite the message, wasn't it?" Shahnnah asked.

"But, Shahnnah, will we go? Will you turn over the Family to someone else? Just on the strength of her dream?"

"Dreams, Cousin. Dreams. She has had several dreams that pertain to us, and now she's had one that told her to tell us. We'd better start packing. And I need to start thinking of who to turn the Family over to."

A ten-day later, after a flurry of packing, unpacking, and repacking; after a round of parties to say farewell; after a huge feast and celebration where much laughter reigned, and small gifts were exchanged, and much, way too much, celebratory wine consumed, Shahnnah and I again climbed onto the wagon, and began to retrace our route of two years ago. This time, I rode next to her, the grass not quite so intimidating.

The night before our departure, I, too, dreamed. Again, my birth mother called to me. Again, I could not understand what she said, but she seemed happy, and excited.

∼❦∼

"Oh, Shahnnah, look how empty Michlin appears. Two of every three houses stand empty and boarded."

"Cousin, more than half the people died in the plague. It will take time to bring in new people, and to have more children. No one wants to move to a plague city."

The streets, once filled with laughing children, now appeared empty, and those homes with occupants remained quiet. Now and then, I would see a curtain move, as someone watched from inside. "They have become suspicious, Shahnnah. I see curtains move here and there, but no one comes out to greet us."

"We might bring another bout of the plague. They fear for a reason."

174

We rode up the hill in silence, and into the Courtyard of the Healers. Even here, the quiet seemed too much. "Shahnnah, something is wrong. Wait here." I jumped from the wagon, and ran into the infirmary. No one. I ran down the hall, all the while calling, "Anka. Hakka. Where are you?" No answer. I went into every room, and every room was neat and tidy, and free of dust, but no one was here. Panic began to seize me.

Laughter. Screams of joy. I turned as Anka came running into my arms.

"You came back! You're here. Oh, my sister, I am so glad to once again hold you in my arms!" She pulled me close, and then held me at arm's length to look at me. "Oh, Hakka will be sorry she picked this day to venture to the mines. Come, our room is ready. Is Shahnnah staying, too? Oh, you are home. At last. At last, my sister, you have returned to me."

Eventually, I stopped laughing and crying long enough to answer some of her questions. I did not tell her of our planned trip, we both deserved the happiness of the moment. We would stay a day or two, but then we must go on, we would take the low road, so we could use our wagon. And avoid The Shales.

"First, a bath. By the time you are through, dinner will be ready and Hakka will be home. Come." Anka led us down the hall to the bath, as if neither of us were familiar with the layout of the building. Then she was gone.

"She won't like that we are leaving so soon. She didn't want you to leave with me in the first place, you know."

"Really? She and Hakka practically forced me to go."

"They hoped you would find your mother. Your birth mother."

"That couldn't happen. She died."

"Yes. But they wanted you to find her name. They love you, Cousin. Your imminent departure will bring great sadness again. Allow them a bit of happiness before you tell them we leave on yet another journey. We have time."

I said nothing, closed my eyes and soaked in the hot water until time to dress for dinner.

Why, I wondered, was everyone so interested in my birth mother? I admit a certain interest—she was, after all the woman who gave me life. But what would her identity mean to me? Unless a cessation of my dreams.

If I find her, will I know the name she gave me? Will I become a different person?

Neh! But this mother bit became tiring at times. Saba is my mother. She loves me; she raised me. Roose is my mother. She loves me and trained me. This Lu who birthed me gave me life— then died and left me.

The fourth night dream seldom intruded in my thoughts, and Lu Mother, as I now thought of her, seldom visited my dreams anymore.

"Cousin?" I hazarded to voice my thoughts.

"Yes?"

"Maybe you can go without me? I am home, with sisters, where my Authority sent me. Neh! I want to stay here. You can go, and tell me what I need to know when you return." My eyes closed. I did not see if she made a face. She said nothing.

※ ❦ ※

"Did you hear about Lengo Ja and Mali? They had a baby girl, and have Authority's blessing to marry!" Anka and Hakka could hardly wait to tell me the news. Further, they could hardly believe it.

"Marry? Are they going to allow Healers to marry?" I stared slack jawed at such a concept.

"Why not? Shamans marry. Why can't healers?" Shahnnah asked, almost with defiance in her voice.

"Because, Shahnnah, healers can't have children. At least, none ever had, until now." I raised my cup of wine, "To Lengo Ja and Mali. And their baby girl!"

176

Everyone echoed my toast, and then with a wicked smile Anka asked me, "Do you know what they named their daughter?"

"No. You haven't told me."

"They named her Jibuli, for her mother, and for you."

I was so shocked I spewed my mouthful of wine across the table.

⤛ 𝄞 ⤜

Semp Istan and Ter came to visit. It was decided Shahnnah and I would leave with their caravan to Yaylin in two ten-days. Ter and his deaf friends all went to work for Semp Istan after the Inquiry, and Ter had become master of his own caravan. He taught anyone who showed interest to use the finger talk, so the men could talk with each other and others and were no longer caged within their small community of silence.

As we rode over the low road to Yaylin, both Shahnnah and I began to learn the language, and soon found ourselves included in this silent world.

⤛ 𝄞 ⤜

"The word spelling is easiest to learn, but longest to use," explained Ter. "Soon, you picks up the short forms if you pays attention."

Listening in on others' conversations became something easy to do; I just watched the fingers move, often without realizing I did. I learned Ject Zon tried to boss the wrong people in prison, and ended up in the mines. He tried to buy his way out, then tried to escape, and is now buried and forgotten in one of the deep pits.

"Mem, don't watch so hard. The mens like they privacy." Ter grinned at me.

The mens, as Ter called them, talked about the women they hoped to meet in Yaylin.

177

Chapter Twenty-One

> Wherever you go, there you are.
> Wherever you are, there you are home.
> —*Jonk Zinn, Itinerant Tinker*

"MEMS," SAID TER, bowing to Shahnnah and myself, "this be our last night out. We be in Yaylin tomorrow, about high sun. The mens thanks you for all you did for us on the trip, and has a present for each of you." He turned and motioned Ged to come in closer. Someone added another log to the fire, and the flames danced bright, illuminating Ged and two sticks.

Ged, shy around women approached us with his head down. He held two beautifully carved walking sticks out to us. He did not look at either of us.

"Ged," signed Ter, "look, you be giving them to the wrong ones!"

Ged looked, then blushed, and quickly reversed the sticks. Mine had a sliwa carved into it, one that clearly resembled the one on my cheek.

"Ged," I spoke and signed, "thank you very much. Did you carve this?"

"Yes, Mem," he signed back. "And hers, too."

"Ged, mine is beautiful. You must have spent time in the grass to get this bird like you did." Shahnnah also spoke and signed. Ged blushed a deeper purple.

"Mems," said Ter, "these be from all the mens. They 'preciate you learn their language, and gives them privacy, that you treats them likes mens, not animals."

178

I looked at all the men standing around the fire. Their faces happy and relaxed, not like the first time we met on the high road above us.

"Now, we party. Last night. Tomorrow, Yaylin!" Ter called out and signed, and the men heaped bowls with spicy food and brought them to us before filling their own. After we ate, they brought out their drums and danced for us.

༺ ༝ ༻

"Mems," said Ter, "we be in the gates, now, and the mens must take cargo to warehouse place. I must go with them, but Ged has pass to take you to Healer's School. Again, Mems, we thank you." As each wagon passed, the driver looked at us, smiled, and dipped his head in salute. Ged waited until all had passed, then took us to the School.

As happy as I was to be home, I was also sad to say good-bye to Ged and the men. My life seemed to be nothing but a series of 'hello' and 'good-bye.' And though each hello eventually brought a good-bye, I only wanted the hellos. Shahnnah and I were welcomed, taken to a room, and then to the bath.

"Authority requests your presence an hour before dinner, if you don't mind."

"Thank you, Acolyte. Please, tell her we will be happy to be there."

"Clean robes are here. You may leave yours where they fall." The acolyte stammered, looking for the right phrase. I realized her problem, we had no red robes, and Shahnnah's, as a Lu, was red.

"Lu Shahnnah may wear a purple robe. It will be all right, at least for a while."

"Thank you Jibutu Healer. Please enjoy your bath."

Then we were alone, to enjoy the luxury of quiet, hot water, and perfumed soap.

"Cousin, are they not curious? About me, I mean? About your bald head? Why does no one ask?"

179

"Oh, they are curious, all right. But they will not ask. At least not until after Authority has met with us, and we are in the dining hall. Then, rest assured, they will ask."

"It is so quiet here. Nothing like the family compounds."

"Yes. I think the constant noise of talk and laughter was one of the hardest things for me to get used to at the Nah compound. It was pleasant, but healers are quiet. Patients require quiet to heal."

"What is your Authority like?"

I smiled, "You will find out soon enough. Now, it is time to get out, and prepare to meet her."

⤚✧⤙

"Roose Healer told me you said you were a Shaman-Healer when you woke from your fourth night. She didn't understand what it meant, and holding the prejudice against shamans, denied it, and told you that you did not say it. Authority smiled, paused a few moments then spoke, "I see she was wrong.

"And you, Lu Shahnnah, claim kinship? How can you tell?"

"If you look at our net patterns, you will see they both have one large star. One star means House of Nah. But, no one seems to know who she is. As you know, her mother died shortly after her birth. However, a Dream Seer in my town has told us that my mother, who now lives in Bel Harq with her husband and my brother, holds the key, and that we must find her."

"Authority, I am home. I don't know that I want to leave. I admit, I have some curiosity as to who my birth mother was, and the name she wanted me to have, but—"

"Jibutu Healer, I think this is something you must see through to the end."

"But, why can't Shahnnah go with a caravan, visit with her mother, and send a letter with the information? Why is it necessary I, too, go?"

"I don't know, but I somehow feel it is."

180

Shahnnah smiled as if she had won a great prize. "Besides, she will need to see the net pattern on your skull."

You haven't won yet, I thought. "Authority, at least let us stay for a few months, until the Season of Storms has passed."

"Season of Storms? What's that?" Shahnnah asked.

"It is the time when sand storms rake the desert. Not a fun time to be on the desert."

"Authority?" Shahnnah's eyes glinted, "if we can find a caravan, can we go now? I would love to see such a storm. Besides, I have heard so much about the desert, I can't wait to actually be on it."

"Lu Shahnnah, I doubt we can find a caravan willing to cross, but I shall see if one can be found. Now, it is time for the evening meal. Jibutu, do you remember the way to the dining hall? Do you remember you sit at the long tables, with the healers, and not the round tables with the students?" Authority stood, wearing a smile and walked us to the door.

"Welcome home, Jibutu. I am so glad to see you." After a quick hug from Authority, I led the way to the dining hall.

An eight-day later found us at the sliwa pens of Dedman Pew, Caravan Master. "Cousin, this is not a good idea. This is not the caravan we want. Come, let us return to the school and wait for another one." I pulled Shahnnah aside.

"There may not be any more. Come on, Jibutu, you'd be grumpy too, if you had to deal with those lizards and the desert all the time."

"Shahnnah, I grew up with those lizards and the desert. I don't think I was grumpy because of it. There is something about this Caravan Master that is not right. We do not want his caravan."

"Come on. My boxes are here, and ready to be loaded, as is your box. Why didn't you bring the rest?"

"Because, I plan to return soon, so left everything at the school. All I need is my medicine box, and that is a small one, for the men of the caravan. I doubt they'll ask for help. Please, this is the time to change your mind. This caravan master is not the one we want."

"Oh, Jibutu, come on. Look, you can see forever from up here, the sky is clear, and the desert awaits us."

"You healers comin'? Or we leavin' you here?"

"We're coming, Ser Pew. We're coming." Shahnnah answered with such excitement I couldn't argue.

"Well, git, then. We gots to load your stuff and get going."

The handcart from the school, with all of Shahnnah's boxes and my one, was pushed by one of the men who worked at the school. He helped tie them to the sliwa, then turned to go back to the school. "Safe journey," was all he said.

"All right, ladies, I'm Dedman Pew, I'm master of this caravan, and my word is law. This is a dangerous time to trip, so if I say do something you do it and don't question me. It be storm time, so we travel during day. It will be hot, but easier to see storms. If not storm time, we travel at night, but it be storm time. Understood?"

"Yes, Ser Pew. We understand."

"Good. We walk to the bottom of the hill, then ride on the desert."

"Cousin, if you rub your sliwa like this, between his eyes, he will follow you anywhere." I showed Shahnnah how to rub the sliwa between his eyes and ears. She wasn't sure she wanted to be that close to his mouth, but tried it. The sliwa made a low noise in his throat and she jumped away. I laughed. "That's a rumble of pleasure. He likes you. Rub some more."

Once she mounted it, she said, "The sliwa is easier to mount, if not ride, than the buflo. I can see, Cousin, why you like them. Can they run, or do they keep to this pace all the time?"

"Oh, they can run. Very fast. At carnival, we hold races. Also on hunting trips."

The caravan had been oddly quiet. Never had I been on the desert without song of some sort. "Ser Pew," I asked when he came by, "do your men not sing as they travel? It seems a good way to make the time go."

"No singin'. Bothers sliwa. Dumb lizards don't like song."

I waited until Shahnnah and I were alone to speak. "Something isn't right. Sliwa don't mind singing. In fact, many seem to like it. I don't like this, my sister."

"It will be fine. We'll soon be to Bel Harq and away from him. Oh, this is too much fun to complain about whether or not we sing."

We camped that night in the first oasis. One other caravan was there with their cook pot going. "Hello, I'm the Caravan Master Lor. We have plenty, so please, join us." I looked at the man, and he looked at me, "Why, you be the young Healer. From a few years back. Welcome. I see you got your purple. Congratulations."

We dismounted, and offered some of our food, though Pew seemed stingy.

"I am Healer Jibutu, and if any of you are in need of a Healer, I am available."

"Oh, healer, I think we're all fine. But, I wonder if you could check my lead sliwa?"

"Sliwa? I can check, but probably do nothing. I know about people."

"Please, just come look." I followed the Caravan Master out to where his sliwa were penned. We leaned over one while I checked its foot. "Healer, this is not the time to go to Bel Harq, and Dedman Pew is not the Caravan Master to get you there. Please, come back with me. If it is really important that you get to Bel Harq, I'll take you myself, at no cost, in a three-day. Please, consider."

"Thank you for your offer. I shall consider it." I stood, patted the sliwa and said, "I think your sliwa will be fine. Just a bit of compacted sand holding her toes apart."

That night, I took Shahnnah out on the desert to show her the stars and the night dunes. I told her about the warning and the offer.

"No. I feel the need, stronger than ever, to continue. I almost resent having to stop. Cousin, I know you don't like Dedman Pew. I don't either, but our fates are intertwined in ways I cannot see or decipher at the moment. Please. Bear with me."

"At threat of our lives?"

She paused, and then spoke in a soft and resigned voice, "Yes. At threat of our lives."

"Neh!" I led us back to our sleeping rolls. Why was she being so stubborn?

"Healers, I know a short cut. You see how the road curves to the left here? If we go but straight, across the desert, we will meet up with the road again, and take at least a three-day off our trip. That," Dedman Pew grinned, "will be three days faster to a hot bath and a good bed."

"I don't know, Ser Pew. I think I'd rather—" I didn't like this detour, it didn't feel right, somehow.

"A bath? Three days earlier?" Shahnnah interjected, "Let's go!"

"No one will know we've come this way.... If a storm comes...."

"Healer, I remind you, I am Law on this caravan."

"Yes, Ser." There was nothing more I could say. We headed across the desert.

That night I woke to an unnatural quiet.

"Boran," I mumbled, "please, no storms until we reach safety." I crawled out of my sleeping roll, and walked to the top of the nearest dune. I could not see a guard anywhere, no one to watch for a storm.

I did see the glow of another fire off to the East. It was not the sun. A shiver slid up my spine as frightening as the soft movements of a White Snake.

Chapter Twenty-Two

> Do what must be done.
> —*Lu Shahnnah, Shaman of the Grass*

I HEARD LU SHAHNNAH SCREAM and turned around. We would be lucky to stop our sliwa and take cover before the storm would be upon us. Just before the storm raced more people. I was pleased to see that Dedman Pew stopped to offer assistance to those who rode the edge of the storm, only to discover they were slavers, and did not want our assistance. They wanted our sliwa and us. It was then I realized we had wandered far to the east. And the slavers of Daveen had ridden far out of their territory to the west. And Dedman Pew *was* assisting the slavers.

The fight was short and nasty. I fell and my sliwa fell, dead, on top of me, breaking my leg. The storm raged through the night. I woke before sunup and heard the slavers talking.

"Well, this one's dead. We don't want a stinking shaman, anyhow. They make lousy slaves. But the other one, the one with the purple robe, Pew said she be a healer. They bring good money at market. Look a bit more."

I heard them walk on the sand, calling, and probing. "Healer? We has injured. Where be you? Call and we'll dig you out." Pew called. His men called. They probed around my sliwa, but not under it. They finally gave up the search for me, assumed I was dead and buried under the sand. It was then I heard them cut the belts and remove my healer's box.

"Pew, you take this sliwa and the healer's box back to Yaylin. Tell them you got separated in the storm, and this was all you

186

could find. We'll take the rest and sell it. Meet you back in Yaylin, at the usual place." I didn't recognize the voice; he must have been one of the slavers.

I heard them leave but waited until dark before I worked my way out from under the sliwa. It was a long, slow, and painful process, but I eventually freed myself and crawled out. There was nothing on the desert except three dead sliwa, two dead slavers, and Lu Shahnnah. All were stripped of anything of value, and the bodies left for the sands.

My leg was broken, probably from the sliwa on top of me, but I crawled to Lu Shahnnah and held her head in my lap and cried. Soon, her ghost voice came thru my pain, *How are you called?* I sat a bit straighter and replied, Lu-Jibutunah, Cousin of Lu Shahnnah. Heart Sister of Lu Shahnnah. Then I again heard, or felt, her voice, softly, in my mind, *Then, do what must be done.*

With a jolt, I realized for all the time I spent in the Nah Family compound, I knew nothing of their death rites. Allowing myself the luxury of tears for my cousin and my loss, I used my glass knife and slit her throat, and sang the song I knew:

> Great Boran,
> welcome the breath of this life
> upon your winds.
> Allow it to sing to her people.

> Great Mother,
> welcome my sister cousin,
> Lu Shahnnah, a woman of the Grass.
> Allow her to find
> joy and peace in her sacrifice.

> Great Desert,
> welcome this woman,
> who loved your sands.
> Allow her sacrifice

to feed and nourish those who have need.

Lu Shahnnah,
you may now go
where you are now needed,
free of pain and want.

Your sacrifice has been noted, and received.

Bless.

Once my tears dried, I sang it a second time for the slavers, calling them Nameless Ones. To my shame, I did not cry for them and took some small pleasure in slitting their throats.

Tears are a luxury in the desert. I did not cry long. I looked for something to wrap my broken leg, found nothing but sliwa hide. I still had the ritual tattooing knife on a thong about my neck. The untanned hide would be painful when it dried, but would give my leg some support while it healed. I then stripped Lu Shahnnah and the slavers of their clothing; what was left of their clothing. What the slavers didn't take barely made rags. What I could use, I rolled into my pack, the rest, I left for whoever came next. I crawled to the slavers first.

I crawled back to Shahnnah, held her lifeless head in my lap, and again spoke to her. "My sister, may your gods welcome you, and may they share your company with me now and then. Know you will live in my heart as long as I have one. Return, now, to the earth we both know and love."

I crawled back to the dead sliwa, and slit their throats, as well. The bugs and animals would eat well tonight. Using my knife, I cut a piece of hide from one, and used it to wrap my leg, as straight as I could get it. I knew how poor Ter must have felt after our fall down The Shales.

Our boxes were gone. My beautiful box made by Papa Jib that I used as my medicine box, the boxes of Shahnnah's possessions and our medicines. I had only what I carried on my

188

person—a pouch of dried meat, a pouch of water, my knife, my robe, and my god cards—that was all. The water and food had been taken from the others. By now, the sun climbed high on its sky path and I decided to wait until nightfall to begin my crawl back to Yaylin. I crawled to my sliwa and slept in the shade of his body. If I did not die before, I thought I might make it in a seven-night. I knew where water was between here and there, if the storm had not buried it. Dedman Pew did not realize I could read the desert as well as he. He would be surprised once I returned to Yaylin.

I slept. At moonrise, I woke, shivering with fever. My eyes would not focus. I began my crawl to Yaylin, hoping someone would find me. My leg tried to swell inside the sliwa hide that wrapped it and my foot burned. I slit the hide to relieve the pressure. And I crawled. And smelled lilies, and knew I would soon die. Or, in my fever, I *thought* I smelled them, for I still lived. At some point I came upon a bush and dug beneath it for moisture. There was a small seep, so I dug a depression in the sand, put my robe over me and slept until the next moonrise.

How far had I crawled? I have no idea, but I crawled many nights, far more than the seven I had figured. Eventually, worn to nothing more than rags, I saw a town in the distance. It was not Yaylin, but to my fever-wracked brain, it was salvation. I crawled to the wall and fainted.

I woke to daylight casting harsh shadows through a high window. I was on a sleeping pallet in a small, bare room. A woman sat on a cushion next to me, stitching fabric.

"How are you called?" I tried to ask, but my throat was so dry, it came out a garbled mess.

"Aah, you are awake. Good. Drink." She lifted my head, and held a bowl next to my lips. The tea was bitter, but wet. It was not until I woke later, I realized I had been drugged. This time, I did not speak, but merely watched. She, if it was the same woman, sat on the cushion next to me, stitching fabric. It appeared she stitched a design into the fabric, using colored threads. My breathing must have changed from sleep to wakefulness, for she turned to me.

"So, you are feeling better? Would you like to try to stand? Would you like to go to the baths? Would you like something to eat? I think your leg will support some of your weight."

"How are you called?" I again asked.

This time she answered, "Sa Heen"

"Sa Heen? That is a pretty name. Where am I, Sa Heen? How long have I been here?"

"Here," she answered. "Eat, and I will answer your questions. Then we will go to the baths." She handed me a bowl of soup and a spoon.

"You are in the village of Mulk. He owns the village and all who are in it. I am one of his slaves. You crawled to our gate and fainted. One of the guards saw you in the morning and brought you to me. I am the village healer woman. You have been here a five-day. Mulk says your broken leg will keep you out of the mines, but you are too ugly with all your tats to be a concubine." She laughed a bit, "He says your body is right, but you are just too ugly, even for a blind man." She paused then said, "I think you are lucky. Slave concubines do not have an easy life, contrary to what Mulk says."

As I started to tell her my training, I again 'heard' Lu Shahnnah. I did not talk about my shaman training. "I am a healer, trained in Yaylin. And I am daughter of Jib, the headman of our tribe. Both the school and my father will pay you and Mulk for my treatment."

"You are funny. You are now a slave, and belong to Mulk. He will not bother with a ransom. He wants cash, he wants it soon, and he will get it. You will go to Daveen in a few days, as soon as the riders return. You will go to the market. Best eat and rest while you can."

Slave? I was a slave? My blood ran cold. None of the tribes would be slaves and we did not own them. Abomination!

"Sa Heen? Where are my cards? And my clothes?"

"Nameless One, when you were found there was nothing about you but a bit of rag. Not even enough to call rags. There were no cards."

I was a slave, and now I had lost my god cards and my sand glass ball. And according to Sa Heen, I was nameless. I finished my soup and lay back down. Sa Heen finished her project, helped me up, and we went to the slave baths. The water was tepid, and dirty, but better than no bath. My leg worked, after a fashion. Sa Heen rubbed it in the bath, to help loosen it.

"It will loosen as you work it. Did you tie it? It was a good job. The break healed straight, but stiff. Time, and exercise will fix it. You'll get plenty of exercise as you walk to Daveen."

The next day, I was brought face to face with Mulk. He was a short, squat man, with his hair greased. He smelled of sliwa and old sweat. He needed a bath, and perfumed soap.

"So." He looked me over, like a man deciding the price he would ask, and the price he would get. "Sa Heen tells me you are a Yaylin-trained healer. What is your name?"

I would not tell him my name. My name is too important to me. It is *me*, and *me* is not a slave. "Sa Heen has given me a name. She calls me Nameless One. I will answer to that."

The fat face crinkled into a laugh. "All right, you are now Sa Nameless. Perhaps your new owner will give you a new name. For now, though, Sa Nameless it shall be.

"Sa Heen tells me you are healing well. Can you use that hook at the end of your arm? Or is it just for show?" Before I could answer, he continued, "I have heard that my riders are due into town in a two-day. We shall leave in a three-day for Daveen and the markets. You are ugly as sin, woman. When did the Healers of Yaylin start tatting their skulls? Is this new?"

191

So, he didn't know what my tattoos meant? "Yes, Mulk, they are—" Before I could finish he roared at me, and lashed out with a short whip across my face.

"I am Master. Period. You may never use my name. You are not worthy to use my name. Never use a Master's name. Now, answer my question, Sa Nameless."

"Yes, Master, it is new. I am the first to receive the tattoos on my head as well as my face."

"Odd customs you barbarians have."

Barbarians? We do not buy and sell people. Who is he to call us Barbarians? Neh! I steadied my face so he would not read my thoughts.

"Well, Sa Nameless, rest and eat. The march to Daveen will take a two-night and you will have to carry your own water and food."

With that, I was dismissed, and Sa Heen took me back to the room. It was then I found out it was her room, and I slept on her pallet.

"Please, Sa Heen, let me sleep on the floor. I am used to it. You keep your pallet." She would not hear of it, and as I lay on the pallet, and tried to think how long my leg had been broken, and wondered why it healed so fast. I could walk on it, somewhat, without aid of a stick. The muscles were still tight, but it was healed, much quicker than normal. I slept the night through.

Great sadness accompanied me on the walk to Daveen. Several people were brought, and we were all chained to each other. The children were allowed to run loose; the slavers knew they would not run away from their parents, especially their mothers. The new slaves were either angry or numb. The men were angry, the women numb. The children perplexed, but still they played and ran.

At the slave auction we were stripped and oiled, so our ages would be harder to tell. Husbands and wives were sold separately, and older children were sold from their mothers. There was much sadness at the slave block.

As each slave was bought, they were taken to a table where someone sat with several bowls of liquid. He would reach into a bowl, pull out a small block of wood with needles protruding, place the needles on the arm of the new slave, and hit it with a hammer. The slave often screamed at the harsh tattoo just received.

I had no idea what would happen to me, and was surprised when another slave bought me, an older man. He was tall, and carried himself with pride, and was well known at the market. He bargained my price down to where Mulk claimed he would lose money on me, but the old man insisted, and told him I was so ugly with all my tats and gimp leg, that no one would want me. He paid Mulk a bit more for a light robe to cover me, and led me to the branding table.

"Sa Ach, which do you want for her? Mine? Field? Or...?"

"She will be a house slave, so the usual tat will work."

"Are you *serious*? In the House of Veen?"

"Yes. I am serious. It will not take long and they will see her beauty."

I had been tattooed before, but this burned like nothing else. But I did not scream. The man who bought me held tight to my other arm. Whether to keep me still, or for support, or to keep me from running, I didn't know.

"Do not think of running. There is no place to go. Stay with me. Your new home, while not free, is a good home. I am Sa Ach, Chief Steward to the Noble House of Veen. The Family Veen is one of the founding families of Daveen, so know you enter the service of a truly Noble House. How are you called?"

At the mention of his name, I heard a soft snicker, almost a laugh, from Lu Shahnnah.

"Sa Ach, you may call me Sa Nameless. I no longer have a name."

At that he smiled, and spoke again, as he led me through the alleys of Daveen. "That will not work for me. I recognize your tats, which is why I bought you. You are both a healer and a shaman. You have a name. You know your name. You may not wish to be called by that name, but you must have a name on the registrations books. How will you be called?"

The alleys were narrow and the sides were high walls, I assumed to protect the gardens of the wealthy from whatever sand might blow in—or from prying eyes, but I wasn't sure. They may have been walls to warehouses and places of employment. By now, I was thoroughly lost, Sa-Ach walked quickly and we made many turns. We stopped at a heavy wooden gate. His hand was upon the latch. "How will you be called? I need to know before we enter."

"Call me what you will. I do not care."

He gave a smile, a bit sad, and said, "We will call you Mori. Sa Mori. And when we get inside, and you are registered, and introduced, you will tell me your story." I looked into his brown eyes, and saw—what? Eagerness? Fear? Humor? I couldn't read him, but it was like looking into the eyes of Lu Shahnnah. Again, I heard her chuckle in my mind.

For an old man, he had a grip of iron. His left hand was tight about my right arm. His right hand opened the gate, and several bells rang as the gate swung into them. I was ushered into a court not much wider than the gate, with high walls, and a metal gate a few feet away. A man stared out at us from a window in the wall.

"Sa Ach, what have you dragged home this time?" The guard laughed.

"This is Sa Mori. She will be one of us as soon as you register her and allow us entrance." The grip tightened. My arm began to go numb. I said nothing. Lu Shahnnah said nothing, but I sensed her and a bit of excitement as if she gathered herself to tell a joke.

"You can't be serious. She is the most ugly Sa I've ever seen. You know the Veens want slaves that are pleasant to look at. I think you should take her back to the auction, or sell her to someone else. Truly, I cannot allow her into the house."

"She will stay. Her heart is beautiful and she has great value. The Veens will treasure this one."

The guard sighed, "It is upon your head, Sa Ach," and opened the gate. Under his breath he muttered something about Lady Veen not being jealous of this one. We entered a large court—not a pleasure court, but a supply court. I saw a larger gate; one that carts could come through to deposit goods. There were neither trees nor fountains here, just stone and sheds. We stopped at a second metal gate when the first one closed and locked behind us. It was the most ominous sound I'd yet heard.

"How is she called?" Before I could answer, Sa Ach again squeezed my arm, and spoke. "She is called Sa Mori"

The guard wrote in a book, looked me over again, made a few notations, I suppose about my tattoos, and allowed us to pass.

Sa Ach propelled me forward, through a door and down a hall. "I will introduce you to the kitchen workers. We will get you fed, and when you have eaten and had a proper bath, you will get a decent robe. I fear you may not wear purple here, nor may you wear red. Both colors belong to the Noble Born and for a slave to wear either means slow death."

We entered the kitchen, loud with laughter and the banging of kitchen utensils. Introductions were made around, though it was a blur for me. A young girl took my hand and led me to a stool. Sa Ach brought me a bowl of stew, told me to eat, and said he would be back soon, and to wait. I ate. I waited. And I watched. Though they all were slaves, they did not seem badly treated. The laughter was genuine, and the stew was delicious. Soon Sa Ach returned, and led me to the baths.

195

"You will be presented to the Noble Born tomorrow. After you have rested and bathed and are dressed properly to serve in this house. I told them I bought you, and that you are a healer. I did not tell them you are a shaman. That is between you and me, and for all our lives' sake, it must not be mentioned. Ever. The folks of Daveen are very superstitious and do not like anyone but their priests to walk the pathways of the gods. You must tell no one, nor walk the God Paths while here. Do you understand?" Genuine fear colored his whisper.

"Yes, Sa Ach. I understand. I will not mention it to anyone. I am Yaylin trained as a healer. We keep secrets." I didn't understand why they would want only their priests to walk the God Paths, but I understood not only my life was at stake if I tried to walk those paths here, but the lives of any who may have spoken to me and known, would also face punishment. Especially Sa Ach.

"One more thing. Just because someone is another slave, do not place your trust in them until they have earned it." His voice softened, "And Sa Mori, remember this, always—the Masters only own your body. *You* own your mind."

The bath was hot and the soaps perfumed. I could close my eyes and almost be back in Yaylin. Another woman came in, stripped, and joined me in the bath. She said nothing, but began to massage my broken leg. Her hands were smooth and very strong. I nearly cried as she worked out the knots. She smiled as I winced. "We will do this daily, I think, until your leg is better healed. My name is Sa Sely. I am in charge of the clothing and massages. Sa Ach tells me you are a healer, Yaylin trained. I will bring you a robe, in a bit, with a hood. It will be a lightweight robe and you may wear the hood if you choose. The Noble Born may demand it. They do not like ugliness and I am surprised Sa Ach brought you here. I do not know where you will work—Sa Ach and the Noble Borns will make that decision. Now, soak a bit more and when I return we will dress you."

196

Again I was alone. My leg ached from the massage. My heart ached for my predicament. And Lu Shahnnah smiled in my head.

After evening meals were over, Sa Ach took me to his quarters. He had a small shed of his own, as Chief Steward, and did not sleep in the common slave rooms. His room was small, with a cot, a table, two chairs, and an open cupboard filled with books and scrolls. The table held a lantern, a variety of ink stones and brushes and films. But he had quiet and privacy.

"Sit. Please. And tell me of our sister and our mother."

Chapter Twenty-Three

Life awaits in the desert, if you know where to find it.
Death awaits in the desert, when you least expect it.
Freedom awaits in the desert, for those who live, for those who
die.

—from a Desert Funeral Song

AT HIS DEMAND to be told of Lu Shahnnah and his mother, Shahnnah began to laugh in my skull. Then the laughter subsided, and all I could hear was her saying first in whispers, which, as I hesitated, escalated to screams: *"Touch him! Touch our brother, Achennah! Touch him! You must touch him. It must come from you."*

"Achennah, please, before we start, may I be so bold as to hold your hand a moment? Lu Shahnnah requests it."

Shock rode his face as he recognized his real name, not his slave name. He visibly shook as he asked, "What do you mean, *she requests it?*"

Before either of us said anything, my hand reached out of its own volition, grabbed his, and my world went black. I ceased being. I was neither hot nor cold. I was just, well, I was *Not!* Slowly, the world returned, or rather, I returned to the world. I still sat in the chair, still held the hand of Sa Ach, whose birth name I now knew through Lu Shahnnah was Achennah. But that's all I knew. How long had I been gone?

"Aah, you have returned. That is good. Before we continue, you must speak of this night to no one. Ever. Our lives depend on it."

198

"But, Sa Ach, I do not understand. What happened?" I jerked my hand away from his. I couldn't feel Lu Shahnnah, I felt truly alone. And frightened.

"It's all right, Mori, Timorinah, my sister. It's all right." He stood, walked around a bit, collected some crisps to nibble on, placed the bowl between us, and sat again.

"Timorinah? That is my name? How do you know?"

"Mother named you before you were born. She told me. Listen, I will tell you. Shahnnah was my older sister, and as such, would be shaman trained. Being male, I could not become shaman. Our mother, Lu Ahnah, was not only shaman, but she was, well, different. Most shamans mate, have a daughter, and retreat to raise her. Our mother mated, and fell in love with Achen. When she had Shahnnah, Mother stayed. And then she had me, and to show her love for Achen, named me Achennah. When father died, mother nearly died of grief. I was ten when he died, and Shahnnah had already gone from the family compound for her official training. Timor-I came into our home and comforted our mother in the time-honored way. Eventually, she decided to have a daughter by him. She loved him, though not the same as she loved our father. When I was sixteen, a marriage was arranged between the family of Timor-I and me. We were to meet in Bel Harq." He stopped. Looked long at me, and then continued.

"Mother was almost to term when we began the journey. Our sliwa were loaded with clothing, and gifts for the bride and her family, mother rode most of the way. Timor-I became very excited to return to the land of his birth, and yet remained very solicitous of my mother. A few days out from Bel Harq our Caravan Master, Pew was his name, Dedman Pew, told us of a shortcut. Mother, being close to term, agreed. A storm darkened our skies. Our sliwa drivers started to circle our sliwa when mother screamed, and jabbed her sliwa to run. No one knew what she screamed, only that they saw the fear on her face, and her mouth opened. I started after her, but was held back."

"Did you find out why she screamed?"

"Oh, yes. Before the storm rode slavers from Daveen."

The quiet in the small room became thick and heavy, like a wet woolen blanket.

"After the storm, the slavers took me, and those drivers who still lived. They looked for mother, and Timor-I, but could not find them. I always assumed they died in the sand.

"I tried to contact Shahnnah, but there was no way. And then I saw you in the market. You, who look like my mother and my sister. You, who wears the family net on your skull. Then, when you reached out to me a while ago, Shahnnah came through you to me. She told me all. We talked. She told me of your birth mother, found in the desert, almost dead. She told me of the net placed upon your head. She told me you are our sister and that our line of Ahnah is at an end because I refuse to mate and you can't have children."

I looked into the face of Achennah, my brother, and saw tears begin to tumble down his cheeks.

"But, Mori, now I know. And as bad as it is to be not free, we have each other! It grows late. We will have many nights to talk; tonight is not one of them. I need to get you back to your quarters. Come."

And so, I lost my sister, but gained a brother. And the name my birth mother had tried so hard to tell me. Timorinah.

"Please, why did not Shahnnah come to you earlier?"

"She tried, but I am not shaman trained and could not open to her. You, by taking my hand, allowed me to open. Now, she can come to me as freely as she does to you. She could not explain why it didn't work when I touched you, only that it had to be you who touched me."

Exhausted by all that happened, even my racing thoughts could not keep me from much needed sleep.

"Keep your head down at all times. Never look at a Master unless told to do so, and even then, do not look into their eyes. Ever. Now, be quiet, and let me do the talking. Should Master ask you a question, you may reply, but softly, and reply to the floor, not to the Master. Now, come."

Sa Ach led the way into the House of Veen. I kept my head lowered, but could see the richness of the floors. I would learn to see much more from my side vision, but for now, I marveled at the polished stone floors. Yaylin had polished stone floors, but these were of a stone I'd never seen. They were gray, with coppers and golds and blues and greens, even some lavenders swirled and blotched throughout. I found them quite fascinating, and would have liked to ask Master about them, but, of course, didn't.

"Well, Sa Ach, I hear you've been to market again. What have you brought us this time?" The voice was deep, and melodic. Though it sounded friendly, I heard the cold stone of authority behind it.

"Master, this is Sa Mori. She is a Healer, Yaylin trained."

"She is ugly, Sa Ach, take her back."

"Master, please, this humble slave begs, let me tell you of her."

The pause before the sigh and his, "Very well" seemed limitless. Would I be returned to the market?

"Master, she is a trained Healer. She will keep the slaves healthy, both in the House of my Master, as well as any other houses my Master chooses to share her with. I, I have long known of the Healers of Yaylin, and they are some of the finest in our world."

Again, the long silence as he weighed my fate in the balance of whatever scales he used. I wanted to look up at him, but did not, though I felt him scrutinizing me. "Very well, Sa Ach. She may remain. However, she is not to come further into the house

201

than the back kitchen, and she is to wear a head covering at all times."

"Most humble and appreciative thank you, Master." I felt a hand on my arm, and we turned and left the presence of my new Master, whom I could recognize only by his voice.

"Sa Mori, do not tremble so. Come, we need to go back to the kitchen, quickly."

"And so, Cook, do you think you could let us have the back storeroom for Sa Mori as an infirmary?"

"It's only holding junk right now. I don't see why not. What all do you need? It will be nice to have someone here who can treat burns and cuts properly."

"Cook, I will be glad to do so, and to train Sa Sely to do likewise. I understand she did very well before I came."

Cook snorted. "She did what she could. She was the only one even willing to try."

"Well, perhaps you will allow her to be with me part time, to apprentice with me? That way, you will have two healers available." I smiled, and hoped she saw the sincerity. It would be nice to have a helper, especially one who knew everyone in the house.

"Very well. She can help you clean the store room, and get it ready, and then she can come to you for two hours in the morning, after morning meal."

"Thank you." The storeroom Sa Ach chose had two doors. One door opened to a courtyard, the other opened to the house. I was thrilled at having the two doors. That way, really sick people could come to me through the court and not have to carry their illness through the house to possibly infect others.

Daveen stood on the edge of the desert, as Yaylin did. It, too, had high walls to keep the sand where it belonged, but unlike Yaylin, Daveen had very dark trees with spiky leaves that did not drop in the winter. Daveen was cooler, and wetter, rains

202

often came down the mountains behind us, and soaked the city and a small portion of the desert in front. Flowers bloomed everywhere, and the cactus of my desert became thorny bushes in Daveen's desert.

It took a six-day to clean the storeroom. Sa Ach found some unused paint, and I painted it white. He brought me fabric and Sa Sely and I made straw-filled mattresses.

"Sa Mori, I can get you the regular slave mattresses, if you'd like. Sick people do not need to sleep on straw."

"You are correct, they do not. But if they become very sick, and soil the mattresses, the straw can be burned, and the casing washed and purified. It will cost far less for our Masters, and not spread disease."

"Come, Sa Mori," Sa Ach stood in the door, "we must go into the city. Today is market day, and you will need medicines and supplies. Sa Sely can handle any who come in."

"We can just leave? When we need something?"

"Well, not quite. I have permission, and because you are with me, you will be allowed out. If you just tried to walk out, you would be stopped. Once you are known and trusted, you will be allowed out for business. For now, though, little sister, you are with me."

"You can call me sister out here?" I had never referred to that night, nor had he. His calling me little sister shocked me a bit.

"Yes, but only when we are away from the House of Veen. The walls have ears, so do not speak of such things, even in a whisper. As we walk this morning, I can tell you a bit more about our mother and how I recognized you, though I had never met you.

"Mother was a kind and loving woman. She knew I would be a good brother, and let me tie the net. She gave me whatever colored yarns and baubles I asked for from her shaman's box. It was I, little sister, who made your net. I am so glad I did, for

203

otherwise I would not have known you, though I would have known you belonged to the Family Nah."

"Thank you, my brother. And thanks be to our mother for her kindness and generosity in allowing you that honor in making a recognizable net."

"I am so sorry, Mori, that we had to meet like this, as slaves of the Daveen. At least we are not in the mines."

The bitterness in his voice spoke for both of us.

"We will be free, Achennah. Someday."

"Mori, you must not talk that way. Even to speak of freedom can bring a slow death. No. Accept. Just accept. We can do well in the House of Veen. You will see.

"How? How will I see?"

"Your services as healer will be requested by the other Houses. And when you go, you must not allow shock or surprise to show on your face. You must smile, always. Slaves are always happy in public."

I didn't know whether to laugh or cry. I, who wanted only the name of Jibutu, and eventually took Jibutu, now had an entirely new name thrust upon me. "Timorinah. It, it is a nice name. I am sorry I never had the opportunity to meet our mother, to get to know her."

"Yes, I am, too. It is too bad she died as your father Jib arrived, before she could be saved, or tell him of your heritage."

We walked on in silence, I heard Lu Shahnnah whisper in my head, "Sister. I knew it. Yes, I did." I could hear the contented smile. Then we were at the pharmacopia, and I needed to pay attention to what was available.

"Ser Dada, this is Sa Mori. She is a healer, Yaylin trained, and new to the House of Veen. She will soon be coming here without me, and please know to help her, and to place her charges on the House of Veen's sheet."

"Sa Mori, welcome to my pharmacopia. Yaylin trained? Well, I carry many medicines you are used to, and some not, so please ask. I may know what we have that can substitute for what you want." I looked into the brown eyes of a man filled with humor. Lines around his eyes said he laughed often. "You are most welcome to browse and fill the basket with your purchases, then, when you have finished, just bring them to the front counter where I will tally the cost."

"Thank you, Ser Dada." I inhaled deeply. I felt at home. The smells of herbs and medicines reminded me of my days in the pharmacopia at Yaylin. A pang of homesickness swept over me. I must have swayed, because Achennah reached to steady me. I smiled at him, "I am all right. Just a pang of homesickness for Yaylin." I then began to go down the aisles, checking the bins and boxes, taking this, leaving that.

"Ser Dada, I think this is all I will need for now. I do not know, yet, what I will need in quantity for I have not been here long enough to know the ailments and injuries most common. If you have any suggestions?"

Ser Dada looked over my selection, smiled, and said, "I would add one more item." He reached under the counter and pulled out a small package of sweets. "You will treat children. This is candied jer root, easier for them to tolerate than the raw jer root, and they will like it better." He smiled as he added it to my purchase, tallied everything, and gave Sa Ach a copy.

"When we get back, I will take the tally sheet to my office. When you begin to go alone, you will bring the tally sheet to me. Now, we need to find you a box for your medicines."

It did not take long before I had patients. At first, they were shy, and most were new slaves who were sick with fear over their new status. I had no problem relating, gave them some ground jer root for tea, fresh jer root for severe cases, and listened to them. I offered what consolation I could, but as I was in their same situation, I couldn't offer much. And then the guards began coming in. Soon my little infirmary was known throughout Daveen.

205

"Sa Ach, what do I do? I cannot turn them away, and yet...?"

"No, do not turn any away. I should have thought of this, because it was I who suggested to Master that you be allowed to treat them. Here," he turned away and went to a shelf, and turned back with a pad of paper, "take this. Write the name of each patient, and the House they come from. Also write their ailment and treatment. At every new moon, I shall collect the information, and will present it to Master. If he agrees, we will bill the other Houses."

It was almost like I was back in Yaylin. I never touched money. Soon, I went to the pharmacopia alone, and had an opportunity to see some of Daveen. My life settled into a routine of familiarity. Until the night Cook woke me from a deep sleep by her yelling as she ran to my little infirmary.

"Sa Mori! Sa Mori! You must come. Now! Master needs you!" Her voice called as she ran toward me, it carried an overlay of fear.

"Cook, please, take a deep breath and tell me."

"It is young Master. He is sick. They had the priests in, but he is sicker, and they fear he will not live the night. You must come. Now."

I followed behind Cook, not just into the House of Veen, but into the private quarters. Cook took me to a large room where a small boy tossed on a large bed. Beside it were two distraught people I assumed were his parents, my Masters.

"Sa Mori, put your training to work. If you do not save his life, yours is forfeit."

"Master, I will do what I can. Please tell me what led up to this." They didn't know. He was fine, and then not. As far as they knew, he had not eaten anything not from their table, they could find no bites on him, he had never been out of the sight of either themselves or the slaves who cared for him.

"The first thing we must do is break the fever. Cook, will you please go ask Sa Sely to prepare a large quine tisane, strong, and to cool it as quickly as possible before bringing it?" Before I finished, she ran from the room. I only hope she heard everything.

"Masters, we need to get him in a cold bath. As cold as we can make it."

"Sa Sara, run his bath. Now. Make it cold only." The boy's mother spoke, and a slave I'd never met ran to do her bidding.

"Sa Bors, go to our private cellar and bring as much ice as you can. Now!"

Cook returned carrying a large pail. "Sa Mori, Sa Sely is making a new tisane, but this was on the counter in a large bowl. She poured it into the clean pail so I could carry it."

"Thank you, Cook. Now, I need clean cloths."

His mother began to rebuke me for issuing orders, but her husband shushed her and handed me a clean towel. "Will this do?"

"Thank you, Master. Yes. Please, will you rip it for me? Into three pieces?" I began to wipe the boy down with the tisane. As it evaporated, it cooled his skin. Soon, the bath was ready, and we placed him in it.

"He should have clean bed clothes placed on his bed while he is here. The old ones should be boiled before being reused."

"Sa Mori, who do you think you are...." The Mistress Veen's anger raged against me.

"Wife. She is a healer, she is used to giving orders to save lives. Now, get someone to follow her orders, or go back to our quarters. If Arges lives, you will be grateful. If he dies, she will die." At his last comment, she began to shriek.

"Go back to our quarters. I will remain." Master's voice held more command than I'd ever heard. She turned and ran from the room. I, of course, heard none of that conversation, and did not add to it.

207

The fever finally broke, and Arges Veen, the only Veen I knew who had a name, was removed from the bath, dried, and placed back on his bed. His bed with clean bed covers. His breathing became more normal, less labored, and he slept.

"Master, I believe he will be fine. I will tell Cook what to fix for him for the next few days. He won't like it, but it is what he should have until we figure out what caused it. I will stay with him if you would like; however, he does not know me, having never seen me, and, well, my face might frighten him."

"Yes, Sa Mori, I take your point. All right, you may return to your quarters and your duties."

Grateful the boy lived, I returned to the kitchen and gave the orders to Cook. Before I returned to the infirmary, I pulled Cook aside, "Cook, he acted like he got into a supply of sweet root. If he ate too many, they would make him sick and feverish—uncomfortable, but not lethal."

Cook looked thoughtful for a moment then walked to her pantry and searched behind some jars on the top shelf. She quickly found the one she wanted, pulled it off, opened it, and smiled. "That imp. I kept a supply of it here. It's useful now and then. I wonder how often he came and searched. And what he searched for? I shall keep the pantry locked from now on. Thank you for not mentioning it in front of the Master."

I reached my bed, and slept soundly.

"Sa Mori, are you going to the pharmacopia this morning?" Sa Sely stood in the door to the infirmary. She very well knew I was going out. I went every week at this time, and she frequently accompanied me. I didn't need her help, but she needed the time away from Cook, and I enjoyed her company.

"Of course. Would you like to join me?" She smiled, and we soon found ourselves outside the walls, and for a bit, we could pretend we were truly free.

"Sa Mori," Sa Sely grabbed my arm. "Do not walk so fast. I need to talk to you. Do not change expression, for we may still be watched. Sa Mori, I know you are a shaman. I recognized the markings when you arrived. You have been here now for how many months?"

"I don't know. I never counted."

She chuckled, "No, you wouldn't. It's been almost two years. You are trusted, Sa Mori, that is why no one has turned you in. You are trusted and you are liked, but now we need your help. Please."

"Help? How?"

"We need you to walk the God Paths and find a way out of our bondage. Several people are willing to face death in the desert rather than to continue in slavery."

"I...I don't know. I gave a promise when bought. I—" I couldn't speak. We walked on, "I will think about it. I will let you know soon. Do not discuss it again."

Among my purchases that day were two dried buds of the Death Cactus. Shahnnah taught me to roast them, and chew them for traveling the God Paths. Pharmacope taught me to make a medicinal tea of them to help people sleep, so the purchase was not out of the ordinary.

That night, I walked the God Paths for the first time since leaving Yaylin. It felt good, and I felt welcomed. When morning came, I drew a map, and made two shallow cuts in my finger, wiping the blood on two rags. I put the rags away, not sure why they were needed, but remembered the directions I received during my night's journey.

"Sa Sely, thank you for keeping my secret. And thanks to any others who also know and have remained silent. I have a small gift for you. What you do with it is none of my business, and I do not want to know. Here is a map, commit it to memory, and draw it whenever you need to. Burn this one. And here are two rags. I do not know their meaning, but I do know the first

209

and last person must tie one about their ankles, and that the best nights to travel will always be the darkest nights. I do not know if the way is safe, if they will meet death in the desert or at the hands of slavers or if they will succeed. I do not want to know."

The subject was never brought up again, though every few weeks or so, Sa Sely solicitously inquired if I had cut myself. At which time I did, and handed her rags with fresh blood.

Slaves began disappearing from Daveen. Not many, and none, I am thankful to report, from the House of Veen. There seemed to be no set dates. It was assumed the escapees went into the mountains, for to attempt to cross the desert on foot would be certain death. And slaveholders had long convinced themselves that life as a slave was better than no life at all. After all, were we not always smiling?

210

Chapter Twenty-Four

Much is given to those who ask;
much is denied to those who demand.
—*Wisdom of the Desert*

"SA MORI, how long have you been a slave in the House of Veen?"

"I do not know, Master."

"You do *not know*? Every slave knows, to the day, if not the hour, how long he or she has been a slave. I repeat my question. How long have you been a slave in the House of Veen?"

"Master, it has been some time, but, truly, I do not know. It is not something I enjoy keeping track of. However, Young Master was but a boy of about five summers when I came. And he is now a man."

"Sa Ach told me when he bought you that you were different from any slave I've ever owned. He was right."

I said nothing. His next question flummoxed me.

"Sa, what is your full name?"

I seldom talked directly with Master Veen, and did not know how to read him. He seemed kind, at least as far as a slaveholder can seem. He even seemed to have a bit of genuine curiosity about his slaves. But this line of questioning was new. Why? Was he going to sell me? Try for a ransom? "My full name, Master, is Sa-Mori."

He became quiet, and studied me, seemingly with interest. I remained quiet, and studied the floor. A slave does not look her master in the eye but we slaves learned to look at the floor, and watch our masters from our side vision. Dust danced in the sunlight as it came through the window. A bird screeched from a tree outside the open window. No other movement or sound came into the room.

"You are a Yaylin Healer."

"Yes, Master."

"It was not a question, Sa! Since being in my household, you have kept my slaves and my family healthy." He paused, and then chuckled, "In fact, I understand you have kept the slaves and several of the households of many Noble Borns healthy."

I had. I often went to the homes of other Noble Borns to treat either slaves or families. At first, they tested me, and paid me in coin, though I said payment was between them and my Master. They insisted, and so I took the coin home to my brother, who made a note of it, and accounted of it properly. Word soon spread that I was indeed, honest and that I could heal what sometimes the Priests could not. I heard that those Noble Borns who used my arts were careful not to tell the Priests.

He paused, again. I remained quiet.

"You are from the great desert beyond Yaylin, are you not?"

"Yes, Master."

"Can you read a map?"

I wanted to scream at him, *"Of course I can read a map! I can read the stars, too. Do you think me simple?"* but my reply was meek and subservient. I had healed too many slaves who sassed their masters. Often, I healed them only to have them shipped to the mines, from which they would never return. "Yes, Master."

"Good, come, show me, on this map, where your village is."

"I cannot do that, Master."

"Why? It is a simple command. You have admitted you can read a map."

"Master, with all respect, my people are nomads. They travel. I can show you the area where they travel, but our village

212

moves. There is not enough water in the oases to support a full time village. The tribes travel from oasis to oasis. Each tribe has its own area, so we do not come upon a replenishing oasis, nor do we leave another tribe short of water when we move. I can show you our area, but not our village."

He beckoned me to his desk, and I showed him our area. "None of the tribes remain in one place? That is absurd!"

"No, Master. The tribes move, that way no one area is ever stripped of life. We do have a permanent settlement, of sorts, at Carnival. It is on the edge of the desert, near the Forests of Yaylin. Each year all the tribes gather for a ten-day of swapping stories and goods, and brides. And each year the tribes elect a few families to stay, and keep the pools clean, and offer any assistance as needed to those who come during the off season. Each year, they are happy to stay, and not have to move, but by next Carnival, their boxes are packed, and they can hardly wait to rejoin their tribes."

Why did he want to know this? We were too far for him to think of raiding. Even the great Mulk seldom went beyond the Border of Contention; that area defined by the Yaylin-Bel Harq road. To raid beyond the border, and be caught, was death. Slow death. Slavers, when caught, were usually buried in the sand, up to their armpits, facing a nest of nasties several feet away. Their hands were tied over their heads and sweet syrup was then dribbled on the nest of nasties and a trail made across the sand to the slaver. Once the honey was dribbled on their heads, the bonds that held the hands were cut. It was not a pleasant death.

"Young Master Veen wishes to go into business. He would like to trade with your tribes."

Again there was a long pause. Why our tribes? Surely there were tribes within the kingdom of Daveen. I remained quiet. And, if he wished to enter Yaylin, all he had to do was take a caravan to Bel Harq, then one from there to Yaylin, and then find a guide to the Tribes.

"You will take him."

Death faced me, square, as I prepared my answer.

"No, Master. I cannot take him."

"Cannot? Or will not?" My side vision showed his face turning purple.

"Cannot, will not, it makes no difference, Master."

"You are my slave Sa, you will do as you are told. Be prepared to leave in a five day!"

"Master, I will be prepared to leave. But allow me, please, to ask you a question." Before he could deny me, I hurried on, "Do you wish your son to return from our desert?"

His voice thundered so that dust jumped in the air. "Of course I want him to return."

"Master, I can take your son into the desert. But why should I bring him back?"

Another long pause, as he thought about my question.

"Yes. I see your point. You could take him to your tribe and have him killed. Or made a slave."

At that, I smiled. "No, Master. We do not hold slaves. Ever. It would be easier to leave him on the desert. He is full of himself, but that is hollow, and will not see him through the desert. I know the desert. He does not."

The purple faded from his jowls. Again he seemed lost in thought.

"Sa Mori, would you be willing to take my son to the desert if you are paid? And see that he comes home alive?"

"What is the pay you offer, Master?" This conversation began to interest me in several areas.

"I will pay you enough gold to buy your freedom."

"Not enough. You will grant my freedom, here and now. I will not go into my desert a slave. You will free me, and you will pay for all our supplies."

"Free you? I can't."

"Then I remain Sa Mori, your mostly obedient slave." I was not sure, when dismissed, whether morning would dawn on my live body, or dead one.

That night, Achennah came to the infirmary, where I slept to be close to my patients, when I had them.

"Little Sister, what did you do?" In trying to whisper, his voice came out a hiss.

"What do you mean? Come in. I have no patients, we can talk."

"Look. I bring your papers. You are free. Master said there are no strings; you may walk out the gate tonight. But, he also said he hoped you would honor the bargain. Mori, sister, what bargain? What have you done? He said if you stay, I was to give you this. It is a letter of credit for the market, in his name."

The next day, I visited the Administrative Offices and registered my letter of emancipation, and then I went to market where I ordered a purple Healer's Robe with the red hood of a shaman, though the sewer did not know why the hood had to be red. It was ready in a two-day. On that day, I presented myself at the main gate of Master Veen's home. I asked the guard to announce that Healer Jibutu Timorinah stood at the gate to see Master Veen. The guard, though he had seen me often enough as a slave, did not know me now. He did as told, and soon I was invited in.

I waited in the hall, until Master Veen appeared. "Jibutu Timorinah? I don't believe we've met. How may I help you? We do not need a healer here."

I turned to face him. "I believe you will, as your son wishes to cross the deserts out of Yaylin? He is in need of a guide. I shall guide him, for a fee." I looked him in the eye. He was so startled that at first, he did not recognize me.

"Sa Mori, is it you?"

"No," I smiled. "Sa Mori no longer exists. I am the Healer Jibutu Timorinah."

"You are wearing the colors of the nobleborn."

"Yes, they are my colors by right of training—and my freedom."

And so I moved from the infirmary into the guest quarters at the House of Veen and helped young Arges Veen prepare for the adventure of his life.

"Tell me, Sa Mori, how many slaves do you think we will need?" I ignored his question. I ignored him. The silence grew long. "Excuse me, *Jibutu Timorinah*. How many slaves will we need?" I could hear the sneer as he spoke my name, and I smiled before answering.

"Young Arges, we will take no slaves. If you wish to take servants, you may free them and pay them wages. Slaves will not cross the border. And, if they do, they are freed, immediately."

"Of course I will take slaves. I need them."

"No, Young Arges. You do not." And so our hostilities began. He continued to try to make me his slave, to obey him. And I refused either. His father smiled at the battle of our wills. Sometimes I heard outright laughter.

"You think you're so smart, because you tricked my father into granting your freedom. Well, it can be revoked, you know."

"No, it can't. It has been duly registered. And I did not trick him. You want to make a dangerous trip and he wants you to return alive, and that was the price he paid."

After several days of poring over maps, and discussing routes, we decided to take the overland, forest route to Yaylin, and then get sliwa to head into the desert. The overland route was still blocked by winter snows, so we took our time in buying, packing, and getting prepared. We had a safe conduct pass from the Governor General, and requests of same for Yaylin. The overland route made me nervous, I still didn't like the closeness of the forests, but Arges was familiar with the route, at least to a point. He was comfortable in the dark of the woods. I wondered how he would do in the open of the desert.

Summer was almost upon us when Ser Veen called me into his study. "Healer Jibutu Timorinah, I thank you. I know taking my son on this trip is not going to be easy, but I think he will reach his manhood under your tutelage. It will be a long time before he returns, but I am comfortable in the knowledge you will do your best to keep him safe.

"You asked for no money, other than to cover expenses, but please, take this." He handed me a small pouch, heavy with coin. As a Healer of Yaylin, I had no need of money, indeed, didn't really want it.

"Ser Veen, please, take this, grant Sa Ach his freedom, and pay him to remain as your steward. I think you will find that paid servants, rather than forced slaves, will give you more work with less trouble."

I waited through another of his maddening silences. Even though I was now his equal, I still retained some of my training in his presence. I remained quiet, but I searched his face openly with my eyes. No longer did I look at the floor, unless to admire a beetle crawling across it.

"I have given some thought to doing just that. You have shown me. I am an old and hide-bound man, Healer, but I am capable of learning. With the right teacher."

I returned his smile and assured him that Sa Ach would be such a teacher.

The yamas were loaded and we were prepared to leave at sunrise. Before sleep overtook me, a knock sounded on my door.

"Brother. What a pleasant surprise! Come in."

"Sister, I do not know how to thank you. He did it! I am now free, and will receive a salary. If I choose to attend another family, I may do so. I thought never to see freedom again, until I walked the God Paths."

"Well, my brother Achennah, come in. And do not cry. Even if they are tears of happiness."

217

"I may now, as a free man, marry. Thanks to you, the line of Nah may not be ended, after all."

I laughed with him, "Then, I take it you do not wish to leave with me? Is there anyone in mind?"

"Thank you, Timorinah, for the offer, but I have been here too long, and yes, if she will have me, there is someone. She has flirted often with me, though our stations were not equal. Still, if her father will agree…. If she will agree…."

"Brother, *who*? Who are you talking about? What is her name?" I nearly screamed at him. His hope wandered a path I could not see, but I wanted to share in his happiness while I was still with him.

"Why, Dada's daughter, Mecy."

Of course! I had noticed her flirting with Achennah when her father wasn't there. She was a bit old for a bride, but still young enough for children. She was healthy and intelligent. Achennah would never be happy with a woman of no intelligence. "Oh, what a marvelous choice! Dada always speaks highly of you. I think you will find your wife, and soon. I think Ser Veen will even help, if needed."

"I could never ask the Master, I mean, Ser Veen for help."

"Brother, you can. Ask him if he would put in a word for you. Ask if you can bring your wife here, or ask Dada if he would prefer you live with him. Options open for you, brother mine. Take the ones that look the brightest."

Sa Sely had learned enough to take over as healer. I so wished she could have gone on this trip and stayed at Yaylin. I asked if she'd like to go, and though she said nothing would make her happier, she needed to stay where she was needed for now, and not train for the future.

"Healer, please, would you help me roll a few more rags before you leave?" That was the only request she made, and I gladly bled a bit on several. "Some come back, you know. They wear them both ways, and guide the groups. Some don't come back."

"Sa Sely, take care. What you do is dangerous. Do not get caught."

"I won't. And, if I do, I only know one person at a time, so I cannot be forced to give away information."

"You know the map."

"Yes, there is that. I will be careful. Thank you. Thank you from the many." Tears began to trickle down her cheeks. I hugged her; turned, and walked out, hoping the walls did not have ears that day.

Sunrise found us well on our way. Young Arges, being full of himself, gave orders right and left. Mostly they were followed, but not quickly, nor even joyously. The freed slaves were still getting used to their freedom, and we had all had our fill of the Pompous One, as we called Arges. He, however, remained entirely oblivious to everything but his own self.

Leaving Daveen brought no tears to my eyes, but leaving my brother and the many friends I had made was another matter. I hoped Veen would heed my words, and that Achen, as my brother was now known, would convince him to free all his slaves, and hire them. I will never know, but even a Shaman-Healer is allowed hope. And dreams.

The men laughed when I began to sing some of the old desert songs of my youth. It felt good to be able to sing again, and to sing of home. Even Young Arges joined in. Soon, we all taught each other songs of our youth. And the trail, though I knew it would go into the dark of the forest, did not seem quite so forbidding.

I remembered the yama from Yaylin, and gave each a treat of fruit, and head rubs between the ears. Soon, they would have followed me without leads, though they were not given that option.

"Why do they follow you? They never follow me."

"They follow me because I pet them, and give them treats."

"Why? They are but beasts of burden. Why would you give them treats?"

"Because even beasts of burden need to be appreciated. And if they are appreciated, they will carry heavier loads, and carry those heavier loads farther, without balking. Sliwa love to have their heads rubbed. I wouldn't suggest you offer them fruits, though, or they might bite you. They want meat, and would consider fruit an insult."

"You...you pet sliwa, too?" I laughed as Arges Veen visibly shuddered.

"Yes. They are dry, and warm, and smooth. And they love to be rubbed. If you anger a sliwa, you may die. It is always better to placate a giant lizard than to antagonize him. You may trust me on that one. Or find out for yourself." I smiled what I hoped was a wicked smile at him.

Arges approached me once our throats were tired from singing and a companionable silence settled about us. "Healer, I will strike a bargain with you. If you will no longer call me 'Young' Arges, I will call you Healer. I will no longer use the prefix of Sa."

I smiled, "Will you call the other men by their true names? And not call them Sa, either?"

"I don't know their true names."

"Ask them."

Chapter Twenty-Five

There are many paths to Life.
Some are long and tortuous.
Some are short and easy.
Most are a combination fused with acceptance.
—*Selyandra, a slave in name only*

THE OVERLAND TRAIL STARTED OUT as a gentle upward climb to the south and west. The lowland forests were open, and the trees wore light green leaves that were beginning to unfurl in the warm spring sun. Flowers adorned a few trees, their blossoms pink or white, or a combination. "What kinds of trees are these, Arges?" I asked, but he did not answer. Perhaps my voice did not carry to the head of the column. Perhaps he preferred not to be bothered by such mundane questions.

Eventually one of the men softly said, "Them be nut trees, Mem. 'Cept fer them," and he pointed to trees covered in white flowers that gave off a sweet and heady perfume. "Thems be juice fruits." And then he was quiet. I thought it a good time to start up a trail song of the desert. The rhythm lent itself well to walking, and the yama's ears twitched in approval, though the song soon petered out. We walked in silence, each accompanied by our own thoughts.

Sunlight skipped through these trees, just when a leaf captured a bit, the breeze blew it away, making wiggly shadows dapple the road. The sharp, pointy trees with the spiky leaves were farther up the trail, and higher on the mountain. Arges told me they need more moisture and cooler air.

221

There were eight in our party, six servants, Arges and myself, and the pack yama. I walked at the end of the line to study these strange men and to be of assistance if needed. Arges walked at the front, grumbling.

We walked in silence, only to hear Arges in the front, "I don't see why I, Arges Veen, heir to the House of Veen, must walk like a common man. I am not a common man. It is unseemly. I should ride a yama. I should be carried in a palanquin!"

He muttered, and fumed, providing great enjoyment for the rest of us.

Dun, the last servant in line muttered under his breath, "Him be spoilt, like last week's meat." He then hawked and spit to the side of the trail. The man in front of him grunted approval.

The sun was high overhead when Arges called out, "There is a small meadow just ahead. We will stop there for our noon break."

Arges tried to sound authoritative, but instead sounded petulant. But he was correct. There was a meadow, with grasses for the yama and a creek with fresh, cold water. Our noon meal was cold, but the rest of an hour most welcome to all of us.

"Tell me, Arges, will the road to Yaylin be like this all the way?" If so, it would not be so bad. I could deal with this. Indeed, I found beauty in it. The lacy trees were not so dark and closed, and the road seemed easy enough to travel, gentle in its ups and downs.

"No, Healer, it won't. When we leave here, the road heads almost due south, and we begin to climb in earnest. We must cross the pass into the Mountains of Life before we stop for our evening camp. It is steep and though not treacherous, it is not easy. That is why I insisted on an hour's rest now."

And the road did turn sharply to the south. We barely made the turn before the road began a long and steady climb. After

222

what seemed like hours of walking switchbacks, we reached the summit of the pass. Before us spread more mountains than I knew existed. And the trees were so dark in their greenery they appeared almost black. They were pointy trees, with spiky leaves. What I could see, at least. The sky came close here, heavy with cloud. I could smell the water they carried.

"We will have rain. More than you, desert dweller, have seen in a lifetime. These mountains are so high they force the moisture out of the clouds before it can get to the other side. They leave a little, or Daveen would have no rain at all."

"Arges, why are those mountains white on their tops, neh?" I had never seen anything like it. Tall mountains with black trees up just so far, and then white. Some of the white glistened, where there was no cloud over it.

"For being so smart, Healer, you sure are dumb. That is snow." His sneer at my title did not go unnoticed by me, or the others. I felt the others stiffen at the affront. I smiled.

"I will remember how you called me dumb when we are in the desert and you thirst. I will know how to find water. Will you?" He gave me a rather odd look, but said nothing more, until I asked him, "Why is it white?"

"It's ice. Snow and ice."

"Ah, is that where your father got his loads of ice from, then?"

"How did you, a slave—forgive me, a *former* slave, know of the ice? Did you steal some?"

At that, I had to laugh. "No, Arges, I did not steal it. I used it. The first time was to save your life. You burned with fever and your Priests could not break it. Finally, your father decided to trust me. I put you in a cool bath and told him I wished I could get it colder. He immediately sent for a large block of ice. We broke it into smaller pieces and we packed you in it. You cooled and finally slept a peaceful sleep. That was when your father realized, truly realized, what I was and where I came from."

223

"Some slaves would steal it. Some tried to sell it. Did you ever steal from my family and sell it?"

"No! And I don't know of any who did."

"I know Father let you go to the other homes to heal their slaves and sometimes family. They paid you. I know they did, for I talked to some. What did you do with the money?"

"Yes, Arges, they paid me. And the money went to your father's steward, Achen, Sa Ach as he was then. He counted it into the records and either took it, or gave it back so I could buy food and clothing for those too poor to buy their own." I did not tell him some of the money also went to Sa Sely for those who would walk the night path to freedom. I did not lie, I merely told him only part of the truth.

He had no idea that, as a shaman, I could walk the God Paths. He had no idea I was a shaman as well as a healer. It was through chewing the cactus buds bought from Dada's Pharmacopia, after I roasted them, that I found the path through the desert to the Barren Mountains. A path few could see, that led to a hole in the wards of the mountains to a pass, and freedom on the other side. The Houses of Daveen knew the slaves were leaving, but had no idea where they went. The path was somehow magicked, and the slaves, who traveled at night, were never seen. No one expected the slaves to go through the desert—Mulk and his men controlled the desert. No, everyone was sure the slaves slipped into the mountains, these same mountains we now traversed, covered with dark and forbidding trees.

I smiled as I remembered the gods speaking to me, telling me to cut my skin and place a bit of my blood on two rags. Two rags, not just one. The group leader would wear one around his ankle, and the last in line would wear the other around his. I did not know why, just that a drop of my blood would keep them safe.

224

We made it over the pass and about half way down the mountain, according to Arges, before halting for the night. My breaths were labored; I could hardly breathe in this water-soaked air. I felt I would drown while I walked, and wondered how people could not only live in the forests, but prefer them to the open spaces of the desert. The trees were forbidding and foreboding. Their leaves were narrow spikes and stood so close together, little light filtered to the road. Why would anyone choose the wet of the mountains over the dry of the desert? And yet, I knew they did.

A rough shelter waited at the rest stop; a low-roofed lean-to, covered in old thatch. The men quickly put tarps over the thatch and built a fire with the driest wood they could find in the shelter. They went into the forest for more wood and boughs. I stayed with the yamas. Soon, we had a good fire, wood stacked under the shelter and boughs laid out for our sleeping. The smell of camp stew filled our little area and I made a hot and healthy tea for us all. The men seemed oblivious to the weather. I don't know if it was to keep my spirits up, or if they truly did not find it a hardship. I tried not to let them know I feared I would drown with each breath I took.

The rains came before dawn—loud, powerful, accompanied by thunder and stroked by the fingers of the gods. The wet soon found its way through the tarps and old thatch into our shelter. As we couldn't sleep, we got up, hastily ate a cold meal, and packed our bedrolls and belongings. The yamas were soaked and not cooperative. They wanted to be out of the rain. I didn't blame them, and gave them each an extra fruit and rubs between their ears. Neither did much to mollify them, but they quieted a little.

As the sky lightened in the east the rains stopped and we again began our trek. The trees, in their nasty way, apparently saved all the rain that fell on them and, as we walked beneath them, they would wave and shower us all over again. All of us

225

were cold and shivering, wet and miserable. And we had days to go before reaching Yaylin. I hoped this weather would blow away and it would at least be dry. Young Arges, happy for once, assured me it would not. And wasn't this marvelous, to go adventuring in the mountains and the rain? I assured him I thought not!

"Look!" called Arges. "We are half-way there. There is the pass with the border stone. On the other side of the hill lies the Kingdom of Yaylin."

We began our climb to the summit of the pass. The road seemed to climb straight up with few switchbacks, but nothing like the one we climbed our second day out. From the summit, I looked back at the Mountains of Life—high, rugged, snow-capped. Looking toward Yaylin, the mountains seemed rounder, somehow gentler, not as high, nor as black. Then, maybe it just looked that way because it was *home*.

Arges stopped at the stele that marked the border. "Come on, men, let us see if we can move it a ways into Yaylin." He placed his arms around it. "Come on, it can't be so heavy we men of Daveen can't move it."

I started to laugh. "What's so funny, Healer? Do you think we cannot move this stone?"

"Arges, that is not a stone, it is a stele. It goes deep into the ground. It does not set on top of it. And you will hurt yourself if you try. Why do you want to move it, anyway?"

"Why? Why, to give more land to Daveen, of course."

"Arges, look at it. It is covered in old Mage runes. I suggest you give up your dream, and we continue down the road." At that, he stopped, and truly looked at it.

"Can you read it?"

"Some." I answered. "It says something about there being no further contention over this border." No, I couldn't read it, but Lu Shahnnah could, and did, and told me what it said. It had taken time, but I was finally not only comfortable having her in

my head and my heart, but I welcomed her company and wise
council. Without her, I think I would never have lived to regain
my freedom. She could see farther down the God Paths than I,
and counseled patience at every turn. Now that I was nearly
home, I did not want patience. I wanted to run. I wanted to run
all the way, which of course, I could not. But, oh, how I wanted
to run—or at least borrow the wings of a bird. Any bird. I didn't
care. I just wanted to go *home*.

The forest did seem more open and less wet. And trees with
broad leaves began appearing. The trees I remembered from
Yaylin. Now, after the trees of Daveen, these forests seemed
much more open than my memory of them.

Rains still came, though less frequently and less hard. The air
felt drier, my breathing eased, and at times I felt the warmth and,
I was sure, the perfume of my beloved desert. The road was
gentled in its ups and downs. We walked more westerly now.

At last, the day came when we stopped on the crest of a
hill, and looked down upon the city of Yaylin. It seemed little
changed since I had last seen it. "There," I pointed, "there is the
School of Healing where I lived and learned. There, down by the
river, are the markets. That is where the inns and taverns are
located."

"Is that where we will stay? In one of those inns?"

"No, Arges, I think not. We will go to the School. Unless it
has changed, there will be room for us as well as the yama. There
will be hot baths and good meals. We will go there, first."

"Remember, we are going into the desert. To find your
people."

"How could I forget? I am going home. But we will need a
few days to rest, and the yama, too, need some rest and
grooming. And we will have to find sliwa for the desert."

"We aren't taking the yama?"

"No, we will take sliwa. It will take a few days to locate the
right ones. Do not be impatient. Impatience in the desert kills."

As we began our descent into Yaylin, I heard one of the servants call out in pain. I told the group to continue as I walked back to him. "Mem, I ain't hurt none, I jes' need to talk to you. Alone. See, we ain't servants. We, all of us, we still be slaves. And here, in Yaylin, we be free. Is that right?"

"Yes. It is."

"And if we goes back to Daveen, we be slaves agin. Right?"

"Yes. I think so, unless you received and registered your Letter of Emancipation before you left."

"Mem, can we stays here, in Yaylin?"

At this, I smiled. "I don't know, but we'll check into it. You will not go back to Daveen; that is guaranteed."

"Mem, we was picked 'cause we gots wives and families. Them Veens knows we loves 'em, our families, and will come back to 'em. Mem, our families told us not to come back. We wants jobs, Mem, to earn money to buy our families and bring them out."

Of course! It made perfectly good sense. I began to appreciate, once again, how devious the owners of people could be. "I will see that you all are put in touch with people who handle jobs. I cannot guarantee you jobs, but you will not return to Daveen. That I can promise, and that is a promise I will keep."

"Thanks be to you, Mem."

I returned to the head of the line and Arges.

"What was that about?"

"Oh, nothing to worry about." At least not yet, I thought to myself. The time will come, but not for a while. I was nearly home. That thought consumed my very being. "I will do the talking at the gate, Arges. You will answer questions when asked, otherwise, be quiet, please."

"But, I am leader. I should talk."

"Arges, you are the leader, but you do not know these guards. Now, be quiet unless specifically asked a question." We reached the gate. The blue and gold paint looked new and, to me, inviting.

"Healer. Where are you and these men heading?" The guard smiled at me, and ignored Arges and the men. "Have you been gone for a while? You do not look familiar. I thought I knew all the healers, at least by face."

"Yes, I have been gone. But now I am home, or nearly so."

"Welcome. I'm sure you have been missed. It is always good to have our healers return. Now, where are you and these men going?"

"We are all going to the school. I do not know if we will all stay there, but if these men move into an inn, or another place, I will bring them back to sign the book. I am not sure how long we will be there, but Arges Veen and I will be leaving out the Desert Gate when we go."

"Will these men also leave by that gate?"

"I do not yet know."

The guard straightened his face to a most serious expression and spoke to the men. "This healer vouches for you. Do not let her down. Keep to your manners. If you break our laws, it will not go well with you." And then the gate opened, and I was almost home.

"I suggest you listen to the guard's words, and heed them. The laws of Yaylin are different than the ones of Daveen. Here, if you break the law, if you strike a Citizen, even in self-defense, you can go to jail. You will not be sold into slavery, but I understand jail is not something to strive for. You might prefer returning as a slave to the House of Veen."

Arges smirked at my last comment.

229

Chapter Twenty-Six

Start your day with a sweet, a bowl of tea, and a smile.
Well, at least think about the smile.
—*Graffito from a tower room, Healer's School, Yaylin*

I LED OUR LITTLE CARAVAN to the main gate of the school. The guard, recognizing my healer's robes and tattoos, did not question us, but immediately opened the gate and allowed us into the main court. "You men stay here with the yama," I croaked to the servants, my voice thick with emotion. "Arges, come with me." We walked up the stairs to the large door. I grasped the ring and knocked three times, paused, and then once more. I knew it was useless, as many eyes watched. Still, formalities, like rituals, must be maintained.

My hand touched the door. I was home. I had waited—dreamed—many years for this. The door opened, and a young acolyte stood before us. "Come in Healer, Guest. How may I be of service?"

"Acolyte, please, inform Authority that Healer-Shaman Jibutu awaits her pleasure." My voice gave out. I could say no more. I heard Arges gasp at the addition to my title; he had not known I was shaman as well as healer. My eyes feasted upon the walls, the long hallway. The acolyte looked at me with a rather odd expression, turned, and ran down the hall. She went past Authority's office. So, Authority was in class? Or, perhaps she was in the dining hall? Soon, I heard a scream echo down the hall. "Roose. Find Healer Roose." So, my mother was here? I could barely stand.

"Healer!" Authority walked so fast she almost ran as she came to me, arms wide, robes flapping behind her. She hurried toward me, and I to her, to meet in a tearful embrace. "Oh, child, we thought you dead. The Caravan Master said you were, and returned your box to us as proof. And here you are, you are returned to us." Our tears mingled and stained our robes. A third person joined us.

"Daughter, it is you." Almost as if she feared I was not solid, she stretched out her hand and gingerly touched mine. Assured I was not an apparition, her lips quivered, her eyes filled with tears, and she hoarsely whispered, "You *live*." Then her arms were about me.

"Mother Roose, you are here! I could not believe it when I heard your name called. You are here!" When I looked at her, the shock must have been all over my face.

"Yes, my hair is white. When I heard you and Lu Shahnnah went missing, the gray began. When she was found and only bones near her, we feared some of them were yours. My hair went white and Authority called me home, to school, to teach."

The tears subsided and all the folks who had crowded the hall to witness such an emotional welcome began to fade into the shadows, to return to their duties.

"And who is this?"

I had completely forgotten Arges. "Authority, may I present Arges Veen, of the House of Veen, one of the ruling families of Daveen." I motioned, and he approached. "Arges Veen, I present Authority, head of our school, and Healer Roose, one of my mothers."

"You are welcome here, Ser Veen. Doubly welcome for returning one of ours from the dead."

We stood a bit longer, and I explained our trip and that six men and the yamas waited outside. "Well," said Authority, "they must be tired and hungry." She called, and an acolyte appeared, received orders and left to take the men and yamas to the stables where all would be cared for. Arges and I, along with our luggage, were taken to our rooms, and then to the baths. How I looked forward to bathing in the luxury of school's bath.

"What? We are to bathe together?" I chuckled at the sudden shyness of Arges.

"Yes, if you'd care too. Or, you may wait until I am finished. The human body is open to all healers." My robe, dropped at my feet, waited to be collected by an acolyte. I stepped into the water and sighed at the heat.

"Arges, while we are alone, I must speak to you. I noticed you looking at many of the students. The ones without tattoos. You may look. If any are interested in you, they will let you know, and if it is mutually agreeable, a liaison may take place."

"What? And spread the seed of a Veen to someone who will grow to claim Daveen citizenship? I think not."

"Oh, Arges. There will be no children of your seed by one of us. We cannot have children."

"It's a good thing, as all you Healers are so ugly."

"We are ugly for good reason. When we go out to the tribes, we are allowed lovers, but not marriage. Should any of our lovers be married, we do not want the wives of men who may visit our tents once in a while to become jealous of us. And they are not, for they know their men will return to them and soon bless them with a swollen belly and another baby."

"Healer, may I wash your back?" Two acolytes had entered. One came into the pool to wash my back. The other hesitated before asking Arges the same question. He had the presence to blush, when he realized his remark had been heard.

"Arges Veen, they do a remarkable job of washing backs. I advise you to allow." I groaned with the pleasure of having my back scrubbed and promptly forgot he shared my bath. When I stepped from the pool and dried, a clean healer's robe lay folded on the stool for me. I noticed a clean robe also waited young Arges and our dirty ones had been taken to the laundry.

"Healer, before you leave, what did you mean that you are a Healer-Shaman?"

"I was trained as both a healer and a shaman."

"Why did no one know of that when you lived with us?"

"I thought it prudent not to mention it. To anyone. Why?"

"You would have died. Our Priests do not like shamans. Did you ever practice your, uh, did you ever...."

"No, Arges. Never. No one knew, no one asked." How easily the lie rolled off my tongue. But to admit I had might bring retaliation once he returned home. And retaliation would be indiscriminate, to every slave who ever talked to me, or may have talked to me.

I left him to his own devices. He wanted to be a man grown; he was on his own. I knew the acolyte would take him back to his room and someone would bring him to the dining hall later. The table in my room held a carafe of tea and my favorite cheese and bread. Someone pulled the curtains together and I took advantage of the dark and the peace. I drank the tea, nibbled at the food and promptly fell asleep on my cot. I was home. I was safe.

"Healer. Please, the bell has rung for evening meal. Authority requests you and your guest sit at her table. May I escort you?"

"Thank you, Acolyte. May I know your name?" I sat on the edge of my cot and took the cool and damp cloth she handed me. As I washed my face, I detected a slight odor of the yellow fruit. Refreshed, I handed it back, and stood.

"I am Acolyte Layn, Healer."

"And I am Healer-Shaman Jibutu." I smiled back at her. She blushed, and told me she knew that. That everyone in school

233

knew who I was. It was my turn to blush, though with my dark skin, I'm sure she did not see it. We walked to the dining hall in silence.

"Please, join us. I have also invited your young Arges to sit with us." Authority motioned to her right, in the place of honor. Often, this chair was left empty, waiting for any guest who might join us after meal had started. The honor was not lost on me. And to my right sat Mother Roose. Arges was escorted to the table, and sat across from me.

"We are all most eager to hear of your adventures; however, I think we will wait until after our meal, perhaps in my office, neh?" I smiled at that. Never had I heard of her using the common 'neh?' ending. Or, if I had, I didn't remember it.

The meal was most pleasant, and during it, several students flirted with Arges. He was new and different and in their eyes, exotic. When we stood to retire to Authority's office, several of the women invited him to accompany them for an evening's entertainment. He would be much happier with them than with us in Authority's office.

We sat in comfortable chairs and shared a warm, fermented tisane and sweets. "Now, Daughter, tell us. Tell us everything," urged Authority. I leaned back in my chair, closed my eyes, and began.

They were quiet and saved their questions. I repeated the whole story, before I remembered part of it.

"Wait. Something else happened in the desert. It was while I was delirious with the fever. In looking back, perhaps my leg was infected. I still had my knife and water and my robe I slept under during the day, but I remember little else. I slept, and dreamed. In my dream I was here, in the garden, and smelled the lilies bloom. The scent was so real, and so thick, I remember being sick to my stomach. Then my leg began to burn. My broken leg. It burned up into my body and into my head. It was as if the Sun had dropped her own blood into mine. I would die. Then, my head exploded, and my skull became a million new stars, born from me and sent to the cold sky. I died. Then Moon came, and saw my death, and dropped some of his blood onto me. My skull healed, but the stars remained in the heaven. My head grew cold, and then my body grew cold, and then my leg. I did not realize death was so cold! Especially in the desert. Then I slept.

"When I woke, my water skin was full, and next to me. I drank, and slept, and drank and slept. Until I could again begin my crawling toward what I hoped was Yaylin and rescue but turned out to be Mulk and enslavement."

I thought a bit before continuing, "And, later, after being bought by the House of Veen, when I walked the God Paths, they showed me the escape route through the mountains. The gods also told me to cut my skin and place a drop of my blood on two rags, one for the leader to wear around his ankle, and one for the last in line to wear around his...." I finished by telling them of the 'guards' for the escaped slaves.

The room echoed only the sounds of our breathing. Finally, Mother Roose spoke. "Daughter, we need to go to the desert garden."

"Yes," responded Authority. "I think we should. Now." She stood, Mother stood, and I followed.

"May I ask why?" I ventured.

"We will see," was all the answer I received.

The desert garden smelled of sand and cactus. The center portion of the garden was raised. This is where we keep the white snakes, the Lily Snakes. We walked to the center portion.

"Place your hands on the sand. Move them gently and then stand still." I did as they told. Soon, there was a rustling in the sand and many, if not all, of our captive snakes came to the surface to look at me. "Place your hand out, toward them." I did, and they came to me, and rubbed my hand, their flickering tongues tickling me as they smelled me. Once they finished their caress, they vanished back to the sand. Never had I been so close to them. Never had I seen them do this to anyone. To get that close to one meant death—or so I had been taught.

"Now, Daughter, show me your leg." Mother Roose and Authority both bent to see my bare leg in the lantern light. "Look! There is only a scar of one fang, not two."

"Is that a bite scar? I thought it was the scar of a cactus spine?"

They laughed. A pleasant laugh, one filled with love. "No, Daughter. You were saved by the White Snakes of Death. They must have smelled your cuff and recognized you as one of their own, and in trouble, and tried to heal you in their own way. Tell me, do you find yourself taking fewer fluids than you used to?"

I thought a bit before answering, "Yes. I hadn't thought of it until now, but yes."

"You are now part White Snake. You have absorbed their skin and their venom."

"Am I no longer human?" The thought brought fear, and tears.

"Oh, yes. You will always be human, but now you are more." Authority continued, "You carry their venom in your blood. Had the one who bit you used both fangs, you would be dead. Now, you are healed, and you may handle the snakes with impunity. And when you call them, as you did tonight, they will come."

I knew we used the venom, much reduced, to cure serious infections. Mine must have been terrible.

"There is one more thing. Something beautiful, and yet sad." I turned to Mother Roose, "Remember my fourth night dream, and how Papa Jib told of finding my birth mother and me? Well, her name was Lu Ahnah. Her first-born was Lu Shahnnah, and her second born was Achennah. My name, had she not died or had Father understood her, was to have been Timorinah." And I told them the story of my blood family.

A three-day had passed, and I was again escorted for a tattoo ceremony. This time, it was of my asking. I was to receive an arm 'bracelet" with a design that would incorporate my slave tattoo. I did not want to obliterate my slave marking, as that was a part of my life. Although not a part I would wish on anyone, still, it remained a part of me. The healer who would give me my new tattoo was an accomplished artist and assured me she would not over-mark the existing design.

This time, I sat next to the stone bed. This time, my arm instead of my neck rested on the neck rest so the healer could have access to my arm, and my arm would be supported. I drank a cool tea, and again the room was full of healers. Arges also attended, at my invitation. Mother Roose roasted and ground the cacia bark to powder and handed it to the artist.

I don't know how long it took her. Finally it was done, and I was helped to my feet. The knife used was cleaned by Mother Roose, and the thong that held it placed over my head. Again, I received a Knife of the Healer. Again, there were treats, and drinks, and a party of congratulations.

"May I see?" Arges came to my side. "I'm impressed. That is beautiful. How did you go through it without crying out? Slaves always cry when they get their tattoos and theirs are so small in comparison. Oh, it was the tea you drank, wasn't it? They gave you a drug." He nodded his head and smiled with smugness at having figured it out to his satisfaction.

At the mention of slaves, the conversation stopped. I smiled at Arges and told him, "The pain is not of the tattoo Arges; the pain is caused by the loss of freedom. And, no, Arges, there was no drug in the tea."

I turned to the party and asked for another sweet. Conversation resumed and too soon, the sun dropped over the edge of the earth. We all went to the dining hall for evening meal, then on about our business. My business was a nap.

A ten-day had passed since our arrival at School, and now the time to leave had closed upon us.

"Arges. Your servants desire to be paid." The conversation I had so long dreaded came now.

"My father will pay them on their return." Smugness fairly dripped from his mouth.

"No, Arges. They will not be returning. They have asked me to speak for them." They all stood behind me. As I spoke, I turned to see their nods of affirmation.

"They have new jobs to attend."

"They, they *have* to return. They must take the yama back. And my father will pay them when they do." Anger and fear seemed to fight for dominance in Arges; anger that he'd been hoodwinked by mere slaves, and fear of what his father might do when he returned home without them. "Besides, I don't have any money."

"Arges, that is a lie. You do have money. And you will have more, as school has authorized me to pay you for your yama. If you insist on lying, you will not be taken to Carnival to meet my people. We do not deal with liars. We cut their tongues out and leave them in the desert to live, if they can. No one has yet survived such treatment."

We all watched him. He said nothing, but his mind contemplated his possible fate. "All right. I did tell them they were free and I did hope they would return, where their freedom would be revoked. All right. I'll pay them from the monies for the yama." Anger won out, and he stomped away. The men grabbed each other, then me.

"Oh, Mem, thank you."

"And your jobs? Where are they?" They had told me they had jobs, but not where they were.

"Why, Mem, right here! We've been hired, to a man, to help with the yama." They beamed.

"Mem, one more thing. Can you tell us of a tat artist? One who can erase our slave tats?" I smiled and showed them my new 'bracelet.'

"Yes, I think I can."

"Oh, we don't need none so fancy as yours. It's beautiful, Mem, but too costly for us."

"Don't worry. It will be taken care of. And soon."

"Jibutu. Daughter, will you walk with me?"

"Neh? But of course, Mother Roose. Where shall we go?"

"Daughter, I am sorry for trying to deny what you said after your fourth night. You did say you were Shaman-Healer, but I denied it."

"And it didn't matter, did it?" I laughed and hugged her.

"I have news. About Caravan Master Dedman Pew."

I stiffened at the name.

"He tried to sell others. Only they weren't so easy to subdue. They left him on the desert. They would not slit his throat or remove his clothing. They buried him under sliwa plops."

At that, I burst out in laughter.

"The men assured me it was true. In fact, it was his own men, Pew's men, who helped. They were his slaves and they revolted."

"Never, Mother Roose, has a man so deserved such a burial." Shahnnah's laughter rang in my head.

"Neh. Never." Finally, my laughter subsided.

Our sliwa were purchased, packed, and waiting for us. My boxes, long stored, had been returned to me. I was especially glad to see all my hooks, and was delighted to see the box Papa Jib had made for me so long ago. Pain at leaving school so soon ripped through me, even as I could hardly stand the wait to get back to my desert to be with my people—at least for a little while. I no longer knew if I wanted to live with my tribe forever. I had spent too much time in too many different places. I smiled at the memory of Anka, and wondered if I would ever see her

239

again, and tell her of my adventures. Indeed, there is a world out there neither of us ever contemplated.

"Daughter, are you sure you wish to continue on to Bel Harq?"

"No, Mother. I want more than anything to stay with my tribe. All I have ever wanted was to be healer to the Tribe of Jib. But it isn't what I want that matters, is it? It's what must be done. So after a visit, I shall take Arges and go on to Bel Harq. Lu Shahnnah fairly insists on it. I do not know where we are going, or who we are to see, but she is insisting that my life must be broadened, and when we meet the person, or people we are to meet, she will tell me."

"At least I know you live. You know, a Mage from over the Barren Mountains was here some time ago. She brought a young Mage who we are training and when she left, she took Healer Elen, to train as well. Authority wanted to send you, but we thought you were dead. Perhaps that is the person you are to see."

"I have no idea, Mother."

"Well, when you get to Bel Harq, go to the Governor's Palace, and ask to speak to the Mage. She may be able to help. And, daughter of my heart, when you get to your tribe, perhaps," and here she smiled, "you will finally want your naming ceremony." Tears fell down her cheeks as she hugged me good-by. My tears joined hers. And then the Sliwa Master called us. The time of parting had arrived.

240

Chapter Twenty-Seven

Fortunately, ignorance can be treated.
Unfortunately, stupidity cannot.
—*Healer Leys*

OUR LITTLE CARAVAN of three humans and six sliwa slowly crossed the desert. We had been gone a three-day when the sliwa master decided I knew enough about handling the great lizards that he would not make the trek to Carnival with us. I told him when I bought the sliwa that I was capable, but he didn't believe me. Nor did he trust Arges. Mostly, I think, he did not trust anyone from Daveen.

"Healer, are you sure you will be all right? I mean, with *him*?" The sliwa master's concern, though genuine, was misplaced.

"I appreciate your concern. However, I have known Arges for many years and though he is spoiled and puffed up with his own self-importance, I can handle him. If he gets to be too much, I will leave him in the desert for a time. The desert is a marvelous teacher, is it not?" At that, the sliwa master laughed, gave us an extra skin of water, and left us with five sliwa. Three were packed with trade goods, two were for Arges and me to ride and carry our things.

"Healer, do you think it wise for him to leave us? I mean, what if we get lost? It has been a long time since you were, uh, home."

"Arges, you are right; however, this *is* my home. This desert, these oases, these seeps, these people—they are *mine*! We will not

241

get lost, we will not run out of water and we will reach Carnival in a five-day. *If* you follow my directions." I smiled, but Arges saw the threat. Or, rather, the promise for he had learned I do not threaten. "At any rate, *I* shall reach Carnival. Whether you do or not is up to you."

The days were warm, but not the hot of high summer, so we plodded along, giving the sliwa their lead. Arges wasn't too sure he wanted to travel at night and, frankly, I wanted to see the desert by day. I had missed it for years, and now I gorged on its beauty, its perfumes, the songs of its whispering sands. I was home, truly home.

"Don't you get lonely out here? I mean there are no people. How do you know we aren't lost?" Arges looked around and saw nothing but sand. He asked questions like a child. And, in a way, he was a child. He was used to the dark and dank of the forests, not the light and dry of the desert. He was raised with servants and slaves hovering around him his whole young life. Now he was alone, except for me. He seemed to talk just to hear his own voice, not because he either expected or perhaps even wanted answers. Sometimes I answered him. Sometimes I ignored him.

"No, Arges. I do not get lonely. I am comfortable in my own hide. I like myself. I don't mind the inner dialog I hold in my head. You might try learning to like yourself, too." He sputtered a bit at that, but was quiet for a long time.

We met a fellow traveler on the third day. He, too, traveled to Carnival, so joined us. On the fourth day, we came upon a tribe going to Carnival, and followed along. I explained that Arges came to study the possibility of opening trade with the tribes. They were not impressed.

"Welcome to Carnival!" Old Leys stood in the road, his arms spread wide, a huge smile upon his face. "You are the first to arrive! The market square is cleaned and my tent is open." His face radiated his genuine welcome. The tribe moved on to their normal place. I approached Leys.

"Healer Leys, I am Healer-Shaman Jibutu. We met several years ago, when Healer Roose brought me, before taking me to school." His eyes studied me, carefully. I could see he was nearly blind.

"Yes, I remember you. And you died in the desert. And now you are back." At that, his arms went about me in a tight and loving embrace. "And," he continued, "who might this young man be? This young man who is not of the desert, nor of the tribes?"

"Healer Leys, allow me to present Arges Veen, of the Ruling House of Veen in the city and kingdom of Daveen. He hired me to bring him to Carnival, to possibly sell some of his wares and to discuss with the tribes the possibility of setting up trade between his house and ours."

Old Leys looked at Arges a long time before smiling and responding. "Welcome, Young Arges Veen. If this healer vouches for you, you are most truly welcome."

"Thank you, Healer Leys. I am honored at her vouchsafing me and honored at your welcome."

"Now, will you two youngsters honor this old man by staying in my tent?"

"Healer Leys, I thought you would never ask."

We walked to his tent, and were soon joined by the families who had stayed at Carnival for the year. Tisanes were steeped, and sweets offered. Once the formalities were finished, and the curiosities satisfied, I took Arges to the Market Square.

"Market space is given on a first come basis. So you may pick your place, but once chosen, you may not change it. Your items will be safe, so you may lay them out, and at night cover them with a cloth to keep the blowing sands off. No one will take anything, for stealing is dealt with harshly in the desert. If someone comes by and you are not here, they may pick an item

243

out, and move it to the back of your space, as a way of saying they wish to buy it, or at least bargain for it, and will be back, later."

"Where do you suggest I spread my carpet, and my wares?" Arges looked at the huge square, and tried to decide where the most advantageous spot would be.

"Arges, I have no idea. I only shop at the market; I do not sell. I don't think it will matter. You are a stranger; everyone will come by to see what you have to sell. I tell you this—do not lie to anyone, do not make false promises, and do not try to cheat anyone. To do any of those will be your death sentence. This market is not like the markets of Daveen. Remember that."

"Well, you will be with me, right? To keep me honest."

"What? Oh, no. I am a Healer, and will be in the tent with Old Leys, at least until my tribe comes. Then I will share my time with them, as well with as Old Leys."

"Well, what if someone lies about me? Who will know the truth?"

I sighed. Did this man ever listen with his ears? "Do not worry. Lying is not condoned here. Remember what we do to liars? We cut their tongues out and leave them in the desert. Besides, I am sure, there will be at least one Truth Sayer here to sit in court, should you be accused. She will know a lie from a truth."

"How long will we be here?"

"Until the end of carnival. Usually carnival lasts a ten-day, once the last of the tribes has arrived. You will enjoy it, I think. There will be music and dancing and entertainments. Oh, one other thing. Even if the women flirt with you, I suggest you do not flirt back. If you truly need a woman while you are here, approach one of the healers. To flirt with a desert woman means you are considering marrying her and by the end of Carnival, you will have a wife. Or no head."

He paled at the last. Finally, he stuttered, "But, won't there be a tent set up for pleasure women?"

"Yes," I laughed. "Were you not listening? If you need a woman, you may approach a healer."

"But, but you are all so ugly. And, well, old."

"Arges Veen, it is time you learned some truths. One is that true beauty is not on the face; it is in the heart. The second is that yes, we are older than you. That gives us experience you do not have. Third, you may learn much from a healer, if you so desire. Fourth, healers do not allow diseases to be spread; we treat them. Fifth, when *you* marry, it will not be for beauty, but as a political alliance between the House of Veen and the House of Whoever. You might wish to consider this. Your wife may not be beautiful to look upon, but if you treat her well, she will share her inner beauty with you, and thereby become beautiful. Sixth, you may desire a healer, but you may also be refused."

I turned and walked away.

"Your young man has much to learn, has he not?" Old Leys asked as he and I sat, drinking our bowls of tea, in the shade of the tent.

"Indeed, he does. However, he has learned much already and I think he will live to learn much more. And now, my old friend, tell me of your life. What have I missed at Carnival all this time? How is it you are still here and not back at school?" My questions bubbled from me as water from a newly dug well.

"Ah, I am still here because I prefer it here, and Authority agrees with me. Even nearly blind, I can still heal. The tribes are generous in their gifts to me. I enjoy the relative solitude when the tribes are gone, and the children of the families who stay. And I love the bustle of the tribes during carnival, but am glad for the quiet when they leave.

"And you, Jibutu. What tales can you tell an old man?"

So we passed the hours, treating the few who came to us, telling stories, listening to new stories, and then I glanced to the desert and saw a new tribe approach. My father, Jib, rode the lead sliwa.

"Healer Leys. My father's tribe is here!" I jumped up, excitement making my voice a hoarse whisper, "My father still rides the lead sliwa. I must go. I shall return later, but I must see my family."

"Of course, child. They will be happy to know you still walk the sands with feet of flesh instead of feet of the spirit."

I fairly ran to greet my tribe. They still camped in the same place and by the time I wove my way to them through the other campsites, the tents were unloaded and some even up. Shyness covered me as I approached my father. How would he take to me? I had been gone so long and had already been mourned as dead.

His back was to me as I approached. He directed the boys, my younger brothers whom I've yet to meet, to pull this rope, pound that stake. I stood behind him, drinking in the sound of his voice. My eyes ate hungrily the breadth of his shoulders, the sureness of his stance. His hair, once black now held streaks of silver. The boys looked at me, puzzled as to why a Healer would look so at their father, and went back to work.

"Papa?" I spoke as my hand reached for his shoulder. "Papa Jib. It is me. Jibutu."

At my voice, or my touch, he froze in place before he wheeled around and stared at me. His eyes as hungry for me as mine were for him. We stood and stared at each other for at least an eternity before he spoke.

"Daughter?" he whispered, his voice coarse as sand, "It is you? Truly? We heard you were dead upon the desert. We have mourned you." Then, he turned, and bellowed, "Wife! Saba! Come here! Your daughter has returned from the sands!"

The boys stopped their work and watched. Something important was happening, but they did not know exactly what. My mother ran to us, screaming my name. And then the three of us were holding each other in an embrace so tight, I'm not sure but what our bodies didn't melt together to become one, at least for the length of our embrace.

We laughed, we cried, and again, I told my story.

"I knew," sobbed my mother, "I knew. I told Jib you were not dead, you would return. I *knew!* But he didn't believe."

"That's right, Daughter. She always said our Mourning Ceremony was not right. You lived. But, she is a woman and a mother—and we mourned you anyway." He shrugged, and we all dissolved in laughter, even the little brothers I did not yet know.

In the days of carnival, I enjoyed my new siblings and caught up on old friendships. The healer for my father's tribe was Tems, now a man grown and highly thought of by everyone. He, too, came to the Healer's Tent during Carnival.

"How does that work?" asked Arges. "I mean, your tribe's healer is a male. What do the men do, when, uh…?"

I laughed. "Oh, Arges, the men must care for themselves. Again, Tems is so ugly, that when a wife visits his tent, her husband is not jealous."

"Women? Women can see a male healer? I mean, for *that?*"

"You seem shocked. Of course! All people have needs and problems. It is allowed." So continued Arges's education. "On the desert, women are free and equal, not subservient, as they are in Daveen."

⤙ ⚶ ⤚

"Come, Daughter, Carnival will end soon, and we have had no time to ourselves. Let us walk out to the dunes for a quiet time together."

"I thought it would never happen." I smiled as we walked in silence to the dune crest. "Papa, do you remember my birth mother at all?"

"Barely. She held you toward me, mumbled something I did not understand, and when I took you from her hands, she died."

247

"Do you remember anything of what she mumbled? It is important. Please, think about it." I watched him. He searched my face, saw the great need I felt, closed his eyes, and journeyed back through his memories.

"I am sorry, Daughter. It made no sense to me, something like, "Tuh, Tehmoh," I'm sorry, child."

"Papa, could it have been 'Timorinah'?"

"*Yes!* I believe that is what it was. By Boran, I'm sure. Timorinah. Why? How did you know?"

And so I told my father the whole story of Lu-Shahnnah, my capture, of Achennah, of my journey.

"Arges' family held you slave? He will feed the desert before the sun rises!"

"No, Papa. It is over. He has learned much, and will learn more. He is to be treated only as you know him, not as he was. Hopefully, it will be the beginning of the end of slavery in Daveen. If you feed him to the desert this night, it will lower our tribe to the level of Daveen."

He looked at me for a long time; saw the honesty of my words, and agreed. We continued our talk on the dune until the eastern sky lightened, and then walked back to our respective tents.

Carnival came to a close, and the tribes began to leave. Before my tribe left, Jib invited Arges and me to evening meal with the tribe. They would leave shortly after, as the desert was becoming too hot for day travel.

"Daughter. We, of your tribe, present you with a new healer's box and a new personal box."

To much cheering, my mother and her brother brought out two new boxes for me. When I accepted them, I felt an extra weight. Inside each box was something small and personal from each family. There was a new bowl, carved with the White Snake, in an intricate design from my father's tent. My aunts gave me fabrics; my uncles gave me tools they thought I might use. A knife of silver, a spoon of stone, writing brushes and ink stones. These were gifts often given at birth. "Yes, Daughter. Birth gifts, for you have been reborn to us. And, Daughter, do you not think it is time for you to take a new name? To have a proper Naming Ceremony?"

At that, everyone laughed, for they remembered my naming ceremony of many years ago. The ceremony where I was to have chosen a young woman's name. Traditionally my woman name would have been something of desert—a flower name, a star name. But I loudly proclaimed I would keep my baby name, Jibutu, Daughter of Jib. My mother had stood embarrassed at my outburst, and after a stunned silence, everyone had laughed and all was right with my world.

"Daughter, everyone knows you are the Daughter of Jib. Even if you take a new name, you will forever be, in this tribe at least, known as Jibutu."

I looked at everyone who stood around me. They all smiled and nodded their encouragement. I looked for Mother Roose, but of course, she was not there. "Yes, I will take the name Timorinah."

Everyone cheered, they chanted the new name so they wouldn't forget, and we partied until the time of departure was upon us.

When we reached the healer's tent, Old Leys wanted to see the gifts. "They are beautiful. May I add a small token of my own?" He presented me with a beautifully carved drinking bowl. The stone was green unlike any I'd ever seen. The carving around the outside was a pattern of interlocking circles. It was one of the most beautiful works of art imaginable.

"Healer Leys, this is beautiful. I thank you for honoring me with it. May I ask where it came from?"

He laughed at my question. "Yes, Healer, you may. It came from my home. I carved it before entering School."

"I shall treasure it always."

249

Arges reached for it, and after careful examination stated, "This is the work of an artisan. Healer Leys, I think you missed your calling. You could have been a master carver. Why, bowls like this would bring in top price."

"Yes, Young Arges Veen. I could have been a master carver. It has been a hobby of mine for years. But, I wanted to be a master healer. Healing was the only thing I ever wanted to do. As a healer, I have no need of money. I continued my carving, even after becoming a healer, and gave them to people I thought would enjoy and appreciate them." Leys paused a bit before continuing, "If you have not noticed, young man, all healers are devoted to the healing arts. To become a healer is to give up much, it is not something to be entered lightly."

We took our leave of Healer Leys, said our farewells to Carnival, and again set forth on our journey.

"So, Arges Veen. Carnival is over, and you still live. You must have comported yourself well. What do you think, now, of my people? Did they welcome you and your wares? Do you have contracts for next year?"

The full moon gave the desert a blue hue. The black sky and bright stars combined with the blue light of the moon to bring an almost-chill feel to the air. We traveled toward Bel Harq.

"Yes, Healer Timorinah, I tried to behave myself. Your men carry long and evil looking knives. I preferred to buy them, not wear them someplace inside my body.

"As to what I think of your people, well, I would like to spend a year traveling with one of your tribes. Do you think I might? Eventually?"

"I cannot speak for them, Arges Veen. However, I see no reason why you can't ask, at next Carnival. It is a hard life and you would have to hold your own, but I see no reason why you couldn't do that. The hardest, for you, would be the taking of orders. You would have to do that, you know."

250

"Yes. I know. Perhaps I can spend a year with the Tribe of Jib? Would you speak for me?"

I smiled. "Yes. Perhaps."

"As to selling my wares, yes, I sold most. Or actually, I traded most. And I have contracts for next year. I may have to come with three extra sliwa to carry everything away."

"You can always come with coin, and buy the sliwa you need from the tribes. They usually have several they wouldn't mind selling."

We stopped at several oases along the way, and kept our water skins full. Many had people, so we mixed our food with theirs, and Arges had a chance to trade more of his wares from Daveen. Our trip toward Bel Harq was leisurely and pleasant.

"This is an oasis you must remember, Arges. Here our road changes course and we join the caravan road. When you come next year, I suggest you come the desert way, rather than the overland way. Join a caravan to Bel Harq from Daveen and hire a guide at Bel Harq to bring you to Carnival."

"How will I know an honest guide? How will I know someone won't take me into the desert, steal my goods, and leave me to die?"

"Arges, have you not listened to me? Have you learned nothing this trip? Desert folk do not steal. We *have* no thieves." There were times I wanted to shake him and scream in his face.

"How is that so? I know you've told me, but there are always thieves and cutthroats and men of evil design."

"Yes, there are. And those tendencies show up early in childhood. If they are not treated and cured by one method then they are treated and cured by another. The desert is not merciful."

"You mean, you send children to the desert?"

"If necessary. Most of them go on their own, in search of riches that don't exist. We tell tales of a city in the desert where robbers go—called by many names, directly under the Blue Star,

251

there. Do you see it? The city exists only in stories, but the lure for the malcontent is strong."

The eastern sky glowed green, then faded to blue as the sun rose. It warmed our faces, and gave the sliwa a spurt of energy. "I think we can go on for a bit. We are nearly at the base of the trail up to Bel Harq. We will camp there and go up tomorrow, starting with first light."

"Does nothing grow upon these mountains? At night it is hard to tell, but now, seeing them in the light of day, they look, in fact, to be barren."

"Nothing grows upon them, I've been told, except on the plateau on which Bel Harq sits. There, I've been told, trees and shrubs, all planted, grow. Nothing grows on the mountains otherwise. The mountains hoard their water, giving it sparingly. Or, at least, so I have been told. We will set up camp and stay awake as long as possible, so we can sleep tonight. Tomorrow will be a long day, neh?"

Chapter Twenty-Eight

Those scarred by pain are forever marked;
they owe a debt to those who still hurt.
—*Lu Ahnah, the Lost Shaman*

"THAT IS A LONG CLIMB, Healer. It's a good thing the road has so many turn-backs to it."

"Why, Arges Veen, I am surprised you are not used to such climbing, spending as much time in the forests as you do. Perhaps you are not suited for desert living? The clean and clear air that contains no moisture?" I laughed at his huffing and puffing. Though, I admit, my knees were glad we reached the top.

Arges ignored my not-so-subtle teasing and looked out over the desert, "The forests have trees, and shade. This road is exposed but the view is magnificent. Where is Daveen from here? Can we see it?"

We stood at the top, waiting our turn at the gate. "No, I think not. Nor can we see Yaylin, though surely, from here, we should be able to see the whole of the world, neh?"

We were hot from our climb, and the guard surely was hot in his uniform, but he remained patient and friendly. "Mem, Ser, if you go around that way, follow the wall, you will come to the Daveen gate. Outside the gate is a pen with water for your sliwa. You may leave them there, and enter through the Daveen gate without their burden." Yes, he was friendly, but I understood, too, that it was more order than suggestion. He had heard our conversation about Daveen and recognized Arges as being a citizen of Daveen.

"Come, Arges, we will go that way. Then, we can enter Bel Harq and not be burdened by having to herd our sliwa." I led the way, before he could complain. The trail was wide here, though the edge was sharp, and it was a long way down. I would be happy to get to the other gate and to leave our lizards.

My father had attached straps to my boxes and built me a frame so I could wear them on my back if need be. "Do you wish to camp here for the night, or go in and find an inn?" I longed for an inn, and a bath, but did not wish to leave Arges quite yet. While in his father's house, I had heard many tales of the slave pens at the bottom of the Daveen road. I wanted to go down with him, to see for myself. And to make sure he saw them.

"Let us go in. I could use a real chair for my bottom and a good meal." I removed the frame and strapped my boxes to it.

"I agree. I shall take my things with me, then tomorrow, I will leave them at the inn and walk down the road to the bottom of the hill with you."

Two boys at the pen agreed to watch the sliwa and their packs for a coin. Arges paid, with no haggling over the price. The guard gave us directions to an inn he said was clean and fairly priced. They had two rooms available, for which Arges paid. Or rather, tried to pay.

"Young man, I will take for your room, but the healer here, her room is paid for by the school in Yaylin." He turned to me, "Healer, would you please sign our bill before you leave?"

"Of course." We went into the dining room, where Arges again paid for his meal, mine was added to the bill.

"I did not know. You never pay?"

"Sometimes, for small things, but no, the school pays our bills, or the villages, if we are assigned to a village or tribe. We do not require heavy expenditures and it is known that healers carry little to no coin, so we are safe from anyone who would think to relieve us of whatever we might have."

"From what you've told me, those folks don't survive long, anyhow. I mean, with your city under the blue star and all."

I smiled. "That is true. However, sometimes, we end up in countries where there is no city under a blue star, or its equivalent." We ate a hearty meal, drank cool teas, and enjoyed bread and jam for dessert.

The next morning, we were up before the sun, and partook of a light meal of cheese and bread and fruit. The proprietor agreed to keep my room for me, and to safeguard my boxes. We joined the throng at the gate and watched as the sun blasted over the rim of the world.

"Here," said Arges to the boys who guarded his sliwa and wares. "You have earned another coin. Now you each have one. Many thanks to you both." He turned to me, "And here, Healer, is a coin for you. Something to spend at market." He awkwardly handed me a small pouch. "Please, take it. Payment for my tutoring." He smiled at that and we began our downward trek.

"Healer, if possible, I think this is harder, going down, than it was coming up."

"Indeed, I think you're right. But it balances, neh?"

"Yes, it does. Now, why are you coming down with me?"

"When I lived in your father's house, I heard many tales of the slave pens at the bottom of this road. As you know, once a slave reaches Bel Harq he or she is free. They are free if they can get into the city. Well, to keep them from reaching sanctuary, the Daveens built huge pens at the bottom, and both they and the road are guarded. See, we come upon a guard at the next turn-back. He faces down, not up, neh? He is not interested in who comes down, only who tries to go up.

"I want to see these pens for myself. And I want you to see them, too." I fear my voice held more anger than I meant to share. Arges remained quiet until way past the guard, and then we talked of nothings for a long time.

"What is that noise? Do you hear it?"

"Yes, Arges. I do. I have been listening. It is the voice of despair, emanating, I fear, from the pens." And indeed, it was so. The pens had little shade, and little water, and forcing the slaves to be so close to freedom, and yet so far from it, broke my heart. And there was nothing I could do to alleviate their pain.

Arges, too, was deeply affected. "I...I had no idea. The slaves at market.... The slaves at my father's house...."

"The slaves at market are in fear for their lives and are in shock, so are quiet. The slaves in your father's house are well treated. Still, if you asked them, which they would prefer, to be a slave in your father's house or to be free even if poor, I think all would take the freedom."

We stopped along the road, on the flat of the desert, and shared our last meal together. "I leave you now, Arges Veen. I hope you make it safely back to Daveen and the house of your Father. If you question the route, I suggest you wait here and join a caravan to cross the desert. But if you stay on this road, you will be fine.

"You have learned much. I think your father will be proud of you."

"And you, Healer?" He looked steady into my eyes. "Are you proud of me?"

I stopped at that. Then smiled, "Yes, Arges Veen. I am. You have become a man I would gladly call "Friend"."

With that, he wrapped his arms around me and gave me a huge hug. "Healer, I say this from my heart. You are one of the most beautiful women I've ever met. I have learned much from you. Not always easily. And, at the time, not always happily, but I thank you. I truly hope we meet again. Friend." With that, he released me, turned away and led his sliwa toward Daveen.

"Arges!" I called, he turned, and I went to him. "Please, will you tell Achen I am safe, and have taken the name Timorinah, and that I thank him for all his training?"

"Achen?"

"Yes. You knew him as Sa Ach, your father's steward. He is still steward to your father, or was when we left, but no longer Sa." Arges smiled, and resumed his journey. I stood and watched him for a while, then turned and returned to Bel Harq and the inn.

Now, Timorinah, said Lu Shahnnah, *rest tonight. Tomorrow, we will go to the markets. Oh, I'm so excited. Aren't you?*

No, I thought. *I'm tired. And you still won't tell me why I'm here.*

Tomorrow. Tomorrow we will find the person, and the reason. She is here, I feel her. But I'm not sure where she stays. We will find her. And then we'll know.

We'll know? You mean you don't know? I, *we*, have come all this way, and *YOU DON'T KNOW WHY? Neh!* Since I could neither laugh nor cry I settled for silently screaming at this ghost who merely laughed in my head. At least *she* saw some humor in this.

Shhh. I knew, once. Things are... well, not so defined on the God Paths. But life goes on, things change, and all I know is that you are needed, here. And we will find out why tomorrow when we meet her.

Lu Shahnnah went quiet. I ate another good meal in the public room of the inn, and retired early. It had been a long day and a long, hard walk. I was lucky have made it back before the gate closed and I had to spend a night on the ground.

[⤜⟆ 𝕎 ⟅⤛]

"Healer, this day is market day. We have three, and you might enjoy walking them. The closest is the metal market, where metalwork is made. The next is the Vegetable market, where fresh fruits and vegetables and pastries, anything edible, are sold, and the third is the Wares market, where you can find for sale what is not available in the first two."

The proprietor explained all this while setting out the morning meal. I reached for a plate when he touched my hand. "May I suggest, you eat a lighter than normal meal if you intend to go to market? There are many good things to sample." His smile was friendly, and I heeded his words of advice. Still, I did eat a small meal with him. His wife was an excellent cook.

I expected the Metal market to be mostly weapons and was surprised to see so many ornamental artifacts. Metal is used in the desert, but not for ornaments, being too heavy to carry when we move about. Everything in a nomad's tent is useful. It may also be ornamental, but it is primarily something to use. There were weapons, of course, with beautifully forged blades. I noticed that small boys and desert men checked them out with equal and great interest. There were also beautiful urns, and hanging baskets, small animals for gardens and decorations. By the time I left and headed for the Vegetable market, the sun was high, and food welcome.

I smelled sweet bread. Bread like my mother, Saba, bakes— bread dripping with nectar and sweet spices. Homesickness for the desert and my tribe overtook me even though I had just left them; I nearly swooned. "Healer, are you all right?" It was the voice of the baker.

"Yes, Baker I am. Smelling your sweet bread made me, well, very much want my tribe and my mother, who also bakes." I smiled, "I think I need one of your sweet breads." I handed her one of the coins Arges gave me.

"Healer, my family is alive because of the healers of Yaylin. Take this bread with the blessing of the Family Ress. It is small in token, but great in love."

"And," I said as I swallowed the first bite, "every bit as good, if not better, than my mother's. Thank you." I ate my bread while walking past the booths.

I stopped in front of a flower vendor, amazed at how fresh the flowers were. "How," I asked, "do you get these flowers across the desert and here in such a fresh state?"

"Healer, they are grown here. The other end of the plateau is farmland. We grow most of the fresh fruits and vegetables for the city. In fact, we grow all. Anything that must come from the desert is dried."

"I did not realize the plateau was that large." We talked a bit, and then Lu Shahnnah began to almost scream in my head.

Hurry! She's here! I see her! Hurry, before she disappears!

Stop screaming! You're giving me a headache. Who is here?

She. The one we seek. I see her, at the other end of the market, and she is walking away from us. She. The one in the midnight blue robe. The Mage. Hurry. Run!

I will not run, not even for you, but I will hurry, so please stop yelling.

I would do anything at that point, to get Lu Shahnnah to stop yelling in my head. The Mage was talking with someone, and did not seem to be in a hurry, so I did not have to run. I had never seen a Mage before, and noticed her robe was similar to mine. Then, the humor of that observation brought forth a chuckle; all desert robes were similar. How many ways to make a robe?

I stood behind her and to the side, waiting for her to finish speaking. As she turned to leave, I spoke.

"Mage? You are a mage, are you not?"

At my voice, she turned. A pleasant woman. And unscarred. I blinked. Several times.

"Yes, I am Mage Mehree. How may I help you?"

"I am Healer-Shaman Timorinah. I was once known as Jibutu. Please, is there a place we can sit and talk? Somewhere private? Perhaps an outdoor restaurant where we might have a bowl of tea, or juice?"

"Yes, I know of several. In fact, one is just back this way. The woman makes wonderful breads. Come." And so we went

259

back to the booth of Ress. We ordered a plate of cheese, and bowls of cool tea, and Ress left us alone at our table. I told Mehree my story.

"And so, Mage, I am here, we are here, and neither of us entirely knows why."

Mage Mehree listened quietly as I told her my story, and then as quietly studied me for several moments. "You are the one Authority wished to send to our Mage School. Since you were thought to be dead, Healer Elen came in your stead. Do you know her?"

"Oh, yes. She was an acolyte when I entered the school. I remember her as a good healer and a good student." I smiled at the memories. "It took a bit for her to decide to be a good student, as I recall."

"Well, she is one now. And one of our Magi is at your school. Wicker. Her magic is that of empath, and she has a great curiosity of the healing arts. It took her a while, too, to decide to become a good student. But once she decided, there was no stopping her." The Mage chuckled at her memories.

We sat in silence, watching the people wander from stall to stall in the market. Shahnnah had quieted down, though I remained aware of her and her interest. My bowl was nearly empty when Mehree again spoke.

"Timorinah, I think I may possibly know why you are here. It is not the reason you were originally coming, but I would like you to meet some people. They have had a rough time and are very secretive about the location of their village, but I think they would welcome you. I believe they could use a full time healer, one they could learn to trust, and I am confident you could easily become that healer. Yes, I think they would welcome you very much. They may still be in the Wares market. They often are the last to close."

We hurried to the last market, the market where woodwork was sold, and weavings, clothes—everything not sold in the other

260

two markets. Most booths were closed, but one, at the end, remained open, though the proprietors packed their wares away, and their backs were to us. "Ah, good. They have not closed yet. Hurry."

By the time we reached the booth, most of their wares had been packed. The woman turned first, seeing Mehree's shadow. "Mage! You are back? We did not expect you until the morrow. And who do you bring?" At the last, her eyes lit upon my face. I watched as recognition dawned. "Mori! Is it you? Truly?" The men turned at her shriek of recognition. And I found myself embraced by four people I had known in Daveen. People I suspected had walked the magicked road as they had ceased to be seen in Daveen. Manners, and one's safety, dictated slaves never enquired about other slaves. Slaves only asked Masters if Masters required anything more. My joy at seeing them free soared to the boundless heavens.

We embraced and hugged and cried and all talked at once, Mage Mehree being totally forgotten in our joy. Eventually, we composed ourselves.

"I see I don't need to introduce you, after all. I just met this healer and thought you might be in need of one in your village, so I wanted to introduce her to you. I see you already know each other."

"Mehree, the story I just told you? About the road through the desert? Well, these people have walked that road. And from what you tell me, not only they, but several others have survived, and are now free citizens of this kingdom."

"Yes, Mori, there are many of us. We will take you home with us when we leave day after tomorrow. Where are you staying tonight?"

"I have a room at the Inn of the Pampered Sliwa."

"Then, Mori sleep well this night and tomorrow's night, because it is a long journey home. We leave at first light, day next. Do not be late."

261

Mage Mehree stood, her smile one of great happiness, "Timorinah, I stay at the Governor's Palace while in Bel Harq. Please, come with me now so you will know where it is. If I am not there, Mage Ahdree will be. You will always be welcome. I would like to introduce you to Ahdree and the Governor. Please, come now, and also for morning meal." She smiled as we walked into the sudden desert darkness.

Epilogue

There are no problems, only gifts of varying complexity.
— from Sayings of the Desert

AND SO, Joy Moon and whoever reads this to you (Fish? Would that be you?), this has been the story of my travels both before and after leaving Chusett.

The House of Nah continued for a time in, of all places, Daveen. I have met the family of Timor-I, and told them what happened. They are a large and prosperous family, and have hired several from the Hidden Village to work for them.

My journey to the Hidden Village was one of laughter and some tears as I learned who survived the journey from Daveen, who never left on the journey, who made it to safety only to die after they arrived.

The villagers do not want me in a tent, especially away from the village. They still do not trust people, and want nothing to call attention to their location, so they gave me the farthest away cave, and helped me furnish it with rugs and a table and two chairs. I do not need much. The men made a frame for the opening of the cave so I could hang felt panels for privacy, or raise them for fresh air. They also built a frame inside, so I can have two rooms.

As new escapees arrive, we hear more news of Daveen. I learned that Arges had indeed married, and has children. He is the talk of Daveen, apparently, as his wife is pretty, but he treats her as if she were not only beautiful, but as if he feared she may leave him at any time. They have their own house, not far from the House of Veen, and when he and his bride moved in, she brought her personal slaves. He informed her that he would have only servants in his house, no slaves, so he freed them, and hired them as servants. This is very unsettling to the other Houses of the Noble Borns, but he was adamant. Slowly, the other Noble Borns began to see his reasoning and slowly they, too, began freeing their slaves, and then hiring them.

Mulk, of course, was most angry. Slavery had been his meal ticket. He did not appreciate the new order of things, though when Arges brought Mulk in for a visit and a business proposition, even he began to change. Arges Veen, now too busy in local politics and with his young family, needed a business partner to carry on the trade he began with my tribes. Mulk, convinced of a Carnival share of the profits, agreed. He freed his slaves, married one, and hired several others for his caravans. As a master he wasn't so bad, I heard. As a stealer and seller of people, he was terrible.

Trade and the exchange of apprentices between The Hidden Village and the other desert villages continues to grow, slowly as trust remains hard won for my people. The trickle of escaped slaves continues and will until there are no more slaves to escape. Daveen slowly becomes a kingdom of servants and the former masters marvel at how much more work they get for coin. Not only more work, but better work.

Mage Mehree comes to visit, often bringing young apprentices, and often taking with her those who want to leave here for new adventure. Coming and going, she always brings new songs and stories for us all.

And my sister, Lu Shahnnah has finally quit screaming in my head. In fact, she no longer lives with me at all. Or in me. Our brother, Achennah, became quite ill. His wife, Mecy, nursed him as long as possible, but when he left to walk the God Paths, Shahnnah went with him. As much as I enjoy my peace and quiet, I miss her. She promised, when my time comes she will come back, with Achennah, so I will not have to walk the God Paths alone.

Achennah fathered a boy, whom Mecy loves unconditionally. They named him Achendada for Achennah and her father, Dada.

And so, Joy Moon, you were right. I shall not return, nor shall Lu Shahnnah, nor our mother Lu Ahnah, nor our brother Achennah. Please tell Fish I no longer swim, but shall forever remember his love and his lessons.

My friend, know I miss you and all of Chusett and deeply regret the sadness of this letter, hoping only that you will see the joy of closure.

I hear, now and then, the faint, loving voice of my birth mother, Lu Ahnah, no longer lost as she calls my name with love and a smile, *'Timorinah, Timorinah....'*

Blessings to you, Joy Moon, Blind Artist of Chusett, and teacher of Shamans,

I remain your most grateful student and friend, Healer-Shaman Jibutu Lu Timorinah.

Acknowledgements

EXTRA SPECIAL THANKS TO YOU, gentle reader! Thank you for the trust you have placed in my writing and the story you are about to read.

I don't write in a vacuum. While I do write alone, I'm not in a vacuum; I do have air to breathe. And I eventually send what I write out to others to read and respond to. Those others are hugely important, so a Most Special Thanks go to the following in no particular order: my Monday Writer's Group—Maureen McQuerry, Tara Pegasus, Steve Wallenfels, and Jeff Copeland. Patricia Shepherd, John E. Erickson, Dixiane Hallaj, Starr Morrow, Mary Curry, Jeanie Polehn, Lee Warner, William Craig, Richard Badalamente, Marjorie Rommel, Tim Eichorn, Judith Whitehead, Don McQuinn, Thomas Hubbard, Ann Richards, Judy Arndt, Kris Keating, Micki McKinley, Dan Stowens, and the late Jane Roop also made invaluable suggestions and criticisms. Any and all mistakes in this book are entirely mine. My readers did their best to send me in the right direction, but I am stubborn as an old sliwa.

AND A MOST SPECIAL THANK YOU to Julie Hawthorne, an artist and sculptor who co-owns Hawthorne Gallery in Port Orford, Oregon. While going through the gallery one weekend, I came upon the bust, Face of Extinction. It was the first (and only) time I'd seen a representation of Jibutu, and I knew I wanted it for my cover. Actually, I wanted the bust. Julie graciously sent me the photo of her sculpture to use in the cover and gave me permission to use it. No amount of words can express my appreciation for her generosity.

About the Author

LENORA RAIN-LEE GOOD. recently moved from the Pacific Northwest, now lives and writes in Albuquerque, New Mexico. She writes novels, short stories, and radio dramas. Her poems have appeared in various venues including most recently, "*WA129*," the anthology of 129 poems selected by Tod Marshall, Washington State Poet Laureate 2016-2018, and "*Blood on the Ground: Elegies for Waiilatpu*," her chapbook of poems about the Whitman Mission published by Redbat Books in the summer of 2016. Her books are available through her publishers, S & H Publishing and Redbat Books, as well as the usual online booksellers.

IF YOU ENJOYED THIS STORY, please tell your friends and write and post a review on Amazon, Barnes & Noble, Goodreads, and your personal blog and or social media page.

If you didn't like the story, please contact me at lenora (dot) good (at) icloud (dot) com and tell me why. If I don't know where it's broken, I can't fix it.

Many Thanks,
Lenora Rain-Lee Good

Made in the USA
San Bernardino, CA
20 August 2018